FLESH AND BLOOD

DS VICKY DODDS 2

ED JAMES

OTHER BOOKS BY ED JAMES

SCOTT CULLEN MYSTERIES SERIES

Eight novels featuring a detective eager to climb the career ladder, covering Edinburgh and its surrounding counties, and further across Scotland.

1. GHOST IN THE MACHINE
2. DEVIL IN THE DETAIL
3. FIRE IN THE BLOOD
4. STAB IN THE DARK
5. COPS & ROBBERS
6. LIARS & THIEVES
7. COWBOYS & INDIANS
8. HEROES & VILLAINS

CULLEN & BAIN SERIES

Four novellas spinning off from the main Cullen series covering the events of the global pandemic in 2020.

1. CITY OF THE DEAD
2. WORLD'S END
3. HELL'S KITCHEN
4. GORE GLEN

CRAIG HUNTER SERIES

A spin-off series from the Cullen series, with Hunter first featuring in the fifth book, starring an ex-squaddie cop struggling with PTSD, investigating crimes in Scotland and further afield.

1. MISSING

2. HUNTED
3. THE BLACK ISLE

DS VICKY DODDS SERIES

Gritty crime novels set in Dundee and Tayside, featuring a DS juggling being a cop and a single mother.

1. BLOOD & GUTS (a new prequel coming soon)
2. TOOTH & CLAW
3. FLESH & BLOOD
4. SKIN & BONE (coming 1st May 2021)

DI SIMON FENCHURCH SERIES

Set in East London, will Fenchurch ever find what happened to his daughter, missing for the last ten years?

1. THE HOPE THAT KILLS
2. WORTH KILLING FOR
3. WHAT DOESN'T KILL YOU
4. IN FOR THE KILL
5. KILL WITH KINDNESS
6. KILL THE MESSENGER
7. DEAD MAN'S SHOES

Other Books

Other crime novels, with Senseless set in southern England, and the other three set in Seattle, Washington.

- SENSELESS
- TELL ME LIES
- GONE IN SECONDS
- BEFORE SHE WAKES

PROLOGUE

An explosion like gunfire makes her look out of the window. Across the dark beach, the fireworks erupt then fade to nothing, leaving a sky dotted with stars, the moon almost full. Then a yellow glow shoots across the sea, leaving a flickering trail in its wake.

She sips the champagne, which tastes sour like beer. Supposed to be good, but it's nowhere near sweet enough for her. Nothing like that stuff they had in Dubai, but it'd do. A wave of goose-bumps crawls up her arms. Why didn't she wear something warmer than a summer dress?

The next wave of fireworks lights up Derek's face in the darkness. Mid-brown hair streaked with silver, laughter lines around his eyes. Can't see his toned muscles through his tuxedo, but it shapes the jacket in a nice way. His left arm loops around her waist and his right interlinks around hers and they sip each other's champagne. Her silver fox. All hers.

Something thuds behind her.

She breaks free and swivels away from the window. 'What was that?'

Derek frowns at her. 'Didn't hear anything, babe.'

She rests her glass on the windowsill and squints into the darkness.

Another flash, blue this time, lights up the room. The door is still open, showing the staircase leading back down to the beach. The walls are bright as though it was midday, bare stone with a long crack running down the middle. And it all fizzles away to darkness, just the faint glow from the battery lantern that doesn't reach into the room's corners.

No sign of anyone.

His searching hand smooths over her hip. 'Maybe you're nervous because we're not supposed to be up here.'

She nibbles at her lip. A green-and-red flash on the wall and the door. Nobody there. Right? 'It's probably a bird, isn't it?'

'There are terns and shags round here.'

'*Shags?*'

'It's a type of seabird. We did it at school. Swear it's the truth.'

'Shut up.'

'Seriously.' Derek gets out his bling smartphone and taps at the screen, then shows her a photo of a black seabird standing on a rock, its wings spread wide. 'Huh. Cormorants and shags are closely related, apparently.'

'Well, you've got even more surprising depths.'

He brushes aside the short dress and runs a hand between her legs, catching on the fabric of her knickers. 'I'll show you how deep I can go.'

She slaps his hand away. 'Stop it.'

'Come on.' He sets his champagne flute down next to hers on the windowsill. 'This is supposed to be romantic. God knows I've paid enough for it.'

'I know, it's just...' She looks around and she's shivering now. It's right in her teeth and her bones, down in her marrow.

A shimmering pink light dances across the walls. The room feels way too big and too claustrophobic at the same time.

Nobody there. Just her imagination. Probably the echoes of guilt and paranoia from months and months of keeping secrets from everyone. The reality hasn't caught up with her yet. And maybe it never will. At least not until the sparkling engagement ring on her finger has a wedding one alongside it.

'Sorry. It's just...' With a sigh, she picks up their glasses, both now smudged with her red lipstick, and hands him one, then links their arms again. 'This *is* romantic. Thanks.'

Derek leans in to kiss her and she fights against his tongue, always so over-eager. She opens her eyes.

A flash of fireworks catches a figure in the doorway.

She drops her glass and tries to push away from him. The glass smashes on the stone floor and she's rocked forward. Derek's bulk pins her against the wall.

An arm swings a golf club through the air.

SEARING pain behind her eyes wakes her up, biting at her brain. She tries to move, but can't. The back of her head feels like it's resting against the floor. She's freezing, but everything is on fire. She can barely move her legs. Still got her heels on, the clasps keeping them in place. And something is covering her mouth.

It's deadly silent. The fireworks must've stopped. What time is it? The moon has moved, so it must be hours later.

She can just about make out their attacker standing there, an outline in the moonlight coming in from the window. 'You would've thought, wouldn't you?' He's muttering, his voice deep. 'These people. Their morals, these days. You would've thought they'd learn, wouldn't you?' He looks right at her, but she can't see much. And she definitely doesn't recognise him. 'Why don't you people learn?'

She tries to speak but the gag swallows the sound.

He crouches in front of her and a flash catches in the darkness. A knife, thin like a scalpel rather than Derek's hunting knife. He grabs her by the hair and she tries to wriggle but he's way too strong.

His knees crunch against her ribs and he pins her in place. His thumb holds down her left eyelid. He reaches over with the knife, closer to her eye, and she freezes.

Then he cuts at her eyelid and the pain screams loud.

He pulls the knife away and she tries to move but just can't. Can't do anything. She's so useless, so helpless, and it's like her whole eye is on fire. Liquid fills the socket, little drops. Her own blood.

'Get off her!'

The attacker turns around.

Through a curtain of blood, she can see Derek sitting up, halfway across the room. His shirt is bright white in the dark room, but soaked red. 'You small-cocked wanker!'

The attacker gets off her and stands up with creaking knees. He moves towards Derek. Despite all the searing pain in her head, she knows she needs to do something. Now. So she lashes out with her feet, still bound together. Something bites into her ankles, but she makes contact, her toes connecting with material.

And it's just enough. The attacker stumbles and sprawls forward, landing face-down. He spills the knife and it rolls towards her across the uneven floor.

He's not moving, just lying there.

She should do something. She has to.

Derek is looking at her, his eyes pleading with her.

And the attacker is deadly still. Did she kill him? She doesn't know, but she's got to get them out of here.

So she moves her feet over and a trail of blood runs down her thigh. Another push and she edges her butt over. Then she moves her feet again, and she can just about reach the knife. She picks it up and it's like a scalpel. She reaches down and slashes the blade against the rope and it almost cuts clean through, just a few strands binding her ankles together. She tries to pull her feet apart but whatever the binding is made of, it's holding tight, so she presses the blade against the thread now, and it snaps. She lets out a breath. She can move now. Just like in all those stupid exercise classes, she pushes up to her knees, then hops up to standing.

She tries to cut the bonds on her wrists, but Christ her hands are shaking like crazy. One slip and she'll cut a vein, right? Something drips onto the rope. Blood. She's got to hurry, so she cuts at the rope around her wrists, but it's even harder than freeing her feet. Blood drips down and slicks her fingers. She drops the knife. Christ! She reaches for it again, but something strikes her back.

She stumbles and hits the wall. She hits the floor, crunching up her spine.

'Stay still!' The attacker has the knife again, aiming it at her eye once more. She didn't even see him. 'You have to pay!'

Derek hops over to the attacker and throws himself at him, bashing into him shoulder-first. They go down in a pile near the door.

Should she stay and help Derek?

No, the attacker has the knife again. She's got to get out of here. Got to get help.

She surges forward and leaps over them. Something nicks her neck but she can't stop, so she clatters through the doorway and down the stairs, her heels clicking off the old stone.

Blood runs down her chest from the wound in her throat.

DAY 1

Sunday
Sunday, 22nd July 2018

DAY 1

Sunday
Sunday, 22nd July 2018

1

When Vicky shut her eyes, it was like all the noise in her head stopped. The sun lashed at her skin. The sweet smell of the sun lotion. The sound of the two kids laughing and giggling, the jet of water hissing at them.

Cold hit her bare feet, made her open them again.

Rob was grinning at her, his eyes full of mischief. His shorts were very short and he should really have put a T-shirt on in this heat. He raised his hand, palm facing her. 'Sorry!' But he flicked the water again.

Vicky jerked upright and powered towards him. He might have been taller than her, but she was smart. Besides, the bigger they were... She pushed him into the wide paddling pool and water flooded the lawn. The hose writhed around on the grass like a snake.

Vicky grabbed it and directed it at Rob, placing her finger over the end to tune it to a hard blast.

'Okay!' Rob tried to get up, but a carefully aimed shot at his groin sent him tumbling back into the emptying pool.

Through it all, their two greyhounds lay on the grass, oblivious to the mayhem. Peralta looked up, but didn't see anything of interest, so rested his head back on Holt's side, already covered with drool.

Rob was on his feet, arms raised, water sluicing off him. 'You got me, officer.' He stepped over the rim onto the lawn and held out his wrists. 'You better cuff me.'

Vicky looked round at the kids, then back at him. 'No kinky stuff in front of them.'

He stepped out and wrapped her in a soggy cuddle. 'Sure?'

She grabbed the hose and stuffed it down his swimming shorts. 'You need to cool off, sir.'

He leaned in for a kiss and she let him. Eyes shut, standing in the baking sun, his damp fingers caressing her, her hungry fingers grabbing his back.

'Mummy, I'm *star*-ving!'

Vicky broke off with a sigh.

Jamie was staring up at them, eyes wide through his thick glasses. He was going through another growth spurt. Vicky couldn't remember when he'd started calling her "Mummy", but Christ, did she love it. 'I'm starving!'

She grabbed his hand and led him away from the pool. 'Your daddy's going to fire up the you-know-what soon.'

Bella skipped over and grabbed her mother's free hand. She wore that cute flowery swimming costume Vicky had bought for their holiday to Menorca. Hard as she tried to keep it packed away, you didn't get many days like this in Carnoustie. Her hair was down to her bum now and it needed cutting really badly, not that she'd let anyone near it, barely even to brush it. 'Why can't we call it a bar—'

'Shhhh!' Jamie was jumping up and down in fury. 'Everyone knows, Bella! If you say it out loud, God makes it rain.'

'Don't be stupid.' Bella stopped and planted her feet on the grass. A strop was brewing. 'Uncle Andrew said there's no God.'

Jamie shook his head. 'Shut up, Bella.'

Vicky sat them down on the bench. Jamie could just about manage it himself, but she still had to lift Bella up. Only a few months between them, but Jamie had inherited his father's height.

Bella would maybe grow like her, short until her late teens. Vicky grabbed the towel and started drying them. Bella's hair would take two towels on its own, so she did Jamie first. She squirted out sun cream onto her hand and started rubbing it on to Jamie's arms.

Bella was giggling.

'What's up, sweet pea?'

She hid behind her hand, the laughing getting worse. Just like her grandmother when she got a fit of the giggles. 'It sounded like a pump.'

And now Jamie was off, his over-loud roar of a laugh making it next to impossible to apply lotion to his face. And it'd be her fault if he got sunburn.

The toasty smell of charcoal passed on the breeze. She squinted into the sun.

Rob was shrouded in smoke, with bursts of flames erupting from the navy barbecue drum behind him. He checked his watch and looked over. 'Your parents are late again.'

Vicky rolled her eyes at him, but he was facing away. 'Like you didn't expect that.'

'Just glad I didn't light the charcoal earlier. Nobody likes a cold burger.'

'I do!' Bella squealed as Vicky squeezed a blob of sun lotion on her arm. 'Ow!'

'Should've got yourself a gas burner, Robbie.' Vicky's dad appeared round the side of the house, lugging two giant bags full of food. Belly poking out of the bottom of his T-shirt, reading "Car-snooty? Hardly!". Silvery hair peeking out beneath his Dundee United baseball cap, tangerine on black. At least you couldn't see the sweat soaked into the material, though it still reeked even at a distance and over the smell of charcoal. He dropped the bags on the patio and scowled behind him. 'Where the bloody hell is she?'

Feet crunched over the gravel and Vicky's mum appeared, dressed like it was mid-December. Coat, trousers, heavy shoes. And she carried *another* two bags of food. 'This needs to go in the fridge.'

'Just a sec.' Vicky finished brushing cream down Bella's arms. 'Okay, Toots, let's go help your granny.'

'Okay.' Bella hopped down and skipped inside the house after her grandparents.

Vicky took a second to compose herself.

The white-harled walls of the house glowed in the sun. The kids next door were battering a football around. A thud against the fence made Rob look over at Vicky, then back down into the barbecue, shaking his head. Jamie joined him, peering over the edge into it. Rob brushed a hand through his hair, then looked over. 'Sausages first, Vicks. Thanks.'

'Sir.' She saluted the only person in the world she'd let call her that name, then went in the house.

Their house now. Their home.

Her eyes were struggling to adjust to the light inside.

A thick figure was squatting by the fridge, trying to shove a bag of salad into an already overstuffed crisper. 'Cathy, I *told* you that's too much food.'

'George, I'm just trying to—' Mum looked round at Vicky. 'We brought a few things.'

'Four bags isn't a few things, Mum.' Vicky could see now, so she filled the kettle and stared outside at the billowing smoke. The twats next door would no doubt complain soon enough. 'Cup of tea?'

'Gasping for one.' Dad was on his feet, scowling at the fridge. 'Traffic was a nightmare, by the way.' He looked over at Vicky. 'Millions of people in Carnoustie because of the bloody golf and your mother insisted on going to the Co-op.'

'George, if we hadn't gone, you wouldn't have seen Samuel L. Jackson and Bill Murray outside the Spar.'

'It wasn't them.'

'It was so, George Dodds.'

'Mum, where's Bella?'

She pursed her lips. 'I'll find her.' She disappeared off deep into the house.

Dad winched himself up to standing.

Vicky nudged past him and opened the fridge door. All the food she'd spent the morning preparing was buried under a ton of pre-packed rubbish. And who needed three trifles? Vicky managed to ease out the plates and passed them to her father. 'Dad, can you take this to Rob and do all your alpha-male barbecue stuff?'

He took the plates but was frowning at her. 'What do you mean by that?'

'You know what I mean. Can I get you a beer?'

'If you've got any.' He was looking down at the fridge and Rob's chilling collection of cans. 'Czech would be my preference.'

'I'll bring them out.' Vicky watched him leave her kitchen and took another few seconds to calm herself down. The sound of a football hammering off a fence. Male voices talking, young, middle-aged and old. A flushing sound came from upstairs. Hopefully her mother had found her daughter and all was right in the world. A kettle boiling and clicking off.

Shit, shit, shit.

Vicky sprung into action and tossed a couple of teabags into the pot, then filled it up with water. Not exactly her old man's scientific method, but it'd do. She popped the lid back on the pot, then walked over to the fridge. She eased two bottles of ice-cold beer from under the mound of rubbish, then cracked off the lids and took them outside.

'So, who do you fancy, Robbie?' Dad had taken over the barbecue and was controlling the wall of flames like a pro. The smells of burning meat put lie to that myth, though.

'Not so sure.' Rob was standing there with the plates, reduced to helper in his own garden. 'You got any money on it?'

'A tenner on McIlroy, but don't tell Cathy.'

'Brave man. Oh, cheers.' Rob took the beer from Vicky and pecked her on the cheek. He passed the bottle over to her dad. 'Here you go, George.'

Dad raised his bottle in cheers and took a pull. 'Ah, that's the business. Should get your radio out here, Robbie. No chance I'll get to watch the golf on a day like this.'

'I'll see what I can rustle up.'

Jamie was tugging at Vicky's top. 'Mummy, I'm still hungry.'

She crouched down until she was eye level with him. 'Your daddy's just cooking something with Granddad, okay?'

'Can I have some crisps?'

'We haven't got any.'

'Eh.' Dad took another drink of beer. 'Victoria, your mother practically emptied the Co-op of crisps.'

Superb.

A sharp tug at her shorts. 'So can I have some crisps, Mummy?'

'Come on, then.' Vicky led Jamie back over to the house.

'Doubt I'll win, Robbie, but it'd be nice to listen in.' Dad was grinning. 'Mind you, Vicky's the one winning out with the Open on.'

Vicky stopped and looked back, squinting into the bright sun. 'What's that supposed to mean?'

'Well, you're renting out your house for silly money, aren't you?'

'Doesn't make up for not being able to get anyone to rent it the rest of the year, mind. The mortgage is crippling us.'

'Well, hopefully it'll give you a bit of breathing space.'

'Hope isn't going to cut it.'

The doorbell chimed, cutting across the football kicking and the greyhound snoring.

Vicky took the plate from the low wall. 'That'll be my brother, then?'

'Andrew's sitting this one out.' Dad winced. 'Your mother's taking him to Glasgow on Tuesday. Supposed to be seeing this specialist who might be able to help.'

'I thought he was better.'

'Never learns, that boy.' Dad took another glug of beer and grimaced. 'Burning the candle from the middle as well as both ends. Never learns.'

'I'll leave you to it.' Vicky took the plate and led Jamie across the path. She found the least-crap bag and opened it for him. 'Here you go.'

'Thank you, Mummy.' Jamie took the bag and ate the giant crisp.

'You stay here and wait for me, okay?' She padded through the house.

A shadow at the door. Short, and slim. Before she could open it, her phone rang. It was sitting on the console table just inside the porch.

DI David Forrester calling...

Like she had time for that just now. She swiped to cancel it as she walked over to open the door. An old Ford sped off out of their cul de sac, back onto the main bit of Corby Drive. Black and modified for speed, with a tall spoiler.

Who the hell was that?

A card was stuffed into their letterbox. Plain white, folded over. She snatched it out.

"V — I KNOW"

Handwritten in caps. No name or number.

Vicky got that deep panic, like her veins were filled with ice.

She checked her phone again. Should she call Forrester back?

She caught a smell of cooking meat. No. This was Sunday, time for family, old and new.

Rob walked through, his shorts dripping on the laminate. 'Who was that?'

Vicky stuffed the note in her pocket. 'You're soaked through.'

'Your old man needs another beer.'

'Already?'

Her phone chimed. Forrester again, but a text this time:

"I'm your boss. When I call, you answer. Capiche?"

She looked at Rob with a sigh. 'It's work.'

He looked away, his lips screwed up. 'Right.'

Vicky felt that sting in her gut again as she picked up her phone and put it to her ear. 'What's up, sir?'

'Did you bounce my call?' Sounded like Forrester was outside. A crowd chatting and shouting, cut through by a distant announcer.

'It *is* Sunday and I'm kind of busy.'

'Well, you're about to get a whole lot busier, Sergeant. Need you to get out to the coast between Carnoustie and Arbroath. There's a new golf resort there.'

'I know it.'

'Aye, well there's been a murder.' And he was gone.

Vicky dropped the phone back on the table and looked over at Rob. 'Sorry, I have to go to work.'

Rob folded his arms. 'Leaving me with your parents and two kids?'

'I know. It's more like four kids.'

2

Vicky should have been at home, but instead she was en route to a crime scene. Typical.

And the A92 was heavy with traffic. Really unusual for any time, but especially a Sunday. Not every day that the world's biggest golf tournament hit Carnoustie and upended everything.

Vicky pulled off the dual carriageway and swung round the loop until she crossed under the road. She rose out of the pit and headed towards the sea, which was glistening in the afternoon sunshine. Across the waves, the Fife coastline was hazy under the bright sun. Been ages since she'd been over there. Then again, it was Fife.

Just before the road swung along the coast towards the far end of Carnoustie from where Vicky lived, she slowed, her indicator clicking away.

The new LA Golf course was hidden behind five-metre walls that would *maybe* survive an Angus winter. A seasoned cop guarded the entrance, red-faced and struggling with the heat despite wearing as little of his uniform as he could get away with. Didn't even need to see ID, just beckoned her through.

Vicky rumbled across the car park towards the rows of cop cars and vans littering the place, disrupting any attempt at order and instilling the usual chaos. The gleaming hotel building was squat, four floors of white stucco pockmarked with blue windows and balconies. Still had that brand-new look, with the forty or so trees bare and shivering in the heat haze. She had no idea how they got planning permission for this, save for a lot of brown envelopes under a lot of tables.

She pulled up next to the crime scene van, half relieved not to have to wait around for the forensics team to show, assuming it was her on duty.

At least the pathologist's Nissan was there, plugged in to a charger station, the car's lime green glowing in the sun.

Vicky got out into the baking heat. Her trousers were already soaked with sweat. At least she'd decided to keep her summer T-shirt on. She found Forrester's text with its directions — head down to the sixteenth tee. Like that made any sense to anyone. Still, there were enough uniformed officers to indicate the likely path.

A blue BMW pulled up next to her with the window down, blasting out Ed Sheeran. DS Euan MacDonald got out with an unreadable expression. 'Showing a bit too much flesh there, Vicky.' He hadn't got the same memo as her, wearing his navy suit in this weather. And Christ did he fancy himself. Wraparound shades, his brown hair swept up into a quiff, and the sort of stubble that'd scratch like hell if you kissed him. His car lights flashed.

Vicky stood there, tempted to just bugger off down to the beach. 'This way, I think.' She set off away from the hotel towards the thickest congregation of uniforms. 'Forrester called you too, then?'

MacDonald jogged to catch up with her. 'Said he needed his A-team on it.'

'And yet he asked you.'

'Very funny. Any idea where he is?'

'Search me.'

'Is that an invite?'

'Christ, don't you ever stop?'

'You didn't reply to my text.'

'I've blocked your personal mobile.'

'Oh.' For once, he didn't have a comeback for that.

'I'm just messing with you. It's not the law to reply to every text message, is it?'

'True.' MacDonald ducked his head and followed her inside.

The crime scene seemed to be a stretch of golf course by the beach, golden sand spreading out in both directions. If this was nearer civilisation, the place would be mobbed. Two miles west and you'd be in Carnoustie, three or four east and Arbroath. A lighthouse sat maybe half a mile towards Arbroath on a squat mound of black rock fighting against the rising tide.

DC Karen Woods stood guarding their way in. Medium height, blonde hair in a ponytail. 'Strange to see you two turning up together.'

Vicky snatched the clipboard off her and signed them in, but deliberately misspelled both of MacDonald's names. She thrust the clipboard back. 'Don't.'

Karen tossed a crime scene suit to Vicky. 'Calm down.'

Vicky unfolded hers. 'Any sign of Forrester?'

'What do you think?'

VICKY FOLLOWED MacDonald across the pristine golf course. 'This is just the fairway and it's miles better than our lawn.'

MacDonald twisted round to grin at her. 'Every time you mention *him*, Vicky, it breaks my heart.'

'Good.' Vicky powered on towards the huddle standing by the green. Ten bodies in blue suits, and none of them obviously Forrester, so she pulled up her hood and snapped on the mask.

Christ, it was hot.

MacDonald beckoned for Vicky to go first, ever the gentleman.

She eased between the bodies, most of them crouching and cataloguing. A couple of photographers snapped away when surely one would've done. At least they parted to let Vicky see the crime scene.

A young woman lay in a bunker, face down, her blonde hair splayed out. Little black dress, bare legs, Jimmy Choos strapped on for dear life. No sign of what killed her, though the blood soaking into the sand gave a not-so-subtle hint.

And even less subtle was the gargantuan behind of the blue-suited figure nearest the body, on her hands and knees as she prodded at flesh. Professor Shirley Arbuthnott, Dundee's chief pathologist. She turned round and caught Vicky's gaze, and returned her nod. 'That's as close as I can allow you.'

'Fine.' Vicky stayed up on the edge of the bunker, taking in the scene. The perfect grass lining the lip. The wire mesh keeping the structure in place. The damp, coarse sand. And the dead body lying right in the middle.

Arbuthnott lifted the victim's left shoulder to let Vicky and MacDonald see the giant knife wound across her throat. A deep gouge, covered with dark blood. 'My initial hypothesis is that she died of blood loss from this wound. Will need to confirm that up in Dundee, but I'd say it's over eighty percent likely.'

Vicky nodded, keeping her gaze on the lifeless body. Looked young, maybe late teens, early twenties. A glimmering rock on her finger, though, so she was engaged. A tattoo of some Chinese symbols on her bicep. 'Any idea who she is?'

'Trouble with little black dresses is they don't let you conceal anything.' Arbuthnott's cheeks puffed out in a smile. 'Especially my enormous derrière.'

No ID always meant extra work.

Vicky stood up tall to look around. Nothing obvious indicated where the victim had come from, no telltale heavy footprints or tracks. 'Was she killed in situ or moved here?'

'Can't tell. There was heavy summer rain overnight, which appears to have reset any trail she might've left us.' Arbuthnott rested against the bunker's lip. 'Also makes establishing a time of death extremely challenging. All I can give is from about two a.m.

until seven, and there's a good two hours' error margin either side of even that.'

'Any forensics?'

'Not my department.' Arbuthnott slapped the arm of a much-skinnier woman next to her. 'Jenny?'

'What now?' Jenny adjusted her mask, giving a flash of blood red hair against the vampire-pale skin. Bright green eyes drilled into Vicky. 'Hey, look who's here.'

'Hi Jenny. You got anything?'

'Well, no. I've been here five minutes. And no, we don't have an ID.'

'Can you get a photo of her?'

'A photo? She's not got any ID on her.'

'I mean, can you flip her over, snap a shot and I can show it to people to see if anyone recognises her?'

'Oh right.' Jenny stepped out of the bunker to let two of her team in to start erecting a tent over the body. She folded her arms and watched them working away. 'Well, not yet. We need to capture everything as it was found. Even us lot standing here on this sand is upsetting things and the body's been out in the open for a good while. Let's just see what we can find, okay?'

Vicky let out a deep sigh that'd been building. 'Can I have a look at the face again?'

Jenny glanced at Arbuthnott and got a shrug. 'Fine.' She raised a finger. 'But let me, okay? You cops are hashy.'

'Hashy...' Vicky almost laughed, but they were at a crime scene, standing over a corpse.

Jenny repeated Arbuthnott's earlier move, lifting her shoulder up.

This time, Vicky had her phone out on maximum zoom and snapped a couple of shots. 'Thanks.' She inspected them and found the one best in focus.

The woman was definitely early twenties, lacked that teenage puffiness. But the kind of pretty that would stick out in Tayside. Blood covered her jaw, neck and mouth, coming from a wide gash in her throat. But it also covered her left eye.

Vicky held the phone out towards them. 'What's going on with the eye?'

Arbuthnott frowned at it. 'My lord.' She collapsed down to her hands and knees again and twisted the victim's head around. 'Good heavens. Someone has cut at her eyelid.'

'Her eyelid?' Vicky went back to staring at the image on the phone. She zoomed in further, to the point her phone stopped letting her. It was a pixelly mess, hard to determine anything, but there was definitely a dark red mark above the eye. 'Can you check to see if it was from the same knife as the throat wound?'

'I'll do what I can when I get her up to town, but until we have the actual knife, it'll be next to impossible to prove.'

Vicky gave her a smile. 'Just see what you can get.'

'Will do.' Arbuthnott vaulted up out of the bunker with a grace belying her massive arse. 'I'll get someone to collect her soon.' She raised a hand and stared up into the bright blue. 'Rain's on the way.' She gathered her medical bag and scuttled off towards the hotel.

Jenny sat back on the edge next to where Vicky perched. 'Can you imagine?'

Vicky was still staring at the phone. 'What, bleeding out from a throat wound?'

'No, having an arse that size.' Jenny shook her head. 'I mean... Jesus.'

MacDonald was peering over Vicky's shoulder. 'Know what they say in *Spinal Tap*. "The bigger the cushion, the sweeter the pushin'".'

'Gross.' Jenny scowled at him. 'Remember that your skinny-arsed wife works for me.'

'I'm being ironic.' MacDonald held up his hands. 'You know who found the body?'

～

THE GREENKEEPER'S hut was between the fifteenth and sixteenth holes. Pretty fancy too. Solar panels and all sorts of rain-collection devices on the roof, though they looked dry as a bone. A row of golf buggies, all plugged in to the mains, and some mowing equipment that belonged on a farm, not a golf course.

A female uniformed officer appeared at the door. 'What?'

Vicky unfurled her warrant card. 'DS Dodds. Looking for Brendan Doig.'

'Right.' The uniform stepped forward and let the door close behind her. 'He's the head greenkeeper here.'

'Thanks. Can you give us a minute?'

'Thing is...' Her mouth puckered up. 'He's not doing too well.'

'In what way?'

'Well. He found the body first thing, but he told me he froze. Took him like an hour to come round. He had some sort of PTSD episode.'

'Poor guy.'

'Yup. Said he'd found his uncle's body when he was a kid.' She stepped aside to let Vicky past.

Brendan Doig was sitting at a table. He was all skin and bone, the lithe physique of a marathon runner, but with a big-jawed face that looked several sizes too big for him. He was staring into space, his lips twitching.

MacDonald whispered to Vicky, 'I worked with an Edinburgh cop who suffered from this. Let me.'

'Be my guest.'

MacDonald took the seat across from him and waited for him to look up. 'Hi.'

Brendan looked away.

'Mr Doig, my name is DS Euan MacDonald and I need to ask you a few questions about the body. You okay?'

'Hardly.' Brendan's voice was a lot deeper than Vicky expected. And he was clearly struggling, his eyes wheeling around in his head.

'Sir, I gather you discovered the body?'

He gave a vigorous nod, like he'd snapped into the present. 'Just found her lying on the sand.'

Vicky's sight had adjusted to the light. The walls were lined with three rows of lockers, most of them covered in pin-up shots from American porn mags. 'You recognise her?'

'Nope.' He stared at Vicky. 'I was just working. Why should I have to see that?'

MacDonald raised his eyebrows. 'Sir, I want to thank you for calling it in despite the obvious trauma.'

Brendan shut his eyes and tilted his head back. 'Right.'

'Sir, it'd help us immensely if you could take us through your morning.'

Brendan drew a breath and nodded slowly. 'Boss is piling on the pressure to get it perfect, so I was cutting the fairway on the sixteenth. I mean, it's close to burning to a crisp and you've no idea how much watering it's needing. And I just saw her lying there.' He tugged at his hair. 'I mean, a dead body? Like that?'

MacDonald sat next to him and smiled. Gave the guy a few seconds' attention. 'What's your boss's name?'

'John Lamont. He's the owner here. I report directly to him, but he wants to bring someone in to manage this place once things are up and running.'

'Okay.' Vicky scrawled the name down. 'Why is he applying so much pressure?'

'Supposed to be opening up tomorrow, but there's a pro-celebrity match. Some actors and that annoying fat comedian off the telly. But it's not working well, I think the subscription numbers are low. Don't know what he thought would happen. He's got Carnoustie a few miles away and St Andrews over the Tay. Had this big opening ceremony last night during the Open, to cadge punters in, but I don't think it worked as well as he hoped. And he's the kind to sweat the small stuff.'

So the victim could've been a guest.

Vicky took the seat next to MacDonald. 'Were you at this event, Mr Doig?'

He laughed. 'Hardly. He put on a free bar in the function room upstairs for the staff while the VIPs were wined and dined. And of course, I had to bugger off early to get the course shipshape today.'

Vicky didn't want to risk traumatising the guy further by showing the face. 'So you didn't see her?'

'Nope.'

Still, a little black dress and three hundred quid shoes meant it was probable she was a guest. Just not likely to be a local.

3

Up close, the hotel looked less finished than when Vicky had arrived in the car park. All the bits of unpainted wood, smoky glass, lights not working, snagging or whatever they called it.

And where the hell was MacDonald?

I should just get in there and do this myself.

Sod it, she did.

The hotel interior was a riot of activity, a din of out-of-tune whistling and blaring radios tuned to different stations. Bright lights. A wide atrium with a dark granite desk, curtained off behind. Probably supposed to look like it was in London, New York or Paris. But it was in the middle of nowhere on the Angus coast. Whoever owned it, well he was trying to show the world how big his dick was. And the whole place smelled of turps.

Vicky weaved between two joiners lugging big planks of wood across the shiny floor and stopped at the reception desk. Nobody about, but someone had been there working. Two desktop computers hummed away, though there were no chairs. She rang the bell and waited, checking her phone for messages. Nothing, except Rob sending her a photo of Jamie wearing Bella's hair like a wig. Another glance behind her and no sign of

MacDonald. The joiners were nailing the planks together at right angles. She had no idea why or what they were attempting to build.

The curtain swooshed open and a female receptionist appeared, smiling, but her eyes betraying a deep feeling of harassment. And the place wasn't even open yet. She tilted her head to the side. 'Can I help?'

'DS Vicky Dodds.' She flipped out her warrant card and held it for a good inspection, then put it away. 'Need to speak to the owner.'

The receptionist cleared her throat. 'Well, Mr Lamont is incredibly busy.'

'It's John Lamont, isn't it?'

'That's correct. He's having a crisis meeting with our contractors.' She gestured behind Vicky. 'As you can see, our fish tank is way behind schedule.'

Another glance and Vicky still couldn't see how on earth that was anything other than some wood stuck together. She smiled at the receptionist. She wore a badge but it didn't have a name, which made things harder. 'I'm sure your boss is aware of the discovery this morning.'

'And Mr Lamont is aware of how much time it is occupying.'

'Excuse me?'

'Well, we need to get the greens shipshape for tomorrow or—'

'Listen to me, I'm not asking you, I'm telling you.'

The receptionist raised her eyebrows. 'Mr Lamont gave explicit instructions to—'

'Kathy!' MacDonald breezed past Vicky and leaned against the dark stone desk. 'Didn't know you were working here.'

A genuine smile filled the receptionist's face. 'Mac! Good to see you!'

'And you.' MacDonald gave Vicky a clear-off gesture with his head. 'So how's it shaping up here?'

Vicky gave him some space. She was too big to fight him on it, and fighting seemed to be getting them nowhere near speaking to Lamont.

Vicky got out her phone. Another text from Forrester, "Call me." So she did.

And he didn't answer.

Superb. Best case, he was driving. But there were way too many worst cases.

MacDonald sauntered past her, striding like a guest just after a breezy check-in. 'John Lamont is waiting for us.'

Vicky followed him over to the lift. 'How?'

'All it took was a bit of charm, not your flavour of aggression.'

'How do you know her?'

'Know what you're thinking, Dodds. Get your mind out of the gutter. I don't know her in the biblical sense, no.' MacDonald gave a flash of his eyebrows that contained a good chunk of disappointment. 'Used to run the serviced apartments where we stay. Place has gone to the dogs since she left.'

JOHN LAMONT'S office was a corner suite up on the building's top floor. Floor-to-ceiling windows looking across the first and eighteenth holes towards the sea and Fife in the distance. Heavy rain misted over Leuchars and Guardbridge, though it was still sunny this side. Arbuthnott had been right after all. A large telescope looked out towards Carnoustie, probably with enough resolution to pick out people on the high street.

MacDonald walked over to a large banquette in the corner like you'd see on a film in a fancy American restaurant. The curved wall above was dotted with sporting memorabilia. A signed Toronto Blue Jays baseball jersey. A ton of Toronto Raptors stuff, whoever they were. And a muddy Dundee United shirt from their brief glory days back when Vicky's old man insisted on taking both kids to Tannadice, despite mutual apathy.

MacDonald pointed at a couple of basketball shirts. 'You a Raptors guy?'

'Damn straight.' John Lamont was short, maybe five four and broad with it. Typical Dundee physique. Big belly hanging over trousers pulled right up. His accent had that Toronto twang some of Vicky's distant cousins had, the ones whose parents had escaped to the promise of the New World. *Tronno.* 'I'm hopeful we'll win the NBA title next year.'

'We being the Raptors?' MacDonald smiled. 'Now that is hopeful.'

'I'm an optimistic man.' Lamont stuffed his hands in his pockets. 'The kind of people who leave this land behind in search of a new life over the sea, we require an optimistic nature. And it paid off for me. I made a ton of money in Canada.'

Vicky joined them by the display. 'And now you're back.'

'Indeed.' Lamont waved a hand around the vista. 'The LA Golf resort allows me to give something back to my home town.'

'You're from Carnoustie?'

'For my sins.' Lamont grinned. 'Almost lost the accent now, ye ken?' He laughed, though his voicing of the Carnoustie flavour of the Dundonian twang wasn't a million miles off.

Vicky was from the half of the town that had avoided it and just spoke like a generic Scottish person. Even people from Essex could understand her.

Lamont pressed a finger against the glass, indicating a football top, red with black sleeves, all high-tech and much nicer than the Dundee FC shirt Jamie was pestering Vicky and Rob to buy for his birthday. It was mud-smeared and covered with dark ink squiggles. 'When Toronto FC won the MLS Cup in 2016 and again the next year, it reminded me of the glory days when Dundee United won the Scottish Premier Division.' His accent had slipped back in time and place. 'Well, makes you think.'

Vicky smiled at him. 'My dad's a Terrier.'

Lamont laughed. 'I suppose calling them the Arabs isn't politically correct these days?'

'No, it's not. He took me to a few of those UEFA cup matches in 1987.'

'I was there too. Glorious, wasn't it?'

MacDonald snorted, like he was annoyed to be taken out of

the equation by a woman discussing football. 'So what really brought you back?'

'Well, like I say, I wanted to repay my debts. This country taught me skills that I could make use of over the water.' Lamont pointed to a small black and white photo stuffed between sports jerseys. A young couple on their wedding day, her in a flowing white dress, him in a minister's dog collar. 'That and my parents. Mum passed a few years back, but my dad... He got Alzheimer's and I couldn't bear to think of him rotting in a care home in Dundee, so I brought him over to live near us. Took a while, but he passed last year.'

'I'm sorry to hear that.'

'We had some good times. He loved watching baseball. But his death made me take stock, you know? I moved to Canada twenty years ago, but that made me realise how much I missed the old country.'

Vicky gave him a few seconds. 'Sir, we're here to ask about the body on the golf course.'

'I told the young cop, erm, Constantine?'

Vicky grimaced. 'Considine.'

'Right, right, well he came up here and burst in. I was on a call with my contractor. That kid work for you?'

MacDonald nodded. 'Works for DS Dodds here, aye.'

'Well, you tell him from me that we have ways and means of working here.'

Vicky stepped closer to him. She was about three inches taller than him and the closer she got, the brighter the glare from his combed-over bald spot. 'And I have an unidentified dead body in a bunker. That takes precedence.'

'Dude!' Lamont raised his hands in a defensive way. 'I want to help, believe me, but I have absolutely no idea who the victim is. None of my guys do and I asked.'

MacDonald folded his arms. 'You had a big function last night, a gala opening. Maybe the victim could've been a plus one.'

'Look, I'm up against it here.'

'You don't think she was a guest?'

'We, uh, didn't invite many women, no.' Lamont was avoiding Vicky's gaze. Good for him. 'I mean, she could've been a local from Carnoustie or Arbroath, but there weren't any gatecrashers, not that I've heard of. And I deliberately built this place away from the town so as not to attract that type.'

'That type?'

'Look, she could've been someone here for the Open. We had a few movie stars pitch up last night and of course we're going to let those guys in.' His eyes were gleaming. 'The press has been extremely favourable today. When you get an A-list movie star showing up at a party in Angus, the papers put it on their front page.'

MacDonald wasn't relenting though. 'We're going to need to speak to your staff, sir.'

'Buddy, didn't you see what it was like downstairs? I've got this place opening up, twenty assholes working to install a goddamn fish tank and a ton of exotic fish turning up at six.'

'Going to need a list of all your contractors.'

'That's a lot of people.'

'And I've got a dead body on your sixteenth hole.'

'Fine.' Lamont charged across the office as fast as his little legs could carry him. He sat behind a computer that was set about three or four inches higher than he needed, like a little kid on Santa's knee. 'Oh, she could even have been working for the caterers.'

Vicky hovered over his shoulder, hoping that would irritate him. 'Where are they based?'

'Arbroath, Abbey Catering. They're *excellent*.'

The only other explanation Vicky could think of for her small black dress, aside from her being a prostitute. She jotted it down. 'Okay, that's a start.'

He looked deflated. 'Only a start?'

'Were there any prostitutes here?'

'Wasn't that kind of party.'

'I'll take that under advisement.' She sat on the edge of his desk, close enough that he couldn't look right at her. 'Here's what's going to happen. You're going to provide a full list of contractors, including staff.'

'I'll see what I can dig out, but things are chaotic right now. We had to get a load of workers in over the weekend because of the severe number of flaws in the work done so far. My lawyers are going to be inundated with lawsuits for a long time to come.'

'Sure they'll enjoy the work. And all I'm hearing is excuses.'

'I've got to open this place tomorrow.'

'No chance that's happening. You've got a murder victim on your sixteenth. The sooner we identify her, the sooner we catch the killer, the sooner you can open.'

That seemed to perk him up. 'Okay. A list of contractors? Done.'

'Thanks.' Vicky stood up. 'And we're going to need a full list of these employees. Every single one.' She left a long pause. 'And a guest list from this function, including plus ones.'

'Oh, come on.'

'I'm not sure how your A-list movie stars will appreciate a police car sitting out front twenty-four-seven.'

4

Vicky stormed out of the hotel entrance into the blinding light. A maroon Subaru had boxed her in. Superb.

MacDonald was keeping pace with her. 'Hate to see you really pissed off.'

'What do you mean?'

'Supposed to be a charm offensive in there.'

'You'll see me pissed off, Euan, mark my words. And it was effective, wasn't it?'

'Suppose.' MacDonald stopped to laugh. 'Your dad really an Arab?'

'No, he's Indian.'

That got him. 'Wait, what?'

'From Kolkata, Calcutta as was.'

'But you're—'

'Euan, Euan, Euan...' Vicky turned back to face him and the monstrous hotel. 'His parents were jute wallahs, you idiot. I was picking you up on your use of Dundee United's racist nickname.'

'Hardly racist.'

'Ask someone from the Arabic world how they feel about it.'

'Season ticket holder at Tannadice, for my sins.'

'You've got a lot of sins.' Vicky got out her phone and checked the display. 'Still nothing from Forrester.'

'Predictable. What's the plan?'

'You got any ideas? Feels like I'm supplying them all.'

'Should separate.' MacDonald thumbed behind him at the hotel. 'If I take lead on the hotel and the contractors, you can work the other angles. Crime scene, that catering firm. When we get the guest list, we'll split it, assuming we haven't IDed her by then.'

'Right.' As much as she wanted to disagree, Vicky knew that no waitress would wear three-hundred quid heels to work. An escort might, though. 'He seemed rattled when I—'

'Noticed that too. Think she was an escort?'

'Ask around.'

'Will do. Look, we're—' MacDonald glanced over her shoulder and winced. 'Oh, here we go.'

'Come on, Kaz, you're being a dick!' The doors of the Subaru were open and DC Stephen Considine was over the passenger side, his red hair glowing like a fire. Thin but not especially tall, kind of like MacDonald's ginger Mini Me. 'I signed this out, so I should drive it.'

Karen just shook her head at him. 'If it's not a cock replacement, then what is it?'

Considine didn't have anything in response.

Arguing like a pair of children. Now where had Vicky seen that? Oh yeah, at home. Every. Single. Morning.

MacDonald held up a closed fist to Vicky. 'You want to play paper, scissors, stone for them?'

'Girls are better than boys.' Vicky set off towards the Subaru and held out a hand to Karen. 'Keys.'

VICKY KICKED down and overtook the coach, zooming along like it was no effort at all, then slid back in to pull under the railway bridge. Along the Arbroath seafront, past the old nightclub, the still-open arcade, the football stadium and Tutties Neuk pub. Time was, the park would be jumping with families out enjoying the sun, but now it was filled with teen gangs looking to cause trouble. At least policing them was no longer her problem. 'You can see why Considine is so upset about losing this car.'

Karen laughed. 'After what he did to the last one?'

'Exactly. He's lucky he didn't have to pay for it himself.'

'You know he bought himself one?'

'A Subaru?'

'They're expensive too. Wonder where a single DC gets the money.'

'He lives in Forfar, Karen. It's hardly costing him a fortune there, is it?'

'True.'

Vicky shot over the empty roundabout, heading for the main road through Arbroath, not that anyone in their right mind would want to visit the decaying town centre.

'The air conditioning already needs fixing, I swear.' Karen reached over to push the dial up again, beads of sweat on her forehead. 'So sleazy MacDonald was charming the receptionist?'

'Said she used to run the desk at the serviced apartments he lived in.' Vicky pulled up at the roundabout, gripping the wheel tight. Traffic hurtled around it, mostly boy racer cars like nothing ever changed in this part of the world.

'Where he was living with his fiancée while he was sleazing on you?'

'Something like that.'

Euan MacDonald had a habit of getting under her skin. She was thankful for Rob. God knows she'd been a complete dick to him, but they were building a good life together. So why the hell couldn't she stop thinking of kissing MacDonald? As much of a prick as he was, it still got to her.

A souped-up Nissan whizzed past and she pulled away, the Subaru igniting its afterburners and rocketing round. She turned off and headed up the back road towards the abbey.

Old Arbroath was changing. The red stone abbey, a glorious ruin, was surrounded by equally red stone buildings, all dating to some golden time in the town's past. Higgledy-piggledy was the only way to describe it. Old houses of all shapes and sizes, some three-storey, but mostly two, with the ground floors now turned into offices and shops, with flats above.

Abbey Catering was a small single-storey building jutting out of the front of a tall old house, wedged between the local MSP's office and a hairdresser.

Vicky got out and for once was glad to be in Arbroath. The sea breeze cut through the heat. Felt almost blissful. Over the road, most of the ancient abbey was wrapped in scaffolding and there was a new visitor centre she couldn't remember from the last time she'd been there. Which must've been at school, forever ago. 'Come on.' She crossed the pavement and opened the door.

Abbey Catering was a hot mess inside. Thumping and clanging and clattering, all at the boiling point of water. Vicky had expected an office, but she got five people making small party food.

The nearest figure, a man with a mask covering his mouth, was squeezing a mixture into tiny quiche cases. Looked like fifty or sixty on that tray alone, and he switched to the second tray as another masked figure whisked the first one off to a giant oven near the back. The air wilted when the door opened, then the heat haze diminished as it was shut with a slam.

'Can I help you?' A woman stood by a side door, fists resting on her hips. Short and stocky, with greying blonde locks dangling loose from a hair net.

'Police, ma'am. DS Dodds.' Vicky held out her warrant card. 'Looking for the owner?'

'You've found her, hen.' She tilted her head back. 'Come on ben the hoose.' She swivelled round and walked through the side door.

Vicky followed, but gave Karen a frown. 'Ben the hoose?'

'You've never heard that?'

'Obviously not, otherwise I would've understood what she meant.'

'I forget you're a Teuchter.'

'Hardly.'

'It's common Scots for "come on through".'

'Right.' Vicky entered the office, a small room with three desks in a U-formation, each one stacked high with paper files.

The owner was standing by the middle one. Her chair was taken up with a microwave, buzzing as a plastic bowl spun around inside. 'Who you looking for?'

'That's the problem.' Vicky stayed near the door, letting Karen case the room. 'A body was found this morning at LA Golf.'

The owner was more interested in working the microwave. 'That so, aye?' She opened the microwave and took out a plastic tub then rested it on top of a stack of paperwork that looked like it was all going to topple over. 'Microwave is the best way to cook a haggis, trust me.'

'You mind paying attention to me?'

'Huh?' She looked up from dragging a fork through the mixture. 'Hen, I'm stressed out of my head here. I've got eighteen functions tonight alone. Had thirty-two last night. I'm the one who has to bear the brunt of everyone wanting to cash in on the Open in Car-snooty.'

Made Vicky think of her old man's comedy T-shirt. 'We're wondering if a member of your staff is the *murder victim*.' She stressed the words, but the owner put the haggis back in the microwave. 'You mind if I take a name?'

'Mine? Oh, I'm Abby Taggart.'

'Okay, Abby. Did you cater last night's event at LA Golf?'

'Aye. And you know how many casual staff I've had to take on?' Abby shook her head and sighed. 'Who you looking for?'

'Any young, blonde women?'

Abby laughed. 'That your kink, hen?'

Vicky got out her mobile and showed the photo to Abby. 'Do you recognise her?'

Abby took the phone and squinted at the screen. 'Christ, that's...' She swallowed hard. 'Are you sure you should be showing me this?'

Vicky nodded. 'We need to identify her. Urgently.'

'Okay, well it's hard to tell underneath all that blood. But I had three girls there last night look like her. All local lassies.'

VICKY KNOCKED on the door and stepped back to take another look. A big Victorian house with bay windows and a long front garden. 'Seems a bit weird to be working for a caterer.'

Opposite, Keptie Pond glowed green in the afternoon sunshine. One of the few parts of Arbroath that Vicky could ever remember and it was now filled with algae. She was sure her mother had mentioned something about it, but seeing it was different.

The door opened to a chain and a woman peered out. Young, blonde hair, bright green eyes. 'They're in Crete, so come back in a week.'

'Kelly Lawson?'

'Who's asking?'

'DS Dodds.' Vicky flashed her warrant card. 'Are you Kelly Lawson?'

'I am.' She was still alive, which was a start. She could definitely pass for the victim, though. 'Look, my folks are away on holiday, so I shouldn't be—'

'Were you at the function at LA Golf last night.'

'Aye? What of it?'

Vicky took out her phone and showed it to Kelly. 'She work with you?'

'Nope.'

'Do you recognise her at all?'

'Afraid not.'

'Not even from the party?'

'Sorry.'

KAREN KNOCKED on the door and stood back. 'So why aren't we doing the Carnoustie address first?'

'Because of the golf.' Vicky checked inside the house, a brutal seventies thing not unlike her own house, the one she'd fluked out by renting to someone for the golf but which was no longer her home. No signs of life, though. 'Be about an hour getting parked in Carnoustie, so it's smarter to do this one, right?'

'Suppose.' Karen knocked again. 'Still, Ramsay Street.'

Just at the start of Monifieth, a side road that Vicky must've passed hundreds of times in her life and yet this was the first time she'd driven down it. 'When me and Andrew were kids, we used to sing the *Neighbours* theme tune when Dad drove past here. And now Bella and Jamie have started doing it.'

'Is that still going?'

'Rob still watches it. Every day.'

'Christ.' Karen thumped the door. 'No answer. Shall we go to the Carnoustie one?'

'I want to eliminate this first.' Vicky took another look inside. The house was one room deep and she could see movement out the back. And bingo — she could smell a barbecue. 'Come on.' She walked over to the side gate. 'Hello?'

Nothing.

She released the catch and walked along the slabs, the smell of roasting meat getting stronger with each step. 'Hello?'

A tall woman stood facing them, her blonde hair in pigtails and wearing a Baby Spice dress, all short and pink. She was snogging a shorter man, hands down his pants. Her eyes widened and she pushed away from her lover, and stormed across the grass to them. 'What the fuck!?'

'Police.'

But she swiped Vicky's warrant card away, sending it flying across the grass. 'What the fuck!?'

'Sayrah Douglas?'

'Fuck off!'

Her lover sneaked in alongside her. 'Sayr, these guys are cops.'

'I don't fucking care!' She stomped over to the barbecue.

He smiled at them, his wide face stretching out his thin beard lining his jaw. 'What's going on?'

Vicky crouched down to collect her warrant card. 'Looking for Sayrah Douglas. That her?'

'That's her.'

Vicky walked over to the barbecue and showed the crime scene photo. 'You recognise her?'

Sayrah snatched the phone. She looked like she was going to smash it on the patio or hurl it on the barbecue. But she passed it back. 'No.'

'You don't work with her?'

'I've only just started with the agency, sorry.'

'You did work at LA Golf last night, though?'

'Yeah, but so many faces. That was my first gig, and Abby stuck me in the back room.' She checked her watch. 'I'm supposed to be working a party at the DCA tonight and I'm back at Tesco tomorrow, so I need to get on.'

Her boyfriend joined them. He took a look at the photo and flinched. 'Christ. What happened to her?'

'She was murdered.'

'Bloody hell.' He frowned at Sayrah. 'This who Kirsty was talking about?'

'Kirsty?'

Vicky frowned at him. 'Do you work for Abbey Catering too?'

'I'm a sommelier, yeah.' There was a nice-looking bottle of Gewürztraminer on the table. Someone knew what they were doing with white wines, even in Monifieth. 'I don't recognise her, but did she have a tattoo here.' He rubbed at his left bicep. 'Like a puffin or something?'

Vicky got a flash of the image on the victim's arm. 'Go on.'

'Well, it was pretty distinctive. And Kirsty Henderson was talking to us about it, said she wanted to get one, but then she's an ink fiend. Swear she came out of the womb all sleeved up.'

Vicky gave him a smile. 'Do you know if this Kirsty Henderson knew her?'

'Think so. I mean, this woman was on some guy's arm. Kirsty said she thought she was like an escort. Recognised her from some previous gigs.'

5

Queen Street in Carnoustie was mobbed and Vicky had to double park just to get anywhere half a mile from the address. The street was at a good thirty-degree angle so she checked the handbrake was on twice before she got out and walked over to the flat.

Karen got there first and pressed the buzzer. 'See the Gewürz-traminer on the table?'

Vicky checked her phone. Nothing from Forrester or MacDonald. 'I did.'

'My Colin found out Lidl had their one in. Bought six cases of it. Four quid a bottle.'

'Is it any good?'

'Remember last Saturday, the state him and Robert got into?'

'Rob. And yes, I do. Christ.' Vicky pocketed her phone. 'So, if she's a prostitute?'

'That's a whole heap of shit, isn't it?'

'Damn right.' Vicky looked down the hill towards the beach, over the silver-grey railway bridge, a massive horde of people charging along the road towards the train station. The distant rattle of the course announcer was almost lost to the crowd noise, half roaring, half gasping.

Someone jostled her from behind. 'Sorry!' A sunburnt golfer in plus fours and a hideous jumper, walking off up the hill.

Vicky sighed. 'Bloody golf fans.'

'I don't get it.' Karen watched the guy walk up the steep street. 'So how does her being a prostitute agree with that gleaming rock on her finger?'

'Maybe it's just for show.'

'What, someone didn't put a ring on it?'

'Indeed. Wouldn't be the first woman to pretend to be engaged just to avoid wee wankers trying to chat her up.'

The door clicked open. A tall man stood there in shorts and T-shirt, clutching a pint can of Stella. His short hair was still curling like crazy, and long sideburns ran down to his jawline. 'What's up?'

'Police.' Vicky showed her warrant card. 'Looking for a Kirsty Henderson.'

'She's not in.' He slurped from his can. 'You mind if I get back to the golf?'

'She does live here?'

'Aye, aye.'

'You her flatmate?'

'Just feels like it.' He laughed, then let out a burp. 'I'm her boyfriend. And I haven't seen her today.'

Vicky felt a sting in the back of her neck. 'When did you last hear from her?'

He burped into his fist, but the stale beer spread across to her anyway. 'I'm working nights at the Ashworth's in Arbroath, just got back and I'm doing bugger all other than watching the golf.'

'So when did you last see her?'

'Yesterday.'

'Any idea where she might be?'

～

VICKY STOPPED OUTSIDE THE PUB. The 19th Hole, far from Carnoustie's best, but not its worst. 'I had my first drink in there.'

Karen smirked. 'When you were ten?'

'Very funny.'

The door opened and a young drunk in a turquoise tracksuit stumbled out, his skinhead glowing red from sunburn. He shielded his eyes from the glare. 'Christ on a bike.' He staggered off along Kinloch Street, probably in completely the wrong direction, though he looked like he was taking about three at the same time.

Vicky walked over to the door and the racket was almost deafening. No bouncers, though, so she pushed through into the bar. The place hadn't changed in twenty-odd years, and it was absolutely jumping. Not just the golf crowd, but the usual Sunday afternoon boozers sensing an opportunity for a party. The golf played on the big screens in three of the corners, but barely anyone was paying attention.

'Coming through.' Vicky weaved her way through the crowd towards the bar. Like the rest of the place, it hadn't changed, still serving the same old tired selection of beer and spirits. Probably sold wine by the box. Even had those bags of peanuts on the wall that gradually revealed a topless woman. Keep it classy, Carnoustie.

And the barman looked as worn out as his stock. Greasy hair slicked back, his pale pink polo shirt plastered to his back, his wiry back hair poking out of the collar and giving that most sexy of looks. 'Vicks?'

She frowned at him and had to wipe off about thirty years of bar meals and alcoholism to trigger his name. 'Craig?'

'Glad you recognise me. You're looking gorgeous as ever.' He gave her the old up and down, lingering on her chest, then smiled wide. 'That boy caught up with you?'

'What boy?'

'Lad in here asking for you.'

And the note burnt heavy in her pocket. 'No, I'm looking for Kirsty Henderson.'

'And here I was thinking you were wanting to speak to me.'

'Have you seen her?'

He pointed across the bar to a group of women chatting up

some golf fans, Americans judging by their apparel. High-end Nike stuff and the shiny white teeth that North Americans thought were healthy but were mostly just fake.

And it didn't take Sherlock Holmes to deduce which one was Kirsty Henderson. The lone blonde in a crowd of brunettes and redheads, sitting next to a real quarterback type. Handsome guy with a loud voice that carried, the kind of generic American accent you heard all the time on TV. 'I mean, you try hunting a guy with a red hat across three states.'

Kirsty leaned her head back and roared with laughter, though Vicky didn't see any humour in it. Kirsty brushed fingers through her hair, and even the back of her hand was covered in tattoos. Seemed to run all the way up her arm. And Vicky realised she was on the other side of a generation gap.

'Well, she's smashed but alive.' Karen charged over, nudging a drinker so that about half of his pint spilled onto the floor.

'Fuck sake.' His local accent warped the words into a violent weapon. 'You going to replace that?'

Karen showed her warrant card. 'Police, sir.'

'Aye, so am I. Just cos I'm off duty and you're not doesn't mean you can barge through like that. And I'm a sergeant so you can take your Brains Department pal here and buy me a pint of Export, thanks.'

Karen just handed him a fiver. 'Here you go.'

With a shake of the head, he buggered off to the bar. Kind of place where five quid bought two pints. In 2018. And he still had most of that one left.

'Brains department indeed.' Karen took it easier as he barged through the rest of them. 'Kirsty Henderson?'

Fingers wrapped round a glass filled with a dark liquid, she scowled at them. 'You the cops?' She was way past smashed, on the expressway to banjaxed.

Vicky glanced at Karen and caught her frown. 'How did you know that?'

'Kier texted us.' She got to her feet, then drunkenly tumbled into the quarterback's lap. 'Sorry!' She pushed herself up to standing, and rested against the pillar, looking at them with pissed eyes. 'What do you want?'

Vicky showed her phone. 'Recognise this woman?'

'Nope.'

Vicky felt a surge of disappointment in her guts. 'You worked at the party last night, right?'

'I did.' She coughed like she was going to be sick. 'Stuck-up place, full of wankers.'

'Someone told us you recognised her.'

'Who told you?'

'Sayrah Douglas?'

'Who?' Clicking her fingers like it could help her remember, but it meant she wasn't propped up, then a final sharp click. 'That new girl, shagging that hot sommelier. Right. Ken who you mean now.'

Vicky took her arm and steadied her. 'Did she work for Abbey Catering?'

'No. This lassie, she's a hoor.'

'A prostitute.'

'What I said.' She burped, but didn't follow it up with any second hand alcohol, at least not yet. 'I've seen her on the arms of a lot of men at events. People who pay for the fantasy of a beautiful woman like me giving them the time of day.'

'You see her often?'

'Two or three times, but not for at least a couple of years until last night.'

'She with anyone?'

'Some bloke. Don't know him. She had an engagement ring on, though. Maybe she's not on the game any more.'

'You speak to her?'

'Once, in the ladies. She asked me for a tampon. I gave her one. That's it.'

'And you don't know her name?'

'Correct.'

'Okay, thanks for your time.' Vicky took her phone back and

bumped through the crowd. She gave the barman a thumbs up as she passed through the entrance.

Best way to think of him. The barman. Don't humanise him with a name.

Down Kinloch Street, the drunk from earlier was sitting on a wall, leaning back and singing, tears streaming down his cheeks. 'Who's that lying over there?'

Vicky's phone throbbed. She saw a missed call from Forrester, alongside a text — "Get back to the crime scene."

~

VICKY POWERED ACROSS THE GRASS, arms folded, scanning the crowd for Forrester.

Karen caught up with her. 'Vicky, was that an ex or something?'

Vicky took one look at her and saw that she didn't have much of a choice, so she stopped and let out her breath. 'Craig Norrie. My first boyfriend, back at high school. Total dickhead.'

'Riiiight.' Karen was laughing through her long exhalation. 'What the hell did you see in him?'

'My taste in boys was as bad as my taste in men.'

'Your love—'

'Doddsy!' Forrester was charging towards them. Hard to miss his long arms and legs, even in a crime scene suit. He had tugged his mask aside and let his white hair out, long and impeccably styled, if you happened to live in the mid-eighties. His face was lobster pink and looked like he'd been held headfirst in a pan of boiling water for a few minutes.

Karen frowned at him. 'You okay, sir?'

'No, I'm bloody not.' Forrester touched his face and grimaced. 'Hurts like buggery.'

'How do you know what buggery hurts like?'

Forrester scowled at her. 'Sure you haven't got somewhere to be?'

'Right, sir.' Karen took the Subaru's keys from out of Vicky's hands. 'I'll see if anyone at the hotel knows anything about that prostitute.' She scuttled off towards the car park.

Vicky fixed Forrester with a hard stare. 'I was looking for you earlier.'

'Right, well, I was at the golf. Followed Casey and Stenson first thing, then I was going to follow Noren and Simpson because nobody's getting near Tiger and Molinari, but then I got this call, didn't I, and I tell you, trying to get away from the tenth hole when the crowd following Tiger bloody Woods is coming towards you... Waste of money and the lad didn't exactly have fun.' Forrester patted his head. 'You got any suntan lotion?'

'You look like you're way past that.'

'Lost my hat, didn't I?'

'I've got some stuff in the car. It might help.'

But Forrester didn't seem to be in a hurry to get any. 'So, you think this lassie was on the game?'

'Not in those terms, no. One of the caterers thinks our victim might have been an escort.'

'Might have been?' Forrester snorted. 'Okay, so I take it—'

'Jenny's running her prints now. We'll see if she's been on our radar before.'

'Well, good effort.' Forrester's smile looked like it hurt, but he was still nowhere near the worst of his sunburn. 'Mac's up at the hotel. Sounds like he's getting hee haw from them.'

'If there's anyone who knows about high-class escorts, it's him.'

'You've really got it in for that boy, haven't you?' Forrester smirked at her. 'I know what you think you're getting at, but he was seconded to the Met's Trafficking and Prostitution Unit for six months a few years back.'

'Never knew that.'

'No, he's got hidden depths. Anything to suggest that the victim was working at this event last night?'

'Karen's digging into that too.'

'Fine. What's your take on the boy running the place? Lamont, is it?'

'He's an annoying dick.'

'Great, another one. Thanks for the insight.'

Vicky shrugged it off. 'Look, we've got an unknown victim. We need to ID her, then we'll have stuff to work on.'

'Speaking of which, what's going on with Jenny Morgan?'

'Why?'

'Well, it's just... I don't know. Look, she's a mate of yours, but she's being a right arsehole to me.'

'I'll speak to her, then. Any idea where she is?'

Forrester pointed down to the crime scene, still dotted with blue-suited officers working away. At least they'd erected a tent over the bunker. On the far side, the sun caught a concrete path leading down to the beach, halfway between them and the lighthouse. 'She was going to check out the launch for Lamont's yacht.' He chuckled. 'But it's more of a dinghy. Not the first rich man to overstate the size of his equipment.'

~

THE LAUNCH LOOKED ALMOST white in the blinding glare. No sign of Jenny Morgan or of anyone on her team.

Forrester was lurking a few metres away, talking into his phone. Sounded like he was on with DCI Raven, his boss. The fact that he wouldn't make eye contact with Vicky clinched it for her. And when Raven got his claws in, it was usually only a matter of time before Forrester was turned up to eleven and making Vicky's life a misery.

Vicky hopped up onto the top of the launch and scanned around.

A speedboat was moored at the jetty and Lamont's boat sat out in the bay. As little as Vicky knew about boats, it was pretty impressive. Two storeys tall and seemed plenty big enough, at least to get all the way to Greece in one go. Assuming you could get to Greece from Scotland. But it looked all locked up. And empty.

Whether anyone had been there last night was another matter.

Maybe Lamont had been entertaining on board? Maybe he'd hired their mysterious escort?

Wait, what was that? At the far end of the launch, just by the speedboat was a dark mark.

Vicky walked off towards it. Not just one, but a few of them, dots connected to wider triangles. Christ, it was a footprint, red and bloody, just by the waterline. And the victim wore heels; they'd make that pattern.

Pretty much at high tide just now, so anything else must've been washed away.

But there were dots of blood either side, likely from their victim. And the angle... It was pointing towards the woods they had to pass through to get here from the bunker.

Did the victim run away from something?

Forrester was facing away from Vicky, ignoring anything but his phone call.

Vicky got out her phone and called Jenny Morgan.

'What's up?'

'Where are you?'

'What have I done now?'

'Have your guys been over the launch?'

'The what?'

'Where the speedboat is.'

'Right, not yet. Why?'

'I've got a bloody footprint here.' Vicky stared at it. The waves were in danger of washing it away. But she could trace the line of travel, and spotted where the victim might've fled from. 'Have you got anyone at the lighthouse?'

'Not yet.'

'Hurry, okay?' She killed the call and waved at a nearby uniform as he turned back around. 'Pot Noodle! Come here.'

The big lump trudged towards her, his swinging arms almost touching the scrub at the edge of the beach. 'What's up, Doddsy?'

'Stay with this footprint.'

'Rightio.' He hopped down onto the sand and lumbered towards her.

Vicky sprinted off in the direction of the lighthouse, her shoes slapping off the damp sand, and made her way to the rocks looming out of the beach. At high tide, the concrete path was inundated. She splashed across towards the bedrock the lighthouse rested on. The lighthouse blocked out the sun, but the doors were hanging open. And bloody footprints led out of the door, the same pattern as on the launch, coming from upstairs.

She got out her mobile and called Jenny. 'Hey, need you to get someone out by the lighthouse. Got a trail of—'

Something smashed, sounded like it came from inside. Sounded like glass, maybe.

'Just get here.' Vicky pocketed her phone. Maybe this wasn't a crime scene to be investigated, but an active attack?

She didn't have a choice, did she?

Vicky climbed the steps, covered in moss and clearly old. The place was dark and cold, and was humming with electricity. The blood trail led her up to the top. Something white glowed in the half darkness of the stairwell. An empty bottle. Bleach judging by the smell. And five litres judging by the label.

Another doorway lay beyond, the humming louder now. Must be where the light shone from. A tall window looked back towards East Haven and Carnoustie behind. The stink of bleach was even worse.

A bottle of champagne lay on the sill, with two smashed flutes on the floor next to it.

No doubt the sound that had lured her up here. No sign of anybody causing it, though, just a gentle breeze coming in through the window. Some seabirds sat on the ledge. A more likely explanation.

Vicky stepped in onto rough floorboards. The room was wide and tall, half of it blocked out by machinery and the long bell of the light. She rounded it slowly.

A man lay on the floor, naked except for a pair of jockey shorts. Relaxed muscle and slim, but his face made him seem mid-forties. A knife was plunged into his heart and he stared up at her with dead eyes, his eyelids missing.

6

Vicky held her phone close to her skull, fighting against her teeth chattering. 'Jenny, I don't care. Just send them over now. I need to lock this place down.' She killed the call and stood there, facing towards the doorway and the steps back down.

Her whole body was shaking from the shock of seeing yet another murder victim. She'd been a cop not far off fifteen years and she'd lost track of the number of times she'd discovered a corpse.

She stared at the victim again. The air escaped her lungs like she'd been punched.

This was something else entirely. Brutal, aggressive. And entirely different from a stabbing outside a pub or an escalated domestic.

A man in his forties, older than her, but not too much. Silver hair, but he looked fit and healthy. No wedding ring. And mostly naked, just a pair of hip-hop star jockey shorts hiding his modesty, the rest of his clothes piled up in the corner. He looked about the same age as Rob. Christ.

Footsteps came from the stairwell, the echoes shortening with each one. 'Doddsy?' Forrester appeared in the doorway, eyes wide, his sunburn seeming to glow in the low light. 'You okay?'

Vicky felt a shiver crawl up her arms. She unpicked her path back to the doorway. 'I just... I just found him.'

Forrester stood there, breathing slowly and squinting in the light as he examined the body from a distance. His eyes grew wider and the blood drained from his face. 'Oh shite.'

'What is it?'

He swallowed hard.

More footsteps came from the stairwell.

Vicky pulled Forrester out of the way. 'David, what's up?'

Forrester waved a hand over at the corpse. 'The eyelids.' His own flickered. He pushed away, skittering down the staircase outside the room.

Vicky made to move but Jenny Morgan appeared in the doorway, flanked by Arbuthnott, crime scene suits hanging over casual clothes, like they were going for a boozy brunch and not on duty at a crime scene.

'Oh here we go again.' Jenny stepped away.

Arbuthnott finished zipping up her suit, secured her mask and goggles, then made her way carefully across the floorboards, retracing Vicky's steps. She knelt alongside the victim and started probing the corpse with her blue-gloved fingers.

Vicky looked over at her. 'You just happened to be here?'

Arbuthnott continued working away at the body, pressing and prodding. Her medical bag tipped over next to her. 'We're taking the other victim up to Dundee for the autopsy. I wanted to check a few things out personally while it was still in situ.'

'I'll leave you to it.' Vicky set off down the stairs, away from another murder victim, and out into the warm air. Two SOCOs were approaching, suited and booted. Vicky stepped away out of their path and spotted Forrester.

He was sitting on the side of the concrete bridge, kneading his forehead.

Vicky had no idea what was going on. She'd never seen him like this, it was like Bella in the middle of one of her tantrums.

Still, she had more options than to just let it play out. She squatted next to him. 'Are you okay?'

He locked eyes with her. The wildness of his pupils, his stray hair and the sunburn made him look like he'd finally lost it. 'I'm hoping this is a suicide pact.'

'You don't run away from a suicide pact.'

'Sometimes you do. Watching someone die in front of you, you might panic and decide it's not for you and—'

'David, what the fuck is going on—'

'It's got to be a suicide. Got to be.'

'You don't cut your eyelids off when you kill yourself.' Vicky grabbed his shoulders and shook him gently. 'Look, whatever's going on here, it'll help if you tell me what's happening inside your skull.'

His jaw kept pulsing. 'If that girl was on the game, maybe she took the boy up here for a bit of action.'

Footsteps clattered from the lighthouse. Jenny, frowning at Vicky. 'Has he stopped taking his meds or something?'

'No idea.' Vicky tilted her head, trying to get him to focus on her. 'Earth to Forrester. Earth to Forrester.'

He shook her free, his wild attention swerving over to Jenny. 'The female victim. Was she attacked up there?'

'I don't know, David. I'll need to check.'

'But her footsteps led from inside the lighthouse, right?'

'That's how Vicky found her, yes. But I still need to check.'

Forrester sighed. 'So someone stabbed her in the throat in there, but she survived and ran off, only to die in that bunker.' His nostrils flared. 'Did her killer follow her?'

'I don't know.' Jenny was tapping away at her smartphone. 'The tide swept away most of the bloody footsteps. There are still some on the steps here.'

Forrester stared up at the lighthouse again, shaking his head.

Vicky led him away from the pool of sick at his feet, catching her nostrils worse than the rancid bleach upstairs. 'David, I need you to talk to me, okay?'

Footsteps descending towards them. Arbuthnott, tearing off

her gloves. 'Well.'

Forrester tried to get past Vicky but she blocked him off. 'Tell me it was suicide.'

'No, this is murder.' She stepped over the walkway to them, easing the crime scene suit off. 'Okay, the female victim died of blood loss relating to a knife wound to the throat.'

Forrester nodded to her. 'The woman didn't die of the same means, did she? This boy was stabbed but she bled out, right?'

'You're several steps ahead of me.' Arbuthnott looked over to them. 'Well, it initially appears to be the case, yes, but...'

Vicky grabbed his arm and pulled him back. 'What's going on here?'

But Forrester only had eyes for Arbuthnott, staring at her like a gambler whose desperate last tenner on a five hundred to one bet hadn't come in like he needed it to. 'Same killer?'

'Way too early to tell.' Arbuthnott looked down at them. 'But I'd say that they've both died from knife wounds. I'll check whether it's the same weapon or not. I'll need the knife itself to be absolutely sure. The eyelids, though...'

Forrester stared at the wall like he was going to start kicking and not stop until one of them was a pile of rubble.

Arbuthnott got out a tablet showing a photo of the female victim and waved a hand across the face. 'Her eyelid was partly cut too. I'm assuming that means whoever did this was interrupted when he attacked her, and she got away with a wound which later proved to be fatal.'

Forrester stared into the middle distance, shaking his head.

'Come on, sir.' Vicky eased him away, letting Arbuthnott go with a polite nod and a smile. She kept her grip on Forrester's arm, only releasing it when they were on the sand. 'David, what the hell is going on?'

'I recognise the MO.' Forrester blew air up his face. 'This is the exact same as an old case I worked in the nineties.'

'The lighthouse?'

'No, the eyelids. And stabbing the victims through the heart.' He made eye contact with her. 'Your dad was the DI on it.'

7

Vicky pressed the doorbell and waited there like it was just another home connected to just another case. But it was her parents' house, the place where she'd grown from baby Victoria to school as Vicks and finally leaving for university as Vicky, only to return and work as a cop just down the road.

The living room blinds were shut. From the death metal roaring out, it sounded like Andrew was home, if nothing else. God knows what else he'd be up to in his bedroom.

She looked back along Bruce Drive to the entrance from North Burnside Street, nowhere near the burn. And no sign of Forrester. This house was on a loop—odd numbers on the outside, evens on the inside—and up ahead, past the entrance, was a small cul de sac, the houses set that bit further back. In the distance, a Nissan bumped up and over into a drive, then an old couple got out, dressed like they were at a rave in Greece in the early nineties, but their arguing words carrying along on the late-afternoon breeze.

'Vicky?' Her dad stood in the doorway, ruddy-faced and frowning. 'Come on in.' And he was gone.

Still no sign of Forrester, so she took a deep breath and

followed her dad inside. 'Thought you'd still be at ours but Robert said you left a while ago?'

'Just got back now, aye.' Dad collapsed into his recliner and put his feet up on the leather footstool, then fixed her with a harsh look. 'Bad form to duck out of a barbecue like that.'

'It's the job, Dad. Sure you understand.' Vicky perched on the left side of Mum's sofa, but she couldn't get comfortable. Never could. 'Can you turn that off?'

'Last round.' Dad took a sip of beer from a knobbly pint glass as he stared at the golf. 'Got fifty quid on McIlroy.'

'I thought you'd stopped gambling.'

'Aye, well, it's a special occasion.' He wiped beer from his lips. 'Why are you here?'

'Well, I'm not here to speak to my father, but to DI George Dodds.'

'Aye, latterly Police Sergeant George Dodds.' He looked round at her, his nostrils twitching. 'What do you want to speak to that clown about?'

A car door slammed out on the street.

Vicky stood up and looked out. 'There's Forrester.'

Dad was on his feet now. 'What's Dongle doing here?'

'Dongle?'

'Long story.' Dad slipped out into the hallway just as the bell rang. 'I'm getting it!'

But Mum still came through. She frowned at the door then at her daughter. 'Victoria, what are you doing here?'

'Hi, Mum, nice to see you too.'

'Can I get you a cup of tea?'

'I'm fine.'

A bellow of laughter from the door and Forrester sauntered inside like they were heading down to the snooker hall. 'Hiya, Cathy. You're looking well.'

'And you're looking... David, I've got some aftersun, if you want.'

'That'd be smashing.'

'How about a cup of tea?'

'Only if it's no hassle.'

'Never is. Kettle's just boiled.'

'Well, in that case, milk and no sugar, thanks. I'm sweet enough.'

Mum smiled. 'Hear that line enough from George.' And she slipped off.

But Dad was clearly smelling a rat. He stood by the stereo, a tower of vintage hi-fi equipment topped off by a turntable, his eyes narrowed. 'What's going on?'

'This.' Vicky got out her phone and held out the photo of the male victim, his lidless eyes staring out of the screen.

Dad reached for his reading glasses on the coffee table and put them on his nose, screwing up his face to examine the image. Then his mouth hung open. 'What the hell is this?'

'Hoping you could tell me.'

Dad took a look at his daughter, then at Forrester, then set off into the hall. 'Better do this through here.' He led the way into Vicky's old bedroom, opposite the living room door, the perfect location to hear his late-night TV and her mid-evening music. It was now a small office, with a laptop computer resting on an IKEA desk and a pair of filing cabinets. The light-blue Anaglypta paint that used to look like water damage had been replaced with patterned wallpaper, though the colours weren't that different. And everything was beige, just like the entire house. 'Have a seat.'

Vicky took the futon, rock hard and cold despite the house's sweltering temperature. Felt like she was getting piles from it already. 'So, I take it that photo rings a few bells?'

Dad slumped in front of his computer and rubbed at his forehead.

'Dad, I need to know about it.'

He took a sip of beer and set it aside. 'I hoped I'd never have to talk about it again, but here we go.'

Vicky looked at Forrester, standing by the door, concern etched on his face. 'Why?'

'Because it was the case that broke me.' Dad reached into the bottom drawer and pulled out a bottle of single malt. He held it up and it was the one Vicky had given him for Christmas. Looked like barely a spit left. 'David?'

'Driving, George.'

'Suit yourself.' He poured out a measure into a glass. 'Vicky?'

'I hate the stuff. Now, this case?'

Dad took a sip of whisky and grimaced. 'Ah, that's the good stuff. Slainte.' He held up the glass. 'They called the killer Atreus.'

'Latin?'

'Greek. Some ancient king or something.' Dad sank his beer in one long glug and clattered the glass down on the desk. 'Atreus was a serial killer who killed all across Britain. Five pairs of bodies over five years from 1989 to 1992, all with their eyelids cut off. Just like in that.' He waved at Vicky's phone, his nervous eyes looking at it like the killer could jump out and attack her. 'The eyelids... Christ.'

'Why would someone do that?'

Dad exchanged a look with Forrester, and let out a laugh. '*Someone* genuinely thought that the killer might be killing vampires, stake through the heart and all that shite.'

'Fair cop.' Forrester shook his head with a hefty sigh. 'Cutting the eyelids meant they couldn't even shut their eyes so the sun could get them or something. I was reading a lot of Anne Rice and Stephen King at the time. And I didn't think it was actually a vampire, just that someone thought they were killing them. This was around the time *Silence of the Lambs* came out, another obsession of mine. I kept thinking whoever was doing this was one of those loony types who saw visions, and he genuinely thought he was killing vampires.' He drifted off with a final shrug.

'So you worked this case too?'

'Aye, but I was a daft wee laddie in uniform, just walking the beat in Dundee city centre until I got sucked into this case. Tayside Police threw as many bodies as they could at it, didn't want the West Midlands shower taking it away.'

'Why them?'

'First victim was in Birmingham, hence those buggers taking precedence. In the end, we all got co-opted on to their case. The others were in Newcastle, Inverness and Carlisle. We found a body in the Ferry in late '92.'

'A serial killer in *Broughty Ferry*?'

Dad looked round at her, his forehead creased. 'You don't remember this, Vicky?'

'I mean vaguely. Mum banned me and Andrew from going up to Dundee for a bit. Had us on a curfew too. And I remember something about a case in the Ferry, but I just didn't connect the two.'

'Well, there you go.' Dad reached over and took her phone. He stared deep into it. 'We had this fancy criminal psychologist from down south. Wild red hair and full of herself. Reckoned the eyelids were removed so the victims would have to watch Atreus as he stabbed them in the heart.'

'Why?'

'Wish I knew. She had a few theories, but they all seemed crap.'

Vicky took her phone back and flicked through the photos until she found the wide shot of the female victim.

Dad's eyes bulged. 'Christ.' He sighed at Forrester. 'David, you should've told me you had two victims.'

Forrester wouldn't make eye contact with Vicky. 'I'm still not convinced by this.'

'And yet you're here?' Dad settled back in his chair and sipped the foam from the bottom of his beer. 'Victoria, Atreus murdered pairs of men and women, where at least one had been married. Our profiler thought it was because they were adulterous.'

Forrester snatched the phone out of Dad's hand and glowered at the screen as he flicked through. 'The press called him Atreus in honour of the figure in Greek mythology who killed his brother and wife after catching them at it.' He passed her phone back. 'Wouldn't be that intellectual these days, would it? Be some pun based on *Love Island* or something.'

Dad sucked in a deep breath. 'My boss at the time, DCI Syd Ramsay, he wanted to investigate it as a separate case, but I insisted it was connected to the other Atreus murders.'

Forrester smiled at Dad, like he was trying to connect with him. 'Vicky, your old man proved that it was connected. He forced the pathologist to work it that little bit harder, and Bob's your uncle, he found a little nick in the cut. Went back through the previous victims and found the blade matched. Exact same knife used on all of them.'

Dad stood up and hefted his beer glass. 'I'll check on the tea.'

Vicky made to go after him.

But Forrester grabbed her arm, his wild eyes telling her to let him go.

So she sat back down on the futon and folded her arms.

'Your old man found a knife at a crime scene. We were going to run prints. Somehow it went missing between his car and the lab.'

'Seriously?'

'Aye. Your dad got suspended for it.'

'Oh, Jesus. I remember him being off work. Mum told me it was because he was ill.'

'Not exactly untrue. Your father wasn't a well man at the time. Signed off on stress, officially, but it was a suspension.' Forrester sighed. 'He was Acting DI, which as you know means he was just a DS getting taken for a ride. Easy for them to shove him sideways. Spent the last couple of years as a beat sergeant in Forfar.'

'I remember. And I've heard stories, but I thought it was voluntary.'

'Hardly. He was no spring chicken, but *Forfar*. He played it smart, though. Got his pension and got the fuck out of Dodge. And you know the rest. Private security gigs to pay off this place.'

'I just remember him being stressed as hell at the time. I didn't know that was why.'

'Stressful time for the lot of us.' Forrester ran his hand through his hair. 'All the people who screwed your dad over are now dead, or as good as.'

Vicky sat back, trying to process it. But she got nothing, other than a horrible feeling deep in her gut. All that suffering he'd gone through and she hadn't known.

Dad stepped into the room, carrying a teacup and plate. He passed the tea to Forrester and gave the plate to Vicky.

A slice of cake. And she was starving. Mum's All-Bran loaf scraped with margarine, exactly what she needed. 'What happened with the knife, Dad?'

He looked over at her, frowning, then away with a sigh. 'I wish I knew. Swear I took it into the lab and handed it over.'

'In Bell Street?'

'Same place you work now.' Dad stood there, hands in pockets, shaking his head. 'Can I see the photo again?'

Vicky passed it over.

He focused on the image and passed it back, but his gaze was on Forrester. 'David, I can't see much on that phone screen. What's your take?'

'It looks exactly the same to me. Same cut marks.'

'What if he's back?'

'George...' Forrester stood up and rested his tea on the desk. 'George, I know you think you can redeem yourself here, but the original killer *can't* be back. Because he died a long time ago.'

8

Vicky's dad shut his eyes and took a deep breath. 'I'll just get my tea.' He left the room again, but Vicky recognised the bathroom door opening. She knew every creak in this house off by heart.

And she knew her old man. He was in there, sitting on the toilet in a fit of rage. And the last thing he'd want was for her to crowd him. But she needed his help and insight.

And all this time, that case had been eating at him. She could remember him as a detective, when she was maybe ten? He was always home late, always away early. Then after that, he was much more present in their lives. And all because he'd been sidelined for a fuck-up.

But the killer couldn't be back if he was dead. Meaning they'd either caught the wrong guy, or someone was copying him.

She sat next to Forrester on the futon. 'Who was he?'

Forrester finished his tea and set the mug down on the floor at his feet. 'Guy called Jim Sanderson from Broughty Ferry. Died before the trial.'

'Anything suspicious about it?'

'Nope, suicide.'

'Did he live near those victims?'

'Aye, but at the other end of the town, though. The bodies were in those posh houses in West Ferry, but he lived in Barnhill. Practically *Monifieth.*'

'If he was from the Ferry, did he know the victims?'

'Alec Mitchell and Susan Adamson.' Forrester sniffed. 'They worked together and were having an affair. We've got copious evidence of it. This was before texts and stuff, but there were a lot of clandestine phone calls between their homes. And Susan Adamson was the sentimental type who kept all her love letters. She was a lot younger than him, just turned seventeen, whereas Mitchell was mid-fifties. Real sugar daddy type.'

'How did Sanderson know?'

'Knew them from church. They attended the same one, but we didn't find any proof that they knew each other.'

'But all the other victims were from other locations. Birmingham and Newcastle and so on?'

'Right, but Sanderson worked for Kjaer Oil. Their head office was in Aberdeen, but he roved around the country training people in various places. Refineries and distribution centres.'

'Some serial killers escalate up to something close to home, don't they?'

'So that course in London wasn't a complete waste of money?'

'I did get something out of it, but the guy taking it was a gloomy sod.' She frowned, some memory flickering in her head. 'He'd worked in Florida with the FBI and they took down a serial killer who had a similar MO to Ed Kemper. The Co-ed Killer.'

'California, right?'

'Correct. This guy taking the course actually interviewed Kemper, like in that show on Netflix.'

'Kemper's still alive? Christ.'

'But he was really interested in the escalation path. Kemper killed five college students and one high school student before killing his mother and her friend. And that was it, all done. He just gave himself up, mainly to talk. He never stopped, just kept blabbing.'

'Sanderson didn't speak to us, though. Denied it all.'

'Did you get the impression that these were practice kills as he escalated to killing on his home turf?'

Forrester exhaled slowly. 'Maybe.'

'What was his mission, though? Mother? Father?'

'We don't know. The profiler lassie had theories, but it all came down to adultery.'

'Adultery?'

'We hadn't caught him because of...' Forrester waved a hand at the door. 'That nonsense. And he was all over the country on business where he trained the managers on how to use this new piece of software. They had offices everywhere, but the kicker was in Invergordon, just north of Inverness. They had a few rigs in the Cromarty Firth. Went out for a beer with the lads a few times. One of them talked about shagging around with a lassie there. Next thing we know, they're both dead in a hotel, eyelids cut off, stabbed through the heart.'

'That's brutal.' And just like the victim inside the lighthouse. 'How did he... I mean, cutting their eyelids off?'

'Two knives. One for slotting into the heart. The other was like a scalpel, fine precise work around the eyelids.'

'I meant why?'

'Oh, right. Well, we don't know. A few ideas, but he never confessed. He was in serious denial.'

Vicky had seen that a ton of times. The most brutal killers, caught red-handed, and they didn't even show recognition that they'd done it, let alone remorse. 'But Dad blames himself because he could've caught him earlier?'

'You know your old boy too well, Doddsy. But it wasn't just him, the powers-that-be blamed him for it, screwed him over and sent him to Forfar.'

'Is it possible you caught the wrong guy?'

Forrester stared hard at her. 'I know what you're doing here.' He sighed. 'I mean, it's physically possible, but we nailed him down.'

'When did he die?'

Forrester winced. 'On remand.'

'So you didn't get a conviction?'

'Nope. We were thinking ten life sentences, no parole.'

'But he died.'

'Right.'

Vicky held up her phone. 'So, this is a copycat.'

'That's the logical conclusion. Some sick bastard using the same MO as the Atreus killings.'

'Any books publish—'

'Tons. At least ten I've read. Another twenty I haven't.'

'Was there a complete match with the MO?'

'Not that I've seen. Even in that bloody profiler's book. Why do you ask?'

'Because it's a good way to find out if it's someone connected to this Atreus guy. If he passed information on, that kind of thing.'

'Okay, I'll speak to Arbuthnott.'

'Want me to speak to the guy who took the course?'

'What, consult with the Met's brightest? God no. Last thing we need is the Met sniffing around here. DCS Soutar, our boss, she used to work down there and she's got previous in bringing them up here to "consult". Usually means them taking over and making us look like the useless fannies they think we are.'

'Can you bring my dad back as a consultant?'

Forrester rolled his eyes. 'This isn't a chance for you to turn back time, Vicky.'

'I just want to find the killer.'

'Right, well, I'll think on it. Problem was, your old man... This is not long after SOCOs switched from actual officers to civilians. The guy who was supposed to process it, he swears your dad lost the knife.'

She knew she was being pigheaded, but she couldn't help herself. 'Look, you should think about taking me off the case. I'm worried this will cloud my judgment.'

'And leave me with Euan MacDonald? Give me a break.' Forrester checked his watch, then glanced at the door. 'Time we headed back to the crime scene and see how much of an arse he's making of things.'

THE HOTEL CAR park was rammed with police cars and news crews. Superb. So Vicky had to park outside on the verge lining the main road. She got out into the cooling evening and set off across the road after Forrester, his pace meaning she was almost having to jog. 'Only a matter of time before those vultures showed up.' He signed them in and gave the crime scene manager a nod, then led her through the gates into the car park. 'You see what's what with Mac, I'll take our friends from the press out of the game.'

'Sure.' Vicky paced off towards the hotel.

MacDonald stood out the front, wearing his mirror shades again, though he'd lost his suit jacket and his shirtsleeves were rolled up to the elbow. He was talking to Considine and Karen, but it looked like they were getting a lashing from him. 'Get on with it, okay?' He nodded at them in turn, then charged over to meet Vicky. 'Where did you get to?'

'Long story.' Vicky gestured back at the hotel. 'Getting anything here?'

'Nada.' MacDonald propped his shades up on his head. 'Forensics've given up on the launch. Sea washed over the evidence.'

Vicky grimaced. 'At least we've got photos.'

'True. Hear they found a body in the lighthouse.'

'*I* did.'

'Seriously?'

Vicky shrugged.

'Tell you, those two are useless.' MacDonald was eyeing Considine and Karen, still arguing like Bella and Jamie in the back of Rob's car on the way to Saturday morning swimming. 'Keep telling Forrester. Need to bring in some better cops.'

'They're not bad, Euan. You just need to manage them better.'

His eyebrows flashed up. 'Seriously?'

'I'm just messing with you. What are they working on?'

'Finding the cleaners. Ten of them supposed to work here, but they've only spoken to three.'

'Aren't you helping?'

'Wish I could. Guy from the lighthouse... company? Is it publicly owned? Anyway, he's turned up, but I've got John Lamont moaning about police cars filling up his car park and there's that event tonight.'

'He can't seriously be opening up.'

'Raven's cleared it. So long as the golf course is shut and we can speak to his staff, he doesn't mind. But I've got to shift the cars on and—'

'Relax. I'll deal with the lighthouse.'

VICKY WALKED across the pristine green of the fifteenth, heading to the lighthouse. The bunker still had its tent up but there were fewer officers around than up at the hotel. She marched on and got out her mobile to call Rob.

He answered it straight away. 'Finally...' Sounded like bedlam in the background. Screeching and running and dogs barking.

'You okay?'

He sighed down the line. 'Bella and Jamie are going apeshit. Your bloody mother gave them sweets.'

'I keep telling her...'

'Bella's just about impossible with all those E numbers, but Jamie's way over the line.'

'Are you coping?'

'Just. When you coming home?'

'I don't know.' And it was the truth.

'Look, Jamie's teasing Peralta something rotten so I better go.'

'Love you.' But her words were lost to a dead line. Vicky pocketed her phone and walked on across the rough towards the beach.

She caught herself smiling, relieved to have found the right man. One right man in a whole sea of wrong.

She hopped down and set off across the bridge, though it didn't seem as bad as MacDonald intimated. Damp from high tide, yes, but hardly inundated. The lighthouse was blocking out the worst of the sun.

It was clearly connected to her old man's case, the one that broke him, but whether it was more than someone just being familiar with the original crimes... She didn't know, but she needed to find the killer.

She walked over to the door and called inside, 'Hello?'

'Archibald Quinn.' A man appeared, rugged face and rugged clothes. 'Pleased to meet you.' He thrust out his hand.

Vicky shook it, baby-skin soft. 'Thanks for joining us.'

'Not at all, I just wish we were meeting under better circumstances.' Quinn peered up at the lighthouse, squinting into the sun. 'I can't believe someone broke in to her.'

Her? Christ.

'You been here before, then?'

'Indeed. We're based up in Dundee, but I supervised the upgrade from manual to automatic in the early nineties. Felt like I was here every day. We grew attached, me and old Oggie here.'

'Oggie?'

'Why yes.' He pointed at the base of the lighthouse. 'She stands on Ogg's Rock.'

'I didn't know that.'

'And why would you?'

'You still work for the—'

'It's a private business now, yes. And I'm part time these days. But when we got the call in, well there was no other option than for it to be me who attended.' Quinn shook his head. 'But it's like someone's violated my wife, God rest her soul.'

'You know how many people have access?'

'I do.'

'And?'

'Me.'

'That's it?'

'Indeed. There are obviously protocols in place regarding back-up and redundancy, but I'm the only person with manual access to her.'

'Any security cameras?'

'No. It's all locked down, so there shouldn't be any need. Nobody should be getting inside her.'

'But somebody broke in.'

'I know. But I'm afraid there's nothing I can add to the story.'

'How about starting with how they got in?'

'I've had a little look and it's not pretty. Power tools were involved.' He waved over at the door. 'That door was designed for use in a nuclear bunker, so to gain access to her, the reprobates have had to eat away at her very fabric.'

'So they used a drill?'

'I'm not an expert on that.'

'Any reason to keep bleach in there?'

'Well, she gets her annual beauty treatment. We employ a firm based in Elie down in Fife to clean her and her sisters.' Quinn looked up again. 'Can I go up and see what they've done to her?'

'It's an active crime scene, sir.' Vicky nodded over at DC Buchan guarding the entrance. Five foot six of ginger nightmare. She heard footsteps climbing down the inside and knew who that would be. 'My colleague here will take a statement from you first, and you can have a look around upstairs once our forensics officers have completed their tasks.'

Quinn seemed to take that in good grace and he joined Buchan by the door, but kept a grim look on his face.

Jenny Morgan powered out of the lighthouse, holding two massive boxes and smiling like she knew all the answers. Jenny smiling was never a good thing.

Vicky stopped her getting past. 'You okay?'

'Sorry. Didn't see you there.' Jenny dropped her boxes and huffed out a sigh. 'It's *melting* inside, Dougie keeps breaking wind and there's a fucking body with his eyelids cut off. Of course I'm not okay!'

'That must be shocking.' Vicky took a box and led her over the concrete bridge back to the beach. 'Anything I can do to help?'

'Nothing.' Jenny rubbed at her eyes. 'Why are you here? Hiding from Mac?'

'Much as I'd love to, no.' She waved over at Quinn, who now seemed to be sobbing. 'I'm dealing with that poor sod who seems to be coping with his wife's death by anthropomorphising a lighthouse.'

'Christ, and I thought you were mad.'

'I am.' Vicky smiled and it seemed to calm Jenny down a notch. 'So, have you found anything up there?'

'That bottle of bleach you found? Looks like the killer cleaned the corpse and the bloody room with it. I hoped we'd get something, but not even a hair. Whoever did it, they knew what they were doing. Wearing a crime scene suit while they were doing it, kind of thing.'

'Arbuthnott finished?'

'Long since. Found nothing. She might get something later on, but I wouldn't hold out hope.'

'What about the female victim? Anything?'

'Don't know. Arbuthnott was moaning about how last night's rain got to her first and didn't seem too happy when her guys were taking the body back to the morgue. And Mac was pestering her to check if it was the same knife as the female victim's throat wound. Nice that you're not the only woman your lover's been pestering, eh?'

'He's not my lover, but he's still pestering, aye.' Vicky stared hard at Jenny, but the way she looked away so quickly, coupled with her daze coming out of the lighthouse, well it was obvious she was hiding something. 'What aren't you telling me, Jenny?'

'Just waiting for you to ask me to dig into the Atreus killing.'

'Right.'

'I heard your dad was involved.'

Vicky gave her a smile. 'Back in the day, a knife went missing. Can you do some digging into what happened to it?'

'Will do.' Jenny hefted up her boxes, stuffed to the brim with evidence bags. 'Better get these back to base.'

'You find something?'

'Nope.' Jenny frowned. 'Wait, we found an invite for a party at LA Golf.'

9

The bulk of the police work seemed to be happening in the hotel's car park. Now the crime scene manager had been moved to the golf course, an enterprising fast food van was frying up burgers, the hot meaty smell hitting Vicky, followed by tangy onion.

Considine was at the head of the queue, laughing at something the server said. He opened the lid of his burger and squirted tomato ketchup down his shirt. 'Shite.'

Vicky only had a shake of her head for him.

His culinary mishap hadn't put him off chewing on his burger. 'Sarge.'

'Have you got hold of the guest list for last night?'

Considine looked at her like she'd asked him to recite *A Brief History of Time* from memory, so he just chewed with a finger in the air. And a dollop of sauce on the ground.

Vicky spotted MacDonald outside the hotel, speaking to a middle-aged woman. That intense stare, the over-laughing, the stroke of her arm. Christ, he was flirting with her. 'I'll let you finish that, Stephen.' She set off away from the van.

MacDonald clocked Vicky's approach, his eyes widening as he

stepped aside to let her into the huddle. 'This is DS Vicky Dodds, a colleague of mine. This is Lisa Johnson.'

Lisa gave her a careful look, like she was appraising her clothes. Vicky's summer T-shirt and loose trousers were a lot less glam than Lisa's leopard-print skin-tight leggings and the loose brown blouse, but at least they fit properly. Her fake tan looked like she was wearing leather instead of skin, pencilled-on eyebrows and botoxed lips like a puffer fish made her smile look *empty*. 'Nice to meet you.' South African accent, out here in the wilds of Tayside.

Vicky had no idea who she was, so she focused on MacDonald. 'Euan, I'm looking for that guest list?'

'You're in luck here. Lisa organised the function last night.' MacDonald soaked up the lingering look from the organiser. 'Considine and co are digging into the attendees list.'

'Our male victim attended.' Vicky showed him a snapshot of the party invite Jenny had found. 'I need to match this to a name.'

Lisa frowned at them. 'Listen, John never furnished me with a full guest list.'

'How can you run an event without a guest list?'

'Finally someone who gets me.' Lisa beamed. 'He wanted to maintain control of the whole thing. I was just paid to arrange the function. Get people to hand out nibbles and drinks, fine.' She pointed at the photo. 'That's a VIP pass, so you need to ask—' She scowled over Vicky's shoulder. 'John!' She charged off.

John Lamont was sucking on a cigarette, more than a bit too close to the hotel entrance. His suit was as crumpled as his face. Eyebrows low, he was staring right at them. 'Lisa?'

Vicky followed her over.

Lisa shook her head at his proffered cigarette pack. 'The police need access to the VIP list.'

Lamont shut his eyes. 'I can't just—'

'Yes, you can.' Vicky waited for him to open his eyes. 'And you will.'

'It's not that simple.'

Vicky got in his face and sucked in second-hand smoke, but

she still stood her ground. 'Sir, are you aware that we found a second body?'

'I am, but that lighthouse isn't my property.' Lamont looked at MacDonald, then Lisa, then back at Vicky with a shrug. 'Fine, there's no point in arguing with you, is there?' He put his smoke between his lips and reached into his pocket for a giant smartphone. He stared at it, then tapped on the screen and turned it round to Vicky. 'This do you?'

Vicky snatched it off him. The high-resolution screen showed some sort of contacts app, with names and photos. She slid down the list, aware of MacDonald's close presence over her shoulder and Lamont's second-hand smoke coiling into her nostrils.

And there he was. The male victim.

She let out a sigh. 'Derek Craigen.'

Lamont's mouth formed an O. 'Derek?' He swallowed hard. 'My God.'

'You didn't recognise him from the photo you were shown?'

Lamont frowned. 'What photo?'

Vicky looked at MacDonald and his eyebrows shot up. Another Considine mess, probably. She looked back at Lamont. 'How do you know him?'

'He's a good guy.' Lamont exhaled slowly, then pressed his cigarette against the bin and dropped the butt in. 'Local businessman, and I'm trying to get him to sign up as an early-access member at the club.'

MacDonald grinned at him. 'Close the deal?'

Lamont nodded. 'Signed him up last night over the sorbet.'

Vicky shot MacDonald a glare to shut him up. 'How well do you know him?'

'Like I say, he's a local businessman. Runs a plumbing company. If you listen to him, it's a big deal. They cover the north east and Fife, but that's the extent of my knowledge I'm afraid.'

Sounded like at least a reasonably-sized deal. Meaning money could be a motive. 'Did they do any work here?'

'Sure. They were contractors for the build. Did all the

plumbing for the hotel. Even installed the swimming pool and the watering system for the golf course, you name it.'

'Are they anything to do with the rework going on inside?'

'I wish they were. No, the joinery was shoddy, whereas Derek's work was sound. The fish tanks have been a complete disaster. Only wish he accepted taking that on, but he didn't.'

Vicky showed him her own phone, displaying the photo of the female victim. 'Do you know her?'

'Sorry, no. I've seen her already.'

At least Considine had done something right. 'Was Mr Craigen married?'

'Think so.'

'You think so?'

'Well, last night, Derek booked in a birthday party for his youngest daughter. It's her eighteenth in August. I'd need to check the date, but Derek booked our Prom package, even though it's not a prom.' He gestured at the phone. 'And if that's Derek's wife, she'd be about five when the kid was born. So I'd say it's not her.'

So who was she? And why did she have an engagement ring?

'Right.' Vicky put her phone away. 'You get an address for him?'

EVEN THOUGH IT SHOULDN'T, it still shocked Vicky to see her old high school missing, all but the swimming baths replaced by a new building. Not that it looked much better than the old Sixties tower.

Considine was in the passenger seat, gripping the oh-shit handle for dear life. Kept glancing over at Vicky, like he was angry with her driving the Subaru. Probably was. 'You used to be a pupil there, right?'

'Correct.'

'Played football against that shower a few times. Had a few handy players, mind.' Considine glanced back that way with a grin. 'Couldn't prevent me from scoring a hat trick, likes.'

Vicky eased past the heavy traffic flowing up West Path, the steep hill climbing up from the town below. Her dad called it Bury's Brae, but she had about six ideas of how to spell it. 'The kids nowadays don't know they're born. They wouldn't know the joys of a sway.'

'A *sway*?'

'The old building was a nightmare. The middle bit was four floors, but there were extensions on the second floor in like three directions, so you'd be having swap classes and hit a ton of traffic. Just like this.' Vicky pulled up ahead, waiting for a hole in the golf traffic. Nothing was opening up, just a steady stream of Audis and BMWs. 'A sway was when the older kids pushed through and pretty much picked up the smaller kids off their feet. You'd sometimes get carried from one end of the B-floor to the stairs at the far end of Maths. And you were trying to get to Music.' Was that gap big enough? Even the Subaru would struggle to get through. 'You went to Forfar Academy, right?'

'Nah, grew up in Brechin.'

Bingo. A bus pulled in at the stop, so Vicky shot past the tail of a Lexus and got onto the street, residential and almost as modern as Carnoustie got, but more upmarket than most at this end of the town. Vicky knew a few kids on this street growing up, but Craigen's address was at the end, hidden behind tall walls, shrouded on both sides by mature oaks and beech.

Vicky parked and got out. Tall wrought-iron gates blocked entry, but an intercom was buried into the wall. She walked over and hit the buzzer.

Considine joined her, scanning the surroundings, eyes narrowed like he was a pro and in control of guarding the president rather than a numpty. 'Boy was married, right?'

'Believe so.' Vicky tried the buzzer again. 'Three kids, the youngest eighteen next month so we should at least hear some music blaring, right? Ariana Grande or something.'

'Don't try and pretend you're cool, Sarge.' Considine smirked. 'And that's assuming they're in. Assuming they even still live here.'

Vicky tried the gate and it held firm. 'I'm still not forgetting the fact that you were supposed to show his photo to Lamont.'

'That was Karen.'

'Stephen, acting like a child won't get you promoted. Okay? You need to demonstrate leadership, not try and blame everyone else.'

'Here, let me.' Considine grabbed the gate and tried to budge it. But it didn't move for his puny muscles.

Vicky inspected the neighbours' houses. Two-storey buildings, white-harled with paved drives and rose beds in full bloom. No sign of anyone in there either.

Considine was still wrestling with the gate. 'Come on, Sarge, give us a hand here.' But the metal grunted and rolled along the wheel and Considine flopped over, face-first.

'Get up, you clown.' Vicky reached out a hand to help him up.

Considine dusted himself off, but mud and moss stains joined the red on his shirt. 'Well, we've got in.' He looked back at the gate like he was going to fight it again and maybe win this time. Instead, he grimaced. 'Ah, shite, it's an automatic. Have we bust it?'

'Doesn't matter.' Vicky barged past and marched towards the house across the drive, old bricks arranged in a grid, mossed over except for a pair of grooves where a car had repeatedly driven up. A lawn on either side, manicured to within an inch of their lives. Sprinklers sat on both, but neither was spraying.

A Range Rover basked in the sun in front of a wide row of cottages turned into a bling footballer's mansion. The old building had been carved open on the south side with a balcony installed on the first floor.

Considine hit the house bell and it chimed deep inside.

Vicky looked through the window into a living room filled with chintz. Bright oranges and purples and browns, like the designer had taken inspiration from a mid-eighties sweet shop. Black electronics equipment all proudly on display. If he was married, then Mrs Craigen certainly let him get away with more man cave antics than Vicky would.

'Nobody in.' Considine sniffed. 'Shall we do a recce?'

'Meet you round the back.' Vicky stepped off away from him, crunching over small pebbles. Her route gave her a decent view of the balcony and its rattan furniture and glass tables. Still no sign of anyone inside.

She passed through the fence at the side and got a cracking view across western Carnoustie, stretching as far as Barry before the heat haze swallowed it up. To the south, the golf course was a mess of Lego-sized people, though the hulking Carnoustie Hotel blocked off most of the fairway, not to mention the apartments springing up around it. Fife was hidden by mist and rain that hadn't stretched this far north.

Vicky's whole world was visible. Her parents' house, Rob's, her old box just off Barry Road.

'Eh, Sarge.' Considine was standing at the rear of the house, frowning at an open back door. 'I just found it like this, I swear.'

'Don't worry, Jenny Morgan will dust it for prints.' Vicky snapped on some gloves. She had no idea what she'd find. Hopefully a wife and kids, but... Well, her luck hadn't been that good recently. So another pair of bodies was likely. She should call it in to Forrester. But she took a breath and stepped inside. 'Hello?'

Nothing.

So she went further inside. 'Police.'

Still nothing.

'Let's split up. I'll go upstairs, you stay down here. And I mean right here.'

The thick slap of a glove being snapped on came from behind her. 'Sure thing.'

Vicky took the stairs slowly. Framed photos lined the walls, though they were arty golf courses from around the world and not family shots. She recognised Carnoustie and St Andrews, but the rest could've been anywhere. Florida, California, Dubai, Mars.

Three doors on the first-floor landing. A glass one to the left showed into a massive games room. A full-sized snooker table, vintage arcade machines and three pinball tables, all flashing away. Leather sofas and a bar running along the far wall. And there was the balcony and the view across the mouth of the Tay. No signs of life.

So she turned round. Ahead was a bathroom, the door open. She peered in, but the standalone bath was empty and bone dry. A stack of golfing and motoring magazines sat by the pan.

Through the other door was a long and wide hallway, leading to another set of doors, with two each of the walls. She tried the first and it was a kid's bedroom. A female teenager judging by the K-pop posters, but nobody inside. And no laptop or any signs of homework. Across was another bathroom, with a shower but no toothbrushes or toiletries.

Curious and getting curiouser.

She went back into the hall and tried the next door. A guest room with stale air. Same story over the corridor, leaving just the door at the end.

Vicky took a deep breath, expecting another body, and opened it slowly.

A huge master bedroom with an eight-foot bed and—CHRIST —a sex swing hanging from the ceiling. A grown-up version of a child's garden swing, angled back and mounted at the perfect height for... mounting. And God knows what else. No other signs of sexual adventure, save the mirrored ceiling. Oh, and a mirrored cupboard, hanging open. A box filled with leather costumes. Man alive, rich men and kinks went hand in gloved hand.

Another door to an en-suite bathroom. Two toothbrushes, both looking slightly damp but maybe not that recently used.

So this whole floor was empty.

Vicky paced back through the hallway and skipped down the steps. No sign of Considine, but she could smell toast somewhere. She followed it through the bling living room to an equally bling kitchen. Black-marble worktops and shiny turquoise units. 'Are you making toast?'

Considine was standing by the galley unit, sifting through opened mail. 'Hardly.' He shook his head but didn't look round at her. 'There was some burnt toast on a plate and it was reeking so I chucked it in the bin.'

'How many times do I have to tell you not to piss about with crime scenes?'

'Sarge, I'm wearing gloves.' But he was still just going through the post.

'You found anything?'

'Nobody here.'

'So now we're missing a wife and three kids.'

'Maybe.' Considine looked up. 'Hang on. This letter is about an apartment in Carnoustie.'

10

Vicky battled her way through heavy foot traffic coming from the Open. Massed ranks of varying speeds from the slowest on the pavement over to the chancers almost jogging in the middle of the road. And honking her horn wasn't doing anything but getting thumps on the bonnet.

Up ahead, the crowds swarmed like ants to cross the bridge over the train line, heading to Golf Street Halt. A tiny stop Vicky had only ever taken once on a train, not that she used it much.

'This is insane.' Considine was scowling like that would clear the masses out of their path. 'How can they get away with this?'

'Because the council thinks that letting a town of fifteen thousand have an extra fifty thousand visitors a day is a good thing.'

'Might as well park here.'

Vicky put the indicator on but nobody was budging. 'Bollocks to it.' She bumped on the right-hand kerb and left the hazards on.

'You're just going to leave her here?'

'Her? You're as bad as that lighthouse guy.' Vicky got out into the street and it felt like she was back at school in the middle of a sway. She held out her warrant card. 'Police! Coming through!'

Nobody paid any attention.

Considine's solution was to charge through, and it seemed to be working, so she followed in his slipstream, grabbing hold of his suit jacket so they didn't get separated. A sharp left turn and they were through into a courtyard.

The flat was in a new development overlooking Carnoustie golf links. Tall modern buildings on three sides, six or seven stories high with couples sitting at balconies, sipping on wines and beers. More than a few barbecues on the go, though that had to be against so many regulations.

'Could do with a nice lager right now.' Considine pressed the buzzer and stepped back, ogling a pair of women in their late twenties looking down at them. He stood up tall.

The intercom crackled. 'Hello?' A female voice.

Considine leaned down. 'Police, ma'am.'

'What do you want?'

'Do you know a Derek Craigen?'

A long pause. 'What is this about?'

'Ma'am, to whom am I talking?'

'Louise Craigen. His wife. What's going on?'

LOUISE CRAIGEN PERCHED on a stool at the breakfast bar, quietly sobbing into her hands. Early forties, with red-and-grey roots bleeding through dark hair. She looked up. A round face that was moderately cute.

Behind her, the apartment looked across the golf course towards the Carnoustie Hotel, the fairways now virtually empty of spectators and strewn with rubbish. Underneath the temporary stands, a mad clean-up operation was in place, a battalion of stewards armed with grabbers and bin bags tidying it all away.

A large TV was mounted on the wall opposite, playing the golf highlights, but Vicky couldn't tell who had won, not that she recognised many of the names.

The kitchen had that high-end showroom feel to it, all glossy countertops and units, expensive appliances. The coffee machine didn't so much look like it could make a perfect espresso but would instead fly you to Rome for a romantic weekend break without the kids.

Music played from another room, the solid thump of an electronic dance track, but with loose shards of melody and out-of-tune teenage singing.

Louise looked over at Vicky, tears streaming down her cheeks. Her ice-grey eyes drilled into Vicky with the most intense stare she'd seen since her school headmaster and a particular judge in Dundee. 'You're sure it's him?'

'We'll need a formal identification, but we're pretty sure, yeah.'

'Have you got like a photo or something?'

Before Vicky could act, Considine shoved his phone in her face. 'Here you go, ma'am.'

'My God.' Louise slumped back in her stool and ran a hand through her hair. She blew out a deep breath slowly, shaking her head. Whatever anger she'd had was now lost too. 'Well. That certainly looks like him.'

Considine looked like he was going to chime in with something, but Vicky's glare finally got to him. God how she wished she had Karen Woods or someone vaguely competent here.

Louise swallowed hard. 'You know, after everything that's happened, the number of times I wanted him to *die*... It's... That phrase, wouldn't wish it on your worst enemy? That.' She kept staring at the phone. 'Someone cut his eyelids off? How did he die?'

Vicky joined her at the breakfast bar. 'Our pathologist hasn't performed a post mortem yet, so we don't know for sure.'

'But you've got a good idea?'

And sometimes you just had to play along with their questions before you got to ask your own. 'Our initial assessment is your husband died from a knife wound to the heart.'

Louise let out a slow breath. 'But the eyelids? Was it Atreus?'

That was straight out of left-field. 'What do you mean?'

'When I was at school, there was that murder in Broughty Ferry. Supposed to be a serial killer, wasn't it? They called him Atreus. He cut people's eyelids off.'

'When did you last see your husband?'

'Not for months.'

'But you've got kids, right?'

'He still sees Teri. Her bedroom's made up in... Derek treats her like a Disney princess, like he can buy her affection. She's our youngest, but she's not stupid.' Louise folded her arms, the tough Dundee wifie image returning. She nodded at the door, at the source of the thumping din. 'She's eighteen next month, going to Manchester Uni in September.'

'She must be smart.'

'Got a brain on her, that's for sure.' A dark look settled on Louise's face. 'Our middle girl, Audrey, she's at Edinburgh but she's working in Canada all summer.' A sharp snort. 'Christ, I'll have to tell her on the *phone*.'

Vicky gave her a sympathetic smile. 'And your other daughter?'

'Pamela. She's at Dundee, a real brainbox too. Doing a PhD.'

'We're trying to find your husband's killer and we need to build a picture of his life.'

Louise nibbled her nail. 'Fine. We met at school.'

'You're from Carnoustie?'

'Aye, he lived on Thomas Street. His parents are both dead. Dad was a heart attack, mum cancer. Not that long ago, either. Might explain a few things too. We had kids young. I was eighteen when we had Pamela. I was at Dundee College, training as a journalist, had to take a year out and go back at nights. When I finished, the recession was biting hard so DC Thomson didn't take many on from our year and I wasn't likely to get a job elsewhere. So I worked as a typist, and Derek's mum looked after Pamela while I supported Derek. He built up his company from nothing.' She clenched her jaw. 'He almost went bust a few times and, Christ, there are a *lot* of people he stepped on as he climbed the greasy pole.'

Considine nodded at her. 'Can you give me a list?'

Louise shut her eyes. 'Fine, I'll pull together a list for you if it'll shut you up.'

'Thanks.'

Vicky gave Louise a few seconds of nail biting.

She stared at Vicky with that intense look again. 'You're from Carnoustie, aren't you?'

'I am.'

'I think I know you from school, but you were a few years below me. When did you leave?'

'2000.'

'Quite a few years younger than me, then.' She clicked her fingers. 'I know what it is. I was your aunt.'

'My aunt?'

'Yeah, at the start of sixth year, we were aunts and uncles to the kids going up from primary. That was it. I was Louise Mitchell.'

Vicky still had no memory of her, not even a vague inkling, but then that would've been 1994, so twenty-four years ago. A hell of a long time. And she'd remember those eyes.

'I'll be Louise Mitchell again when the paperwork goes through.'

'You're getting divorced?' Another avenue opened up. Vicky scribbled a note of it. 'Were you—'

'He was divorcing me.'

'Can I ask why?'

'You can ask, but the whole thing has left me completely bamboozled.'

'Did he leave you?'

Louise steeled herself. 'Hardly.'

'So why do you live here with Teri?'

'That's none of your business.' She looked around. 'We bought this place for my dad. After Mum died, he couldn't cope with our old place up on Carlogie Road. This was a lot more expensive, mind. He died two years ago, and it's kind of got sentimental value.' She shook her head. 'Derek was renting it out to someone, but it turned out it was to himself. He was putting up his slapper in here.'

'And it's just you and Teri here?'

'Right. Only good thing about us being here is *he* hasn't been able to rent it out to anyone for the golf.' She glared out of the window. 'The hardest part is he'd been shagging that tart here. It was a fuck pad.'

Considine frowned at her. 'He was having an affair?'

'Shagging some little scrubber behind my back. I caught him at it with her in our bed.'

'You know her name?'

'Nope, but she was young. Young, but legal. Probably about the same as Pamela. I mean, what kind of man does that?'

'You ever see them together?'

'Once. I was out for a walk with Teri a few months ago, and we saw them having a meal at that Thai place on Queen Street.'

Vicky got out her phone and showed her the photo of the female victim. 'Is this her?'

Louise didn't even need a long hard look at it, just a glance and she was nodding like a dog in the back of a car. 'That's her.' She got up and walked over to the patio doors, but didn't open them, just looked out. 'I don't know much about her, before you ask. As far as I can tell, that whole thing had been going on for two years.' She turned back round. 'I actually take pity on her. She was just like me, way too naïve to see through his bullshit. Now he's a fat old man, and she must've been too enamoured with his money and the lifestyle he could offer.'

'How rich was he?'

'I don't know the exact details, but Derek was well off for Carnoustie. I mean, people in Arbroath call it Car-snooty, but it's hardly Edinburgh or London, is it?'

'Given that you're not divorced, you still inherit your husband's estate?'

She looked around the room. 'I'm not an expert.'

'That house is worth a lot, and this place almost as much. Do you own it all outright?'

'As far as I know.'

Considine snapped his notebook shut. 'Ma'am, I can drive you up to Dundee to identify the body if you want?'

'Sure.' Louise nodded slowly. 'I'll just have to break the news to Teri.'

11

Bell Street police station was Sunday-night quiet, which wasn't that usual for a Sunday night in the middle of summer. Then again, a massive golf tournament down the road didn't attract the same numpties as a Celtic-Rangers football match, which they'd already be looking forward to in late August. Dundee derbies were much more sedate affairs. Tea and flasks rather than knives and bricks.

Vicky swiped through the front entrance just as her phone rang. Considine. 'What's up?'

'We're just leaving now, Sarge.'

'Seriously?' Vicky stopped on the stairs. 'I've already arrived in Dundee.' She set off again.

'Aye, well, her lassie didn't take it that well. I mean, you're lucky I was here to calm the sitch down.'

'The sitch?'

'Situation. Christ. Had more than my fair share of lassies chucking stuff around.'

'I bet you have.' Vicky pushed through the doors at the top and headed along the corridor. 'Give me a call once she's identified the body.'

'Sure thing.' And he was gone with the loud rev of an engine. Letting him have that Subaru would be a big mistake.

The light was on in Forrester's office. As Vicky closed in on it, she heard two voices and the hiss of a filter machine. She opened the door and the dank reek of rancid coffee hit her.

Forrester slurped from a mug, eyes beaming. 'Alright, Doddsy?' Acting like he'd Irished up his coffee too, but it didn't smell of booze so it was probably just the sheer amount of caffeine in it.

MacDonald put his mug straight on the desk. 'Alright.'

'Thought you'd both be at the PM?'

'Just finished.' Forrester tipped some stinking coffee into a fresh cup and handed it to Arbuthnott. 'Just take it black, aye?'

'Sure.' Arbuthnott had been hiding over by the window, shrouded by the glow from the streetlights not quite hitting the alcove. She wrapped her hands around the mug and soaked in the steam, focusing on Vicky. 'The long and short of it, my autopsy confirmed that the female victim died of blood loss from the wound to her neck. The male victim, this Derek Craigen, well, the wound to his heart was the fatal blow.' She took a sip of coffee and grimaced. 'Both would've been *excruciating*.'

'That's it?'

'I don't know what you were expecting? Whoever did this, they clearly wanted the victims to see the other one's suffering. Mr Craigen's eyelids were removed with surgical precision and the nick in the female victim's neck is from a similar instrument.'

'Should we be looking at medical suspects?'

'I mean you could, but there's nothing tying this back to anyone yet. And, well, it's not advanced surgery.'

'You said they were removed with surgical precision.'

'But that doesn't mean they were a surgeon. I could give you five hundred YouTube videos just on this very topic. All it'd take would be a lot of practice, which someone could do on themselves or on animals.'

Vicky had seen more than enough animal cruelty. 'What about the stabbing through the heart?'

'I'd suggest that was to symbolise breaking someone's heart in their relationship.' Arbuthnott shrugged. 'If this is indeed a copycat of Atreus, then there's adultery in the victimology. Someone's heart had been broken, ergo death by a broken heart.'

As good as Arbuthnott was, she was yet again straying into psychology.

'Let's just see, shall we?' Forrester sighed. His sunburn was looking really bad now. 'We're not so lucky on the forensics front. The lassie's body was out in the open so nowt on her. Nails clean, yadda yadda yadda. And this Craigen boy was covered in bleach. Killing someone, then covering your tracks like that. It's brutal, isn't it?'

'No, it's not.' Arbuthnott put the coffee up to her lips but it didn't look like she drank any. 'It's either extremely premeditated, or he's got a sudden flash of clarity after the bloodlust abated. It's common in serial killers.'

'Why didn't he go after her, though?'

'Maybe he did, but a golf course in the dark is very tricky hunting territory. All the woods and bunkers and they're just so bloody big. You'd need daylight to stand a good chance of finding someone, but it's entirely possible. Plus he probably thought she'd run along the beach.'

'You really think this is someone copying Atreus?'

'Same MO.' Arbuthnott glanced at Forrester. 'I mean, whoever killed Mr Craigen certainly knew enough about those old cases to recreate the same torment in the victims. And the shared victimology.' She grinned wide. 'But Jim Sanderson is dead, David. I don't think a ghost killed them, do you?'

Vicky laughed. 'Okay, well, we probably need to find a decent exorcist.'

'I know a couple.'

'Your old man could do with speaking to one, Vicky.' Forrester took a slug of coffee. 'Lot of ghosts around this case. I'll not keep you, Shirley.'

'Thanks for the coffee.' Arbuthnott waddled out of the room and left the door hanging open behind her.

'Born in a bloody barn.' Forrester stomped over to slam it, and focused on Vicky on his way back. 'What have you been up to, Doddsy?'

'Speaking to Craigen's wife. She'll identify the body once Considine pulls his finger out.'

'We know it's him, though, right?'

'Just going through the motions, sir.'

'She a suspect?'

'How did you guess?'

'Because I know you.' Forrester grinned. 'Plus, women murdering their husbands isn't exactly out of the ordinary. Usually poison them, though.'

'Well, she might stand to inherit the house and the business.'

'What's the house like?'

'It's big. About half a million's worth of big.'

'In Carnoustie?'

'It'd be ten million down south. And that's before we factor in a supposedly successful business. And the flat by the golf course will be at least two-fifty.'

'Why do you say supposedly?'

'Well, businesses being what they are, you can never be sure whether it's failing or not until you dig into the books.'

'But if she's going to inherit a fortune, then we've got ourselves a suspect.'

'Right. And according to her, she's staying in the flat her husband put his mistress up in.'

'Christ.' Forrester slurped coffee, his eyes wide. 'So, how do you want to progress?'

'If I may?' MacDonald glanced in Vicky's direction. 'Don't want to cramp anyone's style, but I've got three years in financial fraud. Know my way round a balance sheet and a P&L.'

Forrester seemed to think it through, then nodded at MacDonald. 'Okay, get round there first thing. See what you can dig up.'

'Fine.' But it wasn't. Yet again, MacDonald was taking credit for Vicky's work. She wasn't an ambitious person, but boy did she hate it when the ambitious types trampled over everyone else.

The door opened and a ruddy face peered in, even more

sunburnt than Forrester. 'Aha, the gang's all here.' DCI John Raven crept in, snarling wide and baring yellowing teeth. Usually he'd be clad in a sharp suit, shiny grey and a patterned shirt underneath, but today he was head-to-toe in walking gear, all synthetic blues and greys. Shorts that didn't hide knobbly knees. And socks with sandals. 'Hi-de-ho.' He walked over and sat behind Forrester's desk. 'Any of that coffee on the go?'

'Sure. Can I get you a cup?'

'My gut's still inflamed from the last one, so no.' Raven grinned as he rested his phone on the desk. 'Okey-doke, who's running interference with the press?'

Vicky looked to Forrester, saw MacDonald doing the same.

Forrester rested his mug on his desk. 'What's happened, sir?'

'Some little shite of a journo from Edinburgh turned up.' Raven sniffed. 'I say turned up, but I mean door-stepped me outside my bloody house just as I got back from the sodding golf. I mean, I appreciate you won't be too sympathetic to my plight, but this is my first day off this year.' He shook his head, then focused on MacDonald. 'Son, when you're a DCI, you'll see just how shite it is.'

Vicky stood there, hands on hips. 'You saying I won't make DCI?'

Raven held her gaze, then shifted it to Forrester. 'Anyway, this little turd was asking questions he shouldn't know the answers to. And they always know the answers before they ask them. Asking me about Derek Craigen.' He was struggling to keep his mouth still. 'Anyone care to tell me who Derek bloody Craigen is?'

Forrester shot Vicky a shut-up glare. 'He's our victim, sir. Just got an ID on him.'

'Didn't think to brief me, no?'

'You would've been briefed if you'd answered your phone.'

'I was driving. Traffic was hell.'

'I left a voicemail.'

'The long and winding voicemail that leads to your door. And I haven't exactly had the ten years to listen to it yet.' Raven didn't seem in the mood to take that. 'I need a TL;DR.'

Vicky frowned. 'A what?'

'Too Long; Didn't Read. A bloody summary!'

'Right.'

'Forget it.' Raven flipped up the lid on Forrester's coffee machine and peered in like you would an open sewer. 'Long and short, David, someone's been blabbing to the press. Someone on your team. Before I've got wind of any progress. Any idea who that might be?'

'No idea, sir.' Forrester drank coffee. 'Vicky?'

'Nobody on my team.'

'Mac?'

'Snap.'

Forrester settled back in his chair. 'Sir, we'll keep an eye on it.'

'You do that.' Raven snapped the lid shut and walked over to take a seat. He put his sandalled feet up on the desk and scratched at his red knees. 'So we've got someone using the MO of a serial killer we put away donkey's years ago?'

'We didn't put him away, but pretty much.' Forrester folded his arms. 'Same MO. Same victimology.'

Raven scratched harder on the left knee now. 'These two were having a fling?'

'We believe that Craigen was having an affair with the female victim, just like with all those victims way back when.'

'Right. You got an ID for her?'

'No, but—'

'That's got to be your focus here, David. Okay?' Raven hoisted himself up and walked over to the door. 'Ten o'clock tomorrow, David, you and I have a call with DCS Soutar. You know what Carolyn's like, right? She'll tear you apart unless you've got something solid and send some clowns up from the Met or bloody Edinburgh. Now, I could get Bri Masson in here, but I trust you to solve this.'

'Will the call be in your office, sir?'

'Aye.' Raven looked at Vicky then at MacDonald. 'And I expect someone to have held this journo nyaff's conkers over an open fire.'

'You going to give me his name?'

'Can't remember it, but I texted you it.' Raven got out his phone and checked the screen. 'Shite, it's not sent.' He prodded it. 'Okay. I'll see you later.' And he was gone, replaced with a swinging door.

Forrester slumped back against the wall with a sour expression on his face. 'Well, you heard the man. We need to get on top of this lad.'

MacDonald rested his coffee on the desk. 'Want me to speak to him?'

'If you could. Put the frighteners on him. Cheers, Mac. See you tomorrow.'

'See you tomorrow, Vicky.' MacDonald grabbed his suit jacket. 'Night, Dave.' He left them to it, but didn't shut the door. Sneaky bugger was probably lurking outside and eavesdropping.

Vicky walked over and kicked it shut. No sign he was still out there, but you never knew with a sneaky bastard like Euan MacDonald. 'He's calling you "Dave" now?'

'You know I hate it as much as people calling you Victoria, but it seems to get him to focus a bit.' Forrester grabbed Arbuthnott's empty cup. 'Cheeky cow didn't drink the coffee I made her.' He sniffed it. Then drank it himself. 'Ahhh, that's the ticket.'

'So you're just letting him run my leads?'

'It's just a case of horses for courses. As much as you don't want to admit it, Mac is just better at some things than you.' Forrester held up his hands. 'And you're better at him on most, before you start.'

'He should be focusing on the copycat thing, not me.'

'Right now, I think your copycat theory is bollocks, so you need to convince me. And I can see where this is coming from. You're just like your dad. You both get obsessed and it can be used well, but it can be a bloody hindrance. It's much more likely that this woman's copied the MO to throw us off the trail. Not divorced, right?'

'Correct, but it's in the post.'

'So dig up their financial records, see what she stands to inherit. Okay?'

'Fine.'

'And you've still not IDed the female victim.' He took a swig of coffee and snarled. 'Get yourself home, get a good night's sleep and show Mac what's what in the morning.'

'Right.' Vicky let out a deep breath. 'Well, I'm glad I drove all the way from Carnoustie to Dundee just to go back again.'

12

R ob's house was still lit up, giving her that nice tingle in the pit of her stomach and that smile on her face. Two years now, with him stopping being Robert and her settling on calling him Rob. Over a year living there and she was starting to think of it as hers and Bella's home now.

And his new VW, a real family man's car. Mum and dad up front, two kids trying to kill each other in the back.

She killed the engine and got out of her car onto the driveway. The evening still had some warmth to it, but the breeze had picked up. Her phone thrummed. She checked it. Just a text from Considine:

"Positive ID. CU tomorrow."

In this day and age of predictive texting, he still had to type like he was a drug dealer using an ancient Nokia.

So she replied, "Thanks. See you tomorrow." Not that it'd show him. She put her phone away and found the note from earlier.

"V — I KNOW"

It made her shiver despite the heat. Who the hell could it be? So many people she'd put away over the years and so many she'd pissed off in her private life.

Someone grabbed her right arm.

Vicky lashed out with her elbow and it cracked off something hard, sending shockwaves up her arm. Something thunked off her bonnet. She swung round and saw a pair of shorts and sandals disappear onto the drive.

Breathing hard, she took her time going round the car.

Her dad was on his hands and knees, sucking in breath. 'What did you do that for?' He was slurring and struggling to focus on her.

'Christ, Dad, don't sneak up on me like that!'

He used her car to haul himself to his feet. 'Have you caught the killer yet?'

And Vicky smelled the booze leeching off him. He was hammered. How the hell did he manage to sneak up on her? 'Are you okay?'

'Been knocked on my arse a fair few times, Victoria. I'm fine and dandy.'

She let out a sigh. 'Go home, Dad.'

'Please. I need to know.'

'I'll call you in the morning when you're sober. Do you need a lift?'

'Only if you'll talk to me about this case.'

'Of course I won't.'

'Night then.' He trudged off into the darkness.

Vicky was in half a mind to follow him. A mile from home and at least three pubs she could think of on the way. She should pick him up, dust him down, sober him up and pack him off back to Mum.

The house light flicked on and the door opened.

Tinkle hopped out onto the driveway, the tabby cat with the squattest body in the world, making her weird chirruping sounds like she was trying to attract birds.

Rob stood in the doorway, frowning out. 'You okay?'

Vicky took one last look at her old man staggering round the corner and decided he was big enough and ugly enough to get himself home, pub or no pub. She walked over and kissed Rob on the lips. 'I'm good.'

'That's... unusual.' He led her inside. 'I've just opened a bottle of red.'

'Brilliant.' Vicky kicked off her shoes and padded through to the kitchen in Tinkle's wake. 'Anything to eat? I'm starving.'

'Leftovers.'

'Sounds good. Kids in bed?'

'Yup.'

'I'll just be a sec.' Vicky climbed the stairs and opened Bella's bedroom door. She was asleep and looked so cute. She tucked Bella in and pecked her hair. 'Night, Bells.' Then she went next door and repeated the ritual with Jamie. 'Night, Jay.'

He wasn't her flesh and blood, but he was as much part of her life as Bella was. Two lost kids finding a mother and a father, but also a brother and a sister.

She stood in the doorway, giving herself a minute of just standing there, soaking in the everyday. Not a beach or bleach or a lighthouse or a golf bunker containing a murder victim, just the sounds and smells of home. Bella's shampoo, the only one that didn't make her skin swell up. Some burnt sausages and the sound of the whirring microwave down in the kitchen, then some over-excited golf commentary. And Tinkle rubbing against her ankle like she wanted to be fed yet again.

Vicky nudged the doors shut and climbed back down with Tinkle.

Rob was sitting in the kitchen, watching the golf highlights as he served up her food. Two sausages, a burger, a pork chop, a kebab and a token gesture of salad and couscous. He looked up at her and grinned. 'Here you go.'

Vicky sat next to him and tucked in. She didn't realise how hungry she was until that first bite of sausage. 'How was your day?'

Rob nodded at the TV. 'Well, I didn't get to watch this live as I had to look after Bella and Jamie on my own.'

'Had to?'

'I don't mean it like that. But your parents buggered off not long after you did. And your old man sank four bottles of beer.'

'I saw.'

Rob looked up from his wine. 'Oh?'

'Popped in there later on. Something to do with the case. You know who won the golf?'

'Nope. That's why I'm watching the highlights.'

Vicky reached across and poured herself a glass of red. She put the glass to her lips and the exhaustion hit her right then, but at least she could relax now.

The door chimed.

Something speared Vicky's heart. The note, still in her pocket. Were they back? Or was it her old man, ready for round two? She put her wine down. 'I'll get it.'

'Have your tea.'

'You watch the golf. You'll want to see Tiger winning.'

'Thanks for the spoiler.'

'I'm joking.' She kissed his cheek, then shuffled through the house, mussing up her hair but also making sure her baton was within easy grasp. She eased the door open and stopped dead.

'Evening, Vicks.' Alan stood there, hands in his pockets, smiling like there was nothing weird about Bella's father turning up out of the blue. He'd lost weight, but his sideburns now reached down to his jawline. He wore a short-sleeved shirt showing off overdeveloped biceps, his quiff swept round in a long indie boy fringe, but greying badly. And she still towered over him. 'Is that the annoying guy from *Friends* staying in your house?'

Vicky felt that deep pain in her gut, but it spread to her chest and arms, down both legs. 'They're all annoying.'

'True.' He laughed. 'I remember you used to have a Rachel.'

Vicky stepped out and ran a hand through her hair. 'It didn't suit me.'

'Beg to differ.'

'You left that note, didn't you?'

Alan nodded. 'Sorry, didn't want Mr Lover Man to see me.'

'You could've put your name and number on it.'

'Where would the fun be in that? Besides, my number hasn't changed since you dumped me.'

She folded her arms. 'How did you find me?'

'It's not just you, Vicks, is it?'

'What's that supposed to mean?'

'Well.' He flashed up his eyebrows. 'Just wondering whether I can see my kid.'

Vicky had played this out in her head so many times. Too many times. Far too many. She could play this any number of ways. Deny Bella even existed? Open up, let him into their lives? Or fight him. But in the here and now, it all just crumbled to nothing. 'She's six, Alan, and this is the first time you're interested in seeing your own daughter?'

'It's not like you actually told me I was a father, is it?'

Vicky's mouth was dry. She needed the whole bottle of wine just to dampen it a touch. 'You're still a dickhead, then?'

He just gave a flash of his eyebrows.

She swallowed. 'What do you want?'

'I see you're in a settled relationship again.'

'I'm a stepmother too.'

'You married him?'

'No, but I'm happy for the first time in years.'

'I'm very pleased to hear it. Trouble is, Bella's still my daughter.'

So he knew her name. Christ, how did he find out? Like most cops, Vicky stayed off the internet as much as she could. On Schoolbook, she used her mother's maiden name, Kidd, so no numpties could track her down. And yet one had. The worst one.

'Look, I can't just—'

'You're saying that if I'd just called, you'd put whatever you were doing aside to talk to me and let me speak to her?'

'I'm saying nothing.' But Vicky couldn't afford to be the bad guy here, so she folded her arms again. 'Alan, now isn't the time for this. I need you to go. I'll call you later. Your number hasn't changed, after all.'

He seemed to think it through, then nodded. 'Okay. But don't take your time.'

Vicky watched him go, that same uneven stride. He looked back and blew her a kiss.

What the hell did she ever see in him?

'Who was that?' Behind her, Rob was standing in the doorway.

'Wrong address. Someone looking for a golf party.' She sniffed, and knew it was her tell, but she couldn't prevent herself from doing it. 'Sorry, it's not. It was Alan.'

Rob frowned at her. 'As in...?'

'As in.'

Rob stood up straight and flexed his fists like he was going to chase after him and beat the living shit out of him with his bare hands. 'Thanks for telling me the truth.'

She shrugged. 'This isn't easy, but lying about it isn't going to make it any easier.'

'Why was he here?'

'I have no idea. And I've no idea how he found out about Bella.' Vicky collapsed into Rob's arms. 'I'm sorry I lied.'

'It's okay.' Rob broke off the hug and led her inside by the hand. He sat her down in the kitchen and handed her the wine glass. 'We need to decide on a strategy.'

'I know. I've had years to plan, but now it's here and he's back and... and... Christ.'

'Alan should have access to Bella.'

'I know.' Vicky sipped her wine. 'And I know it'll hurt, but it's the right thing to do. I'll speak to him and see what he wants.'

'What he wants?'

'Knowing Alan, he'll be after something other than seeing Bella.'

DAY 2

Monday
Monday, 23rd July 2018

13

Vicky bit into the toast and chewed as quickly as she could. The back garden sat in gloomy grey, yesterday's sunny glow now replaced by thick haar, the wispy clouds passing across the lawn like an army of ghosts.

And the strong coffee wasn't helping clear her thick head. Just one glass of wine, but she felt like she'd been out for a long session with Karen and Jenny. Orange juice might shift it, so she tried that.

But the small glass of red wine wasn't behind it, more getting woken up at half five by two bodies jumping on a bed. And working a case in boiling heat without eating or drinking much, and just... everything whirring round her head. The truth about her father's career.

And Alan.

Christ.

A blur of energy squealed through the kitchen and thumped its fists against the patio door, then twisted the handle. 'Mummy!'

'Just a sec, Bells.' Vicky bit into the second slice of toast and got up.

But Jamie roared into the room, arms flailing. Tinkle shot off from her hiding place under the table. Bella squealed into Jamie and sent the poor kid flying. His glasses slid across the floor and Bella almost stood on them as she rushed out of the room.

Vicky dropped her slice of toast onto the plate and rushed over to him. 'Are you okay?'

He was nodding furiously, looking around for his specs. 'There they are.' He reached over and pressed them on his nose, then got up and darted out of the room. 'I'm coming for you!'

'Watch out!' Rob stepped aside to let his son past.

Vicky slumped back onto the stool. 'Well, good luck with them today.'

'I'll need a lot more than luck with those two.' Rob came over and wrapped her in a hug, then kissed her on the top of her head, then he broke off and walked over to the filter machine. 'You need a top up?'

Vicky was staring into her cup just as her phone rang. *Forrester calling…* 'Better take this.' She hit answer and put it to her ear, mindful of the small kids wandering around. 'What's up?'

'You guys get the *Argus*?'

'The Edinburgh paper?'

'Aye. Do you?'

'It's 2018, nobody reads newspapers any more.'

'Okay. Well, can you look at the bloody front page on a computer?'

'Just a sec.' Vicky reached over for Rob's tablet, smothered in jam and orange juice. She put her phone down to wipe it clean. Then it unlocked, and she was in and typing "the argus".

The page blared out:

BACK FROM THE DEAD

The main article had a photo of Jim Sanderson smiling in his business suit. Inset was one outside the High Court in Edinburgh; presumably the man in a purple suit talking to a news camera was his solicitor. The page was shadowed by many other articles about Atreus, all hunting for those elusive clicks and that advertising spend.

But the byline underneath crawled under her skin.

Alan Lyall.

Shit, shit, shit.

She picked up the phone and put it to her ear. 'I've skimmed it. What's upset you?'

'There's a lot more in there than what Raven briefed them about last night. Keep an eye on it for me.'

'What makes you think I know anything?'

Forrester laughed. 'Because you and this Lyall lad have a history.'

'A long dead history.'

'Vicky, I need you to speak to him.'

She huffed out a sigh. 'And I need to not speak to him.'

'Pretty please?'

'Is this who Raven was door-stepped by?'

'Obviously.'

'And you asked Mac to speak to him.'

'I did, but I think I need my big guns on this.'

'You don't think that'd be a conflict of interest? It's a no.' Vicky locked the tablet and rested it on the worktop. 'Look, I need to go. I'll speak to you later.'

'Not so fast.'

'What?'

'Thought about it overnight. Can you chum Mac to this Craigen boy's office, see what his workers know?'

'So I'm working *for* him?'

'*With* him. He can do all his analytical Rain Man shite, you can actually get to the bottom of what Craigen was up to. Guys like that, they'll be boasting about the young lassie they're porking.'

'Porking? Haven't heard that in a long time.'

'I'm joking, but that's how these boys think. Loose lips sink ships and all that.'

'Right. I'll call you later.' She ended the call before he could complain again.

'Sounds like another long work day ahead?' Rob passed her a coffee mug, steam spiralling up like the haar outside.

'Probably.' Vicky took one last bite of toast and fiddled with her phone. She had to unblock Mac's contact to text him a curt: "Call Me". 'I get the feeling this case will go on for weeks.'

'*Weeks?*'

She started her second coffee, even though she knew she'd need the toilet all day. 'I shouldn't tell you this, but it's the same MO as a case my dad worked in the nineties.'

'Seriously?'

'A serial killer case. They called him Atreus.'

Rob nodded. 'I know all about that one. Read a book about it. Wasn't there a podcast?'

'A podcast?'

'You know, a serialised radio show distributed by—'

'I know what a podcast is.' But Vicky had her phone out and tapped out a text to Karen: "There's an Atreus podcast. Dig into it for me." Hopefully that'd be enough.

'The Atreus guy died, didn't he?'

'He did.' Vicky put her phone down again. 'Speaking of murder, what's your plan today?'

'I was going to take the little serial killers to Dundee. That science exhibition thingy is doing something about computer games. I know Jamie's not into them, but Bella can't get enough, can she?'

'No, she really can't.'

'Does she get that from her father?'

A horn peeped outside and her phone buzzed with a text. Mac: "Outside, ready when you are."

'Christ.'

'What's up?'

'Just work.' She walked over and kissed Rob on the cheek. 'I need to go. Love you, bye.'

But Rob held her hand. 'You need to control the Alan situation, okay? Bella's needs are more important than our egos.'

'Okay, I'll get on top of it today.' She caressed his cheek. 'And I might get on top of you later, if you're a good boy.'

OUTSIDE, MacDonald was sitting in the pool Subaru, the engine running and the exhaust pluming in the haar.

Vicky shivered as she walked through the freezing cold air. It might be July, but it was still the north-east of Scotland and it was still battered by haar. She opened the passenger door. The living room curtains were twitching.

MacDonald leaned across. 'You're a bit more professionally dressed today.'

She smoothed down her trousers. 'Why are you here?'

'Boss's orders. Told me to take you down to speak to Craigen's business.' MacDonald checked his watch. 'Supposed to be meeting the number two at half seven.'

'Christ, that's early.'

'Tell me about it. You want to hop in?'

'Like I'd want to be stuck with you. I'll meet you there.'

'Oh, right.' MacDonald frowned. 'You know you're not allowed to drive your own car on duty?'

'I'll be fine. I've got good insurance.'

Rob came out onto the front step with Bella to wave her off.

Vicky returned the wave just as Jamie joined them.

MacDonald glanced in the rearview. 'Now there's a beta male right there.'

Vicky didn't even look at him. She shut the door and walked towards her own car, waving at the love of her life.

THE ONCOMING COMMUTER traffic on the long road into Carnoustie was blocking them as they headed for Dundee, not that Carnoustie wasn't much more than a long road.

MacDonald's Subaru was racing through the housing estate to the main road. Boys and their toys...

And where did he get off, accusing Rob of being a beta male? Like he was some amazing catch.

She pulled across the roundabout and headed down Westfield Street. Her old house looked empty. She turned left onto Thomas Street. Bella and Jamie's school sat back from the road, almost hidden by the haar. A new build that used to be a park, though not one she'd frequented much as a kid.

In the distance, a crane jutted out of the mist, swinging around as it put the finishing touches to a housing development that'd just missed the Open and probably wouldn't fill up until the next one.

She caught sight of MacDonald parking outside a sprawling office complex built out of old mill buildings. In Manchester or Dundee, they were elegant buildings, converted into upmarket apartments or museums, but here in Carnoustie they were just big concrete boxes thrown up in the sixties and left to fester until Derek Craigen came along. The roof had been opened out like his home, with a balcony that would have a great view across most of the golf course. The "DC Energy" sign must be big enough to be seen from Fife and, even though it was early, the car park was almost full.

Vicky grabbed the last space and got out.

A man and a woman in business suits met each other in the car park, smiling and chatting as they ambled over to the door. Clearly the message of the boss's death hadn't been relayed to the staff.

MacDonald was already outside his car, wearing his shades in the gloom.

Vicky walked over. 'You know, I've lived in Carnoustie most of my life and I don't think I've been here before.'

'And they say you can't teach an old dog new tricks?'

'Jesus, Euan.'

'I'm joking!' He held up his hands. 'What did Forrester want after I left?'

'A blowjob.'

He looked at her like he believed it, then laughed. 'But seriously?'

'Nothing much.'

'So it was about me, then.'

'No, it was about me.'

'Fair enough.' MacDonald sighed. 'Considine is a piece of work, isn't he?'

'Well, aye, but what's he done now?'

'After you cleared off last night, I went to find him, but he'd foxtrot oscared and left Louise Craigen on her own in the mortuary with her kid. So I dropped her back home.'

Vicky wanted to ask if that's all he did, but that would mean stooping to his level. 'How was she?'

'Not great. She just sat in the back seat, holding her daughter. Teri or something? Must be tough for her. Losing her old man during a shitty divorce. When I turned off the high street towards her flat, she started talking, though. Asked me in for a coffee.'

Vicky looked round at him. 'Seriously?'

'Mind out of the gutter, Dodds.' He shook his head. 'She needed to talk so I went in with her. Kid was with us the whole time. And it all just poured out. All the stuff that clown Considine was supposed to get, I got. A list of business rivals that boiled down to three people in Southend, Newcastle and Perth. Got phone appointments with them later on. Don't think it's a valid avenue, but I'll go through the motions like my old man.'

'What do you mean?'

'Civil engineer. Spent a lot of time in sewers, wading through...' He coughed, then took off his shades and put them back in the car. 'Look, I thought about it overnight and I'm starting to agree with you about Louise being a suspect. If they're not divorced, then she does stand to inherit the lot, the house, the flat,' he waved at the office, 'this business. That's a serious motive.'

'Becoming an expert in family law, huh?'

'Has the boy found anything on the company's financial health?'

'The boy? Considine?'

'Right.' MacDonald smiled. 'He's, what, thirty, but he acts like he's fourteen at most. Being a right little twat about this Subaru too. Had to get in super early to make sure he didn't claim it.'

'And now who's acting like a silly wee boy.'

'Answer's no. The company seems to be in fine health. And both properties were owned outright by Mr and Mrs Craigen.'

'Okay, so let's see if that "seems to be" translates to "actually is".'

14

Jordan Russell's office didn't look like it belonged in seaside Angus, but rather a London hotel or an Oxford college. Oak-panelled walls and a large fussy desk, with no sign of a computer. Like he was teaching in a private school rather than being Chief Operating Officer of a Tayside plumber. Slicked-back hair and the physique of a gym monkey, his chiselled body stretching out his pinstriped suit, with a big moon face and a disc beard surrounding his pale lips. 'Sure you don't want any coffee?'

Vicky smiled. 'Had some for breakfast.'

'Okay.' Russell reached forward and poured smoky black coffee from a silver pot, similar to one she'd seen in that cafe in Harrogate where Rob had taken her last summer. Russell passed a cup over to MacDonald. 'Here you go. Think you'll enjoy it.'

'Thanks. Sure I will.' MacDonald used silver tongs to drop a lump of brown sugar into the cup. 'Can I say this is a lovely office?'

'Thanks. Dez let us decorate our own, no expense spared. Shame about the view, though.' Russell waved at the window, which pointed the wrong way. Instead of the beach and the links golf course, it looked north and up to the hill that ran along the town, the grand old Victorian houses poking out of old trees. 'The roof garden is perfect for watching the golf, though.'

MacDonald stirred his coffee. 'And did you?'

'Not a fan, hence me taking this office.' Russell sat back in his wooden chair, and held his mug in front of him, savouring the aroma. 'This whole thing is hard to take. Dez was a good mate. We did our City & Guilds together, then worked our arses off, a right pair of cheeky bastards, but we built up this business into what you see here.'

'But you don't own the business?'

Russell frowned at MacDonald. 'No, I got swindled somewhere down the line.' He laughed, but there seemed to be some malice behind the humour. 'Dez took on all of the risk himself, including a massive bank loan, but I got a ten percent stake out of it. Come dividend time, though, it's mighty lucrative.'

'And how's business been?'

'Solid.'

MacDonald took a sip. 'Oh that's good.' He rested the cup down on the table. 'Gather you had a contract for the LA Golf hotel?'

'Right. Took up a lot of Dez's time, so I had to focus on most of the day-to-day shenanigans here.' Russell slurped his coffee. 'John Lamont's... exacting, I think that's how you'd describe it.'

'Were there any difficulties between them?'

'Not really, just that Lamont's a property developer, right? But now he's moved onto the client side, I think he's finding stepping back and letting the professionals do their job a little tough. Always happens with those boys. They go over every single detail when it's the big picture that matters. I'm the big picture guy here, and Dez is all about the detail.' He sipped more coffee. 'It's where the devil lives.'

'So I gather. You and him still get on?'

'Stronger than ever.'

Vicky leaned forward, mindful of trying to get him to something resembling a point. 'How well do you know Louise?'

'Well enough. Not sure she likes me much.'

'Oh?'

'Well, me and Dez are good buddies. Back in the day, the

number of times we'd get absolutely panel-beaten in the pub and end up home late. She went ballistic at us once. And she had a point. Actually made me quit the drink. Got in shape.' Russell seemed to flex a pec under his suit. 'But Dez didn't. Always off on trips with the boys. Don't think she liked him being away so often.' He offered MacDonald a refill, but got a shake of the head. 'Shame about what happened to their marriage, though. The kids were finding it tough, as far as I can tell.'

'You think she'll inherit the business?'

'I assume so. They weren't divorced. It's going to be a nightmare if she takes over.' Russell topped up his coffee cup. 'Remember when Dez first met her, though. One Saturday night at the Golf.' He smiled at them, like he was imparting secret information. 'The Golf was a pub. It's now a restaurant, I think, but it used to be the after-hours place in Carnoustie.'

'I remember it well.'

He narrowed his eyes at Vicky. 'You a local lassie?' His accent slipped and lost some of its refinements.

'Born and bred. Well, my parents are from Dundee so I'm not old Carnoustie.'

'Wouldn't recommend it.'

'Do you know who Mr Craigen was currently involved with?'

'No. I mean, we were close, but Dez could be a bugger for the lassies.'

'You mean he had many affairs?'

'I wouldn't say many.' Russell slurped more coffee. 'He kept going on about this... this lady he was seeing, but none of us met her.'

Vicky reached into her jacket pocket for her phone and found the photo of the still-unknown female victim. 'Is this her?'

'Sorry, but if you'd been listening, you'd have heard the bit where I said I've never met her.'

Vicky felt herself blush. Made worse by MacDonald grinning wide. She stuffed her phone away. 'We believe Mr Craigen was at the LA Golf function on Saturday night. Were you there?'

'No, I had another engagement.' Russell hid behind his coffee. 'But I know someone who was.'

BRIAN OGG WAS CLEARLY a golf fan. His office looked across the course towards the Carnoustie Hotel. And he'd decorated his office in the style of Britpop hooligan. Vicky swore that was Geri Halliwell's Union Jack dress in a display case next to Noel Gallagher's guitar. Unlike his colleague, he wore jeans and a Fred Perry. He had a strange conehead that seemed to taper back like that flying dinosaur, and he kept sniffing like he'd already done a mound of coke that morning, or that he'd been using his espresso machine even more than his colleague over the corridor.

He checked a wristwatch, some hulking great slice of bling. 'So I'm the finance director here, yeah.' He had a local accent and an old Carnoustie name dating back from when it was a fishing village, rather than a Victorian resort or Dundee dormitory town. But his soft and slow Angus voice was sliced up by an American twang like he'd worked over the Pond for a while. 'Trouble is, I've got a meeting in ten, so if this could be quick?'

Vicky sat back and folded her arms. 'What's the meeting about?'

'This takeover... It never rains, I swear.' Ogg got up from his desk and walked over to the window. 'Dez is buying a firm in Southend. Essex. Bunch of chancers called MIH. Had his eye on them for ages as a way of growing the business down south.'

Vicky looked at MacDonald and arched an eyebrow so he got the message, then back at Ogg. 'That must be on hold, though?'

'Right.' Ogg leaned back against the window sill. 'As much as I'm trying to slow things down on that deal, there are punitive clauses in the initial deal memo that are binding. I told Dez not to sign it but he wouldn't bloody listen.'

'Do you own any of the business?'

'Ten percent, but the takeover will dilute my holding down to eight. But our profit will more than double.'

Sounded like business was really healthy. Expanding nation-ally. Meaning Louise Craigen would inherit a shitload of money.

MacDonald joined Ogg by the window, acting like he was trying to pin him down to a single location. 'What's your under-standing of who'll take over as CEO?'

'Well, Jordan's next in line. Continuity's important.' Ogg paused for a few seconds, but he couldn't stand still. 'I'm afraid you'd need to speak to the general counsel about that.'

'The general counsel?'

'Our in-house lawyer. She's in London today. Speaking to the Southend shower about this takeover. My meeting is with her, getting on the same page about this whole thing, but Christ, I'm going to have to brief her about Dez.'

'We understand Mr Craigen was involved with someone.' MacDonald held out his phone. 'You recognise her?'

Ogg took a few seconds to examine it. 'What happened to her?'

'I'm not at liberty to divulge too much.'

'Is this what was in the *Argus* this morning?'

'Potentially. Do you know her?'

Ogg handed the phone back. 'That's Marie.'

'Know her surname?'

'Sorry. It's Marie or something.'

'How do you know her?'

Ogg exhaled slowly, his puffed-up cheeks deflating. 'I went to Dubai with Dez last summer. We were supposed to be charming the CEO of this Essex firm, all under the cover of a business conference. But it was a golfing trip. And when I mean golfing trip, I mean a lot of drinking. Or so I thought. I was staying with my brother in Edinburgh and turned up at the airport for the flight, and Dez had his mistress with him.'

'Was this before he split from Mrs Craigen?'

'Dez told his missus it was a business meeting, sourcing cheap pipe. I tell you, he was laying pipe. Barely saw him all weekend. Had to schmooze the boy myself.'

'We gather this Marie was with him at the function at the new golf course on Saturday night. Know anything about that?'

'Aye, I was there.' Ogg stared out of the window. 'Dez was too. Had her with him. Brazen. Got to hand it to the boy.'

'What do you—'

'I mean, it was like they were finally out of the closet, you know? And she was gorgeous. No idea what she was doing with him, then again he's loaded.'

'Did you see anyone speaking to her?'

Ogg looked over at Vicky with a nod. 'John Lamont, aye.'

U p ahead, MacDonald blasted through the national speed limit at the far end of Carnoustie, following the coast road out east. The haar was blowing in off the sea, like a snowstorm battering the road. Everything was back to normal, no evidence that Carnoustie had just held one of the world's biggest international sports tournaments.

Vicky followed as fast as her old car could muster. Out to sea was just a wall of mist with blue sky above, meaning it'd probably burn off by lunchtime.

MacDonald took a hard left between two tall market garden walls.

She followed him up a single-track lane, then across some pebbles towards a house, an old manse, with a double-height bay window on the right, and ornate lines everywhere. A big wooden garden room to the right. And no signs anyone was home. Further over a low set of farm buildings that looked like offices now. The place was bigger than the entire estate Vicky lived on, let alone her home.

She parked the car and got out.

Something told her this place used to be a private member's

gym. Wasn't it owned by that athlete? The woman from Dundee who ran marathons, might even have won a gold medal?

MacDonald breezed past her and crunched over the pebbles towards the house. 'So, you want to speak to Lamont because he should've told us this mistress was there?'

'Don't you?'

'I don't disagree.'

'Are you testing me?'

'Let's call it coaching.'

'And what makes you think that *you* can coach *me*?'

MacDonald didn't say anything, just kept watching.

She let out a sigh. 'Okay. First, given he took her to Dubai last summer, Craigen's relationship with this Marie was serious.'

'Agreed.'

'Her engagement ring means push was coming to shove. The divorce was going to close soon, so she'd have to act now.'

'Don't you think that seems like a stretch?'

'Hence me using words like "possible" and "may well have".'

MacDonald actually laughed at that. 'Surely she'd be taking him to the cleaners?'

'Maybe she's got skeletons in her own closet.'

'Maybe.' He huddled underneath the entrance and rang the doorbell, getting a deep bonging sound for his trouble. 'Go on.'

Vicky stared hard at him, waiting for him to look round before continuing. But he didn't. 'What kind of man does that to his wife?'

'It's the wife you're concerned about? Not their three kids?'

'It's her he directly impacted.'

'There can be any number of reasons, Vicky. She could be a nightmare, he could've been struggling with the kids, his business could be a mess.'

'You think any of that justifies adultery?'

'I'm not trying to justify it. I'm saying men are not exactly complex beasts, sometimes all it takes is something very simple or trivial to justify the most stupid actions.'

'Speaking from experience, right?'

He tried the bell again. 'Quite some place, isn't it?'

Vicky peered through the side of the bay window, but just saw into an unfurnished living room. Stripped wooden floors and white walls, filled up with packing boxes and furniture wrapped in plastic sheeting. 'Don't think I didn't notice the change of subject.'

MacDonald hit the bell again. 'You don't think Louise Craigen is a suspect?'

Vicky didn't even have to think it through. 'Well, clearly she is. There's the financial motive, and Craigen kicked her and her kids out of their home too. Put them up in his shagging pad.'

'But why would she use the Atreus MO?' MacDonald joined her by the window and peered in. 'I mean, kill them or don't, but why torture them like that? And could she really overpower Craigen? He's a big guy and she's tiny.'

Vicky didn't have answers to that.

The door cracked open and a woman stood there. 'Excuse me?' Local accent and fizzing with energy, like she'd drunk a whole case of WakeyWakey or whatever the kids were on these days.

MacDonald walked over, warrant card out. 'Police, ma'am. We're looking for Mr Lamont.'

'He's not in.'

He gave a broad smile. 'You know where he is?'

'Already at work.'

VICKY GOT out and scanned around the hotel car park. No sign of Lamont, but his Lexus was there.

A huddle gathered around the snack van. Didn't look like cops, so probably reporters. Oh, except for Considine and a couple of uniforms right in the middle, laughing and joking as they tucked in to bacon rolls and coffee.

She stormed over to Considine and locked eyes with Alan.

She stopped dead. Obviously he was here. Superb. Just perfect. She caught sight of Lamont upstairs in his office, surveying the scene with a grim look on his face, then he disappeared.

Considine sauntered over to her, his cheeks full like a hamster's. 'Sarge.' Or at least it sounded like that.

'Have you got hold of the solicitors yet?'

He rubbed his sleeve over his lips. 'Not open until nine.'

'But you have spoken to them?'

'Well, the duty solicitor, aye. I'll get up there after my brekky.'

'Thank you.' Vicky smiled at Considine, even though she wanted to scream in his face. 'Let me know how you get on.'

'Right.' He trudged away, tearing another hunk of roll off with his teeth.

MacDonald joined them, hands in pockets, acting all casual. 'What's he made an arse of now?'

'I've lost count.'

MacDonald nodded at someone. 'I'll catch you later.' He set off towards the huddle of reporters, giving a big tall guy a fist bump, then a bear hug.

'Strange seeing you here, Vicky.' Alan stepped back, his big arms folded across his chest.

Vicky wanted to run away and hide, but she looked at him. Thick stubble covered his face, and his fringe hung low, tucked behind his ear. She had to shut her eyes, otherwise she was going to lamp him one. And that really wouldn't look good. 'Knew you'd be here. I see you're still at the *Argus*?'

'For my sins, aye. Edinburgh's a good city to live in. And it's been good for me and my career. After years of adulation, I should think of moving on but I feel I owe them something.' He smiled at her. 'Got a little something for you, though.'

She should just walk away. Right now, right then. The last thing she needed was this arsehole back in her life. In Bella's too. And Rob's and Jamie's. When she'd told him she was pregnant and he chose the big city lights of Edinburgh over her...

And yet, the little creep was dangling a worm right in front of her mouth. Did she really have a choice?

'You can keep your little something in your trousers.'

'Oh, Vicky.'

'What is it?'

'You think I'm going to just give up a lead like that?'

'I'm not going to beg you. Tell me or I'll go.'

That seemed to hit the mark, at least. 'Okay, well I heard that on Saturday night your friend John Lamont ran naked over the golf course.'

'You're going to have to try a bit harder.'

'I'm serious, Vicks.'

'Don't call me that.'

He raised his hands. 'Spoke to the bar staff here and one of the caterers. I wouldn't normally share a name, but between you, me and our daughter, it's one Sayrah Douglas of Monifieth.'

Vicky stood up straight.

'Gather she had someone interrupting a romantic lunch yesterday?'

'If that's her idea of romance, I'd hate to see her idea of a knee trembler outside a nightclub.'

Alan snorted with laughter. 'Classy, Vicks. Classy.'

'So Lamont did this nude run during the party?'

'Right. I mean, you think there's something in it?'

Vicky looked up at the office, but there was no sign of Lamont any more. 'Should I?'

'Not my place to tell you. I'll be adding it to the website around lunchtime. It's amazing the clicks you get from a story like that.'

Vicky couldn't help but think it was most likely a rich man's eccentricity. Lamont had been working hard to get this place open, had a few too many at his own party, then decided to streak across his golf course. 'You go and get your clicks, Alan.' She clapped his arm and walked off to the hotel.

Inside, the fish tank was up and running. Floor to ceiling and filled with water, but no fish in there yet. Not even a castle in the sand at the bottom. Not even sand at the bottom.

And no workmen, either, so the place finally had the look of an actual hotel, even though it still smelled of glue and sawdust. Hard to shift that, even with the cloying air freshener hissing down from the high ceiling.

The reception desk was empty, with an old-fashioned brass

bell sitting there to attract attention. But it meant a clear run at the lift and at Lamont, so Vicky charged through, determined to do this on her own without assistance from MacDonald.

She stopped by the door and called the lift, not looking back at anyone or anything.

'But I can't.' A loud South African accent, like it could cut through ice.

Ignore it. Ignore it. Ignore it.

'So you want me to get a warrant?' Karen Woods, sounding determined and focused. 'Because I'll get one. And it'll show me everything I want, but it'll let me get at everything you really don't want me to find.'

Ignore it. Ignore it. Ignore it.

Vicky turned round. They were the other side of the fish tank, the view obscured from the entrance, but Vicky could see them from here.

The party organiser—Lisa?—shook her head at Karen. 'Listen to me, as much as I want to help, I've got a gala opening tonight that ain't going to plan, honey. At half past three, I've got four Hollywood stars teeing off in front of the world's press and there's still a crime scene.'

Karen looked like she was going to throw the poor woman through the fish tank and stab her through the heart with giant shards of glass. 'Your hotel will be closed for a good while.'

'This isn't helping me!'

'I'm not here to help you.'

Vicky eased her way between them, giving a look to Karen that hopefully read support, but also shut up. She smiled at the organiser, trying to get on her side. 'Lisa, isn't it?'

She gave Vicky the side eye. 'Well done for remembering.'

'Lisa, thanks for your help in identifying Derek Craigen.'

And that seemed to disarm her. 'Okay?'

'The problem is, we still need to identify the woman. We believe that she might be Mr Craigen's plus one.'

'And, as I've told your little friend here, the whole point in a plus one is they're not listed.'

The lift door slid open and Vicky saw her chance. But Lamont stepped out into the hotel, looked right at her, then turned around, hitting the button until the lift shut. At least she knew where he was.

Vicky swept her gaze back to Lisa. 'I hear you, but I need you to help my colleague here to identify her. Whatever you can access to help us will be greatly appreciated.'

'I still need to—'

'Half three tee time?' Vicky smiled. 'If you play ball, we'll make sure your stars are playing ball by then too.'

Lisa thumbed behind her. 'The CCTV is through there in reception. I can take you through it, show you who I know.'

'That'd be great.'

'I'll just set it up.' She sauntered off, her heels clicking off the floor, and passed around the fish tank, distorted by the glass.

'Karen, I need you to find the victim, okay? And check into what Lamont was up to that night.'

'What do you mean?'

'I gather he streaked across the course.'

'What, seriously?'

'Seriously. Could be nothing, but I'm getting a bad feeling about him. And not just about streaking.'

'Will do.'

'You get my text about the podcast?'

'I did and I hope you're joking.'

'Hardly.'

'I mean it's not like I've got a million things to focus on at once, is it?'

'Thanks, Karen.' Vicky set off towards the lift and hit the call button. It pinged, the lift already there. She stepped in and pressed the top floor button, soaking up the yacht rock soundtrack. Was it Steely Dan or the Doobie Brothers? Her old man would know.

'Wait!' MacDonald was charging towards her. 'Hold it!'

She was so tempted to press the door close button like Lamont had done, but she held them open.

McDonald stepped through, his arms pressed against both

doors like he didn't trust them not to shut on him. 'Thanks.' He hit the button. 'Absolute classic song this.'

The door slid open and they climbed up.

Vicky folded her arms and couldn't take it any longer. 'What the hell is it?'

'You not a fan?'

'It's the kind of rubbish my dad listens to.'

'Well, your dad sounds like a good lad. Doobie Brothers, *What A Fool Believes.*'

'That was my fifty-fifty guess.'

'What's the other?'

'Steely bloody Dan.'

'Oh, now there's a band. You've not lived until you've heard *Aja* through a fifty-grand hi-fi.' The lift opened and MacDonald stepped halfway out, blocking the door with his hip and clicking his fingers in time with the music. 'Anyhoo, I've got a little something for you.'

Vicky stepped out of the lift and it already started to descend. 'Story of my life...'

'One of my journo chums out there, Big Fergus, he spoke to the greenkeeper who found the body.' He gave a flash of eyebrows. 'I've sent Buchan and Summers round to validate this, but it sounds like someone paid him to open the lighthouse so they could watch the fireworks display from the Open. It took two hundred quid for him to nick some tools from a work van and hack away at the door.'

'Why didn't he tell us?'

'Because it's illegal?'

Vicky shook her head. 'Right.'

MacDonald grinned wide. 'The description matches Craigen and his mystery woman.'

16

Vicky walked along the hotel corridor, keeping a few steps ahead of MacDonald. Somewhere, someone was using an angle grinder, but the sound was deadened by a few doors. And elsewhere, someone was brewing coffee, a caramel-y sweetness. 'The greenkeeper just told your mate?'

MacDonald was racing to keep up with her. His boots had a slight heel on them that'd hurt like crazy to wear. 'It took Big Fergus a lot of prodding to get even that much out of him. And the greenkeeper didn't go up there with them, before you ask.'

'How did you guess?' Vicky stopped outside Lamont's office and tried the door.

It opened into a reception area, the same one they'd been in the previous day. The smell of coffee seemed to emanate from here, much stronger smelling. The standing desk was manned by a secretary. A local girl plastered in thick makeup, her blonde hair dyed to within an inch of its life. She looked up at them and smiled, even had the perfect teeth of a catalogue model. 'How can I help you?' Definitely local, judging by that accent.

MacDonald walked over and leaned against her desk, the giant silver computer partially obscuring her. 'Looking for Mr Lamont.'

She nodded slowly. 'Police, right?'

'Right.' MacDonald didn't even need to show ID. 'Mind if we go on in?'

'Sure, but just a sec.' She walked over to a high-end coffee machine and handed an espresso cup to MacDonald. 'Saves me a job.'

'Happy to help.' MacDonald took the saucer and led Vicky into the office.

The room's lighting was up full blast.

No sign of Lamont, though.

MacDonald rested the coffee on the table over in the banquette by all the sports memorabilia.

Vicky searched around the place. Lamont's giant desk had the same computer as his receptionist. 'What the hell?'

A suit jacket and trousers hung from a handle to the side of the other door. Then a flush came from behind and it sounded like a tap came on, followed by one of those high-end hand-dryers that seemed to be everywhere.

MacDonald was standing next to her now. 'Is he in there?'

The door opened and Lamont waltzed out of an executive bathroom, all ivory and varnished oak with soft spotlights, just wearing a shirt and bright-orange boxer shorts. He smiled at them like this was all perfectly normal and eased his trousers out from the hanger, then stepped his toes in like he was putting on a crime scene suit. He stepped into a pair of shiny brogues, then took his suit jacket down and brushed off some hairs and dust before slipping his arms in. 'Can't abide creases.'

'So I can see.' MacDonald passed him his coffee. 'Your secretary gave me this.'

'Goddamn it.' Lamont snarled like MacDonald had just splashed it across his face. 'She *knows* it's not supposed to just *sit* there.' Regardless, he took a sip and smiled. 'Good coffee, but I expect *great* coffee every time.' He cracked it down off the desktop. 'How can I help you guys?'

MacDonald gave him a warm smile. 'Yesterday, you confirmed that Mr Craigen was at the function on Saturday with a woman, but you didn't know her name.'

'That's right.'

'Well, we've found out that you were sitting next to her for your sit-down dinner.'

Lamont stared hard at him for a few seconds, then emptied his cup. 'Okay.'

'Okay?'

'Look, buddy. I'm as upset as anyone that Derek Craigen is dead. We grew close as we worked together. He's good people. But I have no idea who his plus one is.'

'See, if I spend an evening with someone, I've usually got their name out of them within minutes.'

'Believe me, I was trying. She just wasn't playing.'

'Marie.'

'Huh?' Lamont looked him up and down. 'I mean, you're a much prettier guy than me. Maybe women furnish you with their names and numbers just like that?'

MacDonald's cheek dimpled as he beamed. 'But you chatted to her, right?'

'Right. I mean, in my line of business if someone doesn't immediately give you a business card, it means they don't want to know who you are. We had a ton of people at that table who were all keen to press the flesh and they took up most of my attention. I was keen to get them to sign on the dotted line for memberships.'

'How much would that set them back.'

'Twenty grand.'

'That's a lot of cash.'

'Not for these guys.'

'So what did you talk to her about?'

'Nothing much, to be honest. She only had eyes for Dez, wasn't interested in me or the other dudes there. Didn't seem to want to chat to the other dates, either. And let me be clear here, they were all wives.'

'So you think Craigen brought a prostitute to this fancy dinner?'

'Oh, come, come. This wasn't that fancy.' Lamont gestured at his open shirt neck. 'Smart but casual dress code.' He spluttered out a laugh. 'It wasn't even black tie. I wanted my guests to relax and let their hair down and open their wallets.'

'And then head up to the lighthouse?'

'Lighthouse?'

MacDonald's turn to laugh. He pointed out of the window behind him. 'See that big building sticking out of the sea there? It's called a lighthouse.'

'I know what a lighthouse is, son, I just have no idea what the hell you're talking about.'

'Someone broke in there to allow some of your guests access to the building so they could watch the fireworks.'

'Huh?'

'We found a bottle of champagne up there. Two glasses. It's where we found Mr Craigen's body, as you know.'

Lamont stared at him, then at Vicky, but he was still processing things. Assessing the risks and pay-offs of various lies, various stories, no doubt.

Vicky leaned her head forward like she was wanting him to confide in her. 'I suggest you tell us the truth.'

'You do, huh?' Lamont shook his head. 'Look, I heard about this excursion but I had nothing to do with it.'

'See our source suggests that money changed hands.'

'Well, your source might be an excellent greenkeeper but he's not irreplaceable.'

'I didn't say it was him.'

'But I know it was.' Lamont gestured at his coffee. 'This whole business has thrown me. You've no idea the amount of stress I'm under. Think I told you the last time we spoke, I'm used to being on the other side of the fence. Doing the work. Paying for it... It's a killer.' Lamont sat there, arms folded enough to crease his suit jacket sleeves. He was going to hate that if he noticed. 'God, my head is thumping today.' He reached over and pressed a button on his desk. 'Rachel, please bring in three espressos.'

MacDonald stood up and thrust his hands in his pockets. 'Trespassing on government property is a crime.'

Lamont didn't have anything for that, just sat there, eyes narrowed, fists balled.

'Streaking across a golf course is illegal too.'

Lamont looked round at Vicky. 'Excuse me?' He switched his gaze between them, then settled it back on Vicky. 'Look, I was drunk and it was my party, so I can cry if I want to, right?'

'Thank you for telling us the truth. We appreciate it.'

The door slid open and his secretary tottered in on too-high heels, carrying a tray laden with cups on saucers. She rested it on the table and tilted her head towards Lamont.

But he wasn't looking at her. 'Thank you, Rachel.' He waited until she left the room, then looked at MacDonald. 'You want to try one?'

'Sure.' He passed a cup across the table. Lamont raised his eyebrows at Vicky.

'I'm allergic to espresso.'

'Is that a thing?'

'Apparently so. I can drink filter and cafetière, but espresso gives me cold-like symptoms a couple of days later.'

'Huh. Well, I had that machine flown in from Milan,' pronounced Mee-lan, 'and it makes the perfect coffee. Sent Rachel on a week-long barista course to make sure she gets it just right.' He snarled again. 'I designed these two offices so that by the time she brought it from the machine to my desk, my espresso was at precisely eight-five degrees centigrade.' He took a sip. 'The perfect temperature.' He tossed the espresso down his throat like it was vodka and he was on a stag weekend in the Algarve. 'Magnificent.' He reached over and hit the button again. 'Rachel, that's the ticket. Keep it up.'

MacDonald drank his more slowly. 'Got to say, that's good coffee.'

Lamont took Vicky's cup and downed it in one go. 'Still just about right.'

'Sir, this displacement activity isn't getting you off.'

'What displacement?'

'I don't care what it is, someone trespassed in that lighthouse. Two people were subsequently brutally murdered.'

Lamont sat back and his arms hung to his sides. 'Look, I knew nothing about it. I've tried buying that lighthouse, but they won't sell it to me. Apparently it's still needed. But it's been built way too close to my hotel, so it's unnecessary and irritating.'

The way his mind worked, it didn't seem to occur to him that he was the one building next to a lighthouse and not the other way round.

'Buying that land and getting through planning was hell on earth. I had to give them access rights across my land. You know how much I spent on course design? I had to throw out designs for three, four, sixteen and seventeen because of a path that needed to run down from here to that goddamn lighthouse.'

'We need the names of the guests who went there.'

'Good luck with that. I can't give you any names, as I wasn't there. As you pointed out, I was half-naked and running across the eighteenth.'

'Just half-naked?'

'Okay. Fully naked.'

Given the lack of forensics at the lighthouse, it offered a plausible explanation. Kill someone, wash the blood off in a bracing dip in the North Sea and prance around your own golf course, tackle out.

'So where did you go on this jaunt?'

'I was a bit worse for wear, it has to be said.' Lamont folded his arms. 'As far as I know, it was the first and eighteenth, with a detour around the second and third.'

'You go near the sixteenth?'

'Not to my knowledge.'

'Anyone who can validate that?'

'Well yeah, sure.'

'So?'

'Well, it's all on CCTV, but how can I trust you guys with it?'

MacDonald laughed. 'Here's the deal. Couple of cops review

the footage, validate it's you. No harm, no foul.' He left a long pause. 'Unless it's not true.'

'No, it's true.' Lamont leaned forward. 'I suggest you take that up with Lisa. She's got a mind like a steel trap.' He pressed the button again. 'Rachel, another espresso please.'

THE LIFT DOORS slid shut and they started the slow descent back down.

MacDonald ran a hand through his hair. 'That was astonishing coffee.'

'Take your word for it.'

'You're *really* allergic to coffee?'

'Just espresso. Never been tested, but one cup absolutely breaks me. I have two cups of filter every morning and it's fine. If I even think about having an espresso it blows me up.'

'Such a shame.' The doors opened and MacDonald gestured for her to go first. 'So, what do you think we should do about this?'

Vicky stepped out into the atrium and realised she had absolutely no idea. 'What's your take on Lamont?'

'You first?'

'Just a rich dickhead.' Vicky looked across the atrium, where the fish were getting fed into the giant tank. 'Well, Euan, what's the plan?'

'I need to find the event organiser.' MacDonald got out his mobile and put it to his ear.

'So you can work your charms on her again?'

'My charms? Believe me, that wasn't me flirting.'

'Right. Well, she was with DC Woods in the security office.' Through the warped glass, someone was waving at her. Considine. 'I'll catch you later.'

'Okay, thanks.'

Vicky walked across the tiles but Considine had already slipped through the doors.

Outside, Forrester and Raven were making best use of the haar to speak to the journalists one by one. An impromptu press conference. And knowing Raven, they'd be watermarking the stories, adding in little nuggets to each one to be able to trace them back to a journalist, to see who was sharing with who.

Forrester was dealing with Alan, both with their hands in their pockets. Laughing too hard.

Vicky caught up with Considine. 'What's up?'

'I was waving for MacDonald, but I suppose you'll do.'

'I'll do?'

'Christ, you need to calm down. Of course I was waving at you.' His smirk soon soured, though. 'Oh, Jenny Morgan was looking for you. She's at Craigen's house just now. Trouble is, she won't speak to me.'

17

Vicky stepped inside Craigen's house and called out, 'Hello?'

No sights, no sounds, just her voice echoing round the empty hallway.

She looked into the kitchen, empty of people, but the counter-tops were rammed with packets of food and bottles of various types of alcohol, all bagged and tagged.

Considine started inspecting it. 'Oh, some nice stuff here.'

'And it's all catalogued, so none of that should go walkies.'

'Sarge, I'm not a bloody tea leaf!'

The stairs crunched and Vicky darted back through.

Zoey Jones was slouching down the staircase, dressed in a crime scene suit, her mask dangling free as she lugged an evidence box almost as big as her. She frowned at Vicky. 'Hey.'

'Hi, Zoey.'

'Mr Craigen, whoever he is, has a *ton* of computers. I'm going to be *forever* going through these.' Zoey rested the box on the floor at the bottom of the steps and showed off a sizeable baby bulge.

As hard as she tried, Vicky couldn't shake off this sickening feeling deep in the pit of her stomach.

Vicky hadn't seen her in at least two years and if anything she looked even younger, despite her pregnancy. 'You shouldn't be lugging IT equipment around.'

'Christ, I'm pregnant, not disabled.'

'Even so. Have you found a mobile phone?'

'Found *three*. Sneaky AF.' Zoey grimaced. 'I mean, one for personal and one for work. But filthy perverts usually have a third for secret shit, right?'

The sickening feeling deepened. 'Can you work with DC Considine here?'

Zoey nodded a smile at him. 'Sure, but my husband told me to speak to him first.'

'Euan. Right. Is your boss around?'

'Jenny? Oh, she's upstairs.'

Vicky shot a warning glare at Considine. 'You stay here and help her out with all that.' She took the stairs two at a time.

Jenny was in the back room, running through a box of evidence and cross-referencing it to a tablet. 'Hey, Vicky.'

'You didn't even look at me.'

'No, I heard you berating poor Zoey.'

'I wasn't berating anyone. And if I was, it'd be you for letting a pregnant woman carry a box downstairs.'

'What?' Jenny sighed. 'She won't take a telling.'

'Never your fault, is it?'

'No, it will be when she falls and has a bloody miscarriage. But I'm not getting in the way of your love triangle.'

'Jenny...'

'Oh, come on. The number of times you've spilled out your heart about Euan MacDonald over a few glasses of wine...'

'He's a creepy bastard.'

'And if you had a type, creepy bastard would be it.'

Vicky ignored her and walked over to the bed. 'You wanted to speak to me?'

'Come on. You'll want to see this.' Jenny led her through the house's upper floor, away from the sun porch towards the master bedroom. 'Here.'

A study lined with bookcases, and a desk in the middle, a

power supply trailing across from the wall but no sign of the laptop.

Jenny walked over to the nearest shelf. 'We've catalogued them, but haven't dusted them or anything.'

Vicky took it all in and recognised some titles from Rob's collection at home. *Mindhunter* by John Douglas. *Zodiac* by Robert Graysmith. *Helter Skelter: The True Story of the Manson Murders* by Vincent Bugliosi and Curt Gentry. Even some Scottish stuff — three editions of *The Schoolbook Killer: The Ghost in the Machine* by William Porteous. An entire room devoted to books about serial killers. Videos and DVDs too. 'Bloody hell.'

'You haven't seen it yet, have you?'

'What?' Vicky searched through the cases. And stopped dead. A whole section on Atreus. Twelve books, twenty DVD cases, and binders stuffed full of press clippings. 'So Craigen was clearly interested in the case.'

'Anyone who grew up in Dundee when that was going on still is, Vicky. But these books are his wife's.'

Vicky frowned at her. 'How do you know that?'

'There are signed copies to her from the authors.' Jenny opened a hardback with a black cover and red writing. *To Kill for Love: The Truth behind the Atreus Killer* by William Porteous. Inside, it was signed:

To Louise,

My number one fan. See you at KillerCon in Glasgow.

Bill X

Christ.

'Thought you'd be pleased.'

'I am.'

'So why do you look like you've just found out that someone's married your love interest and got up the duff to him?'

'Jenny... This isn't necessarily what I wanted to find. Louise Craigen had a clear motive to murder her husband. Inheriting two expensive houses and a successful business after he chucked her and her kids out of here. Enough to make anyone at least think about killing him and his new girlfriend. I just don't get why she'd copy Atreus.'

'Are you pulling my leg? She was *obsessed*.'

'I know that, it's just...' Vicky looked through the bookcase stuffed with folders full of news clipping. 'This is all about that case?'

'We haven't started cataloguing it yet.' Jenny pulled out one folder, bulging at the seams. 'Holy shit. This is all about your dad, Vicky.'

'What?'

Jenny pulled out a page of handwritten notes attached to a USB stick. 'She interviewed him three years ago.'

18

V icky went up on tiptoes to check in the front window but there was no sign of anybody. Not her mum, her dad or her idiot brother.

Shit, shit, shit.

A patch of sunlight broke through the haar and lit up the old dump that was now a burgeoning millennium forest. Not that she'd been here when it was planted. At that time, she was as desperate to get as far away from this town as possible, though Aberdeen was maybe not quite far enough.

She thought she could make out a Rod Stewart song blasting out. Sounded close though, so she gave it another knock, then called through the letterbox. 'Mum? Dad? It's Vicky!'

No response.

No movement, no sounds. Nothing.

Desperate times, though, so she opened her purse and took out the old keyring, and found the one for her parents' door. Slightly bent and she couldn't fit it in the lock.

A shape misted the glass and the door opened. Andrew leered out into the morning gloom, hair standing up on end, and maybe a week's worth of beard on his face. He looked like death warmed up at a very low setting on the microwave. 'You. Right.' And he slumped off into the house.

Vicky shut the door behind her and followed him through to the kitchen. The dull smell of burnt toast lingered in the air. 'Is Dad in?'

Andrew was sitting at the kitchen counter, his dressing gown shrouding the stool he was perched on, and he tucked in to cereal, splashing milk back into the bowl with each spoonful. 'He's in his study.'

'My old room?'

'Right, that.' He chewed slowly. 'You okay?'

'Busy.'

'Right.' Andrew took another splashy spoonful but didn't eat any. 'Be careful. Dad's in his obsession phase again.'

She grimaced. 'What do you mean?'

'You don't remember what he was like.' Andrew dropped his spoon into his bowl. 'When we were kids, there was this time where he was really angry all the time. Barely saw him and every time we did, he was a total dick. Shouting at Mum and me.' He winced. 'Never at you, mind.'

'I remember.'

'You were what, ten? I was seven. Definitely at school. I remember it all.'

'Thanks for the warning.' Vicky exhaled slowly. 'How you keeping?'

Andrew shrugged, staring into his breakfast. 'Catch you later.'

Vicky wanted to help him, but she didn't know how. And boy did she have her own cross to bear, with nails driven deep into her wrists and through her palms. 'Take care, Andrew.' She turned heel and walked through the house towards the din of Rod Stewart.

Dad was hunched over in front of the ancient computer in her old bedroom. *Downtown Train* blasted out, though the voice sounded too rough and ragged to be Rod Stewart. He looked round at her, then nodded and said something lost to the music. He hit a key on his laptop and the noise cut out.

'It's too early for Rod Stewart, Dad.'

'That's Tom Waits!' But Dad was back to his laptop, squinting through his supermarket specs. 'You here to smack me around again?'

'Only if you don't tell the truth.' Vicky stood in the doorway, arms folded like she was a detective sergeant in her late thirties and not a little girl asking her dad for a puppy. 'You didn't think to tell me about you speaking to Louise Craigen?' Her voice sounded thin and shrill.

'Who?' Dad took a slurp of coffee from a giant white mug that he'd got from a toxic sportswear shop. 'Nice to see you, by the way.'

'She interviewed you, Dad.'

'Oh.' Dad frowned, but was lost to his coffee mug. 'She's just a daft wifie.'

'Sexist, much?'

'What?' He looked round at her, frowning. 'What does that even mean?'

'Dad, we've found a load of books about the Atreus killer in her house, and interview notes with you. You didn't think to mention this?'

'Sorry. Why is it important?'

'Dad, I need you to tell me everything. Now.'

He finished his coffee, but held onto the mug. 'Couple of years ago, she was doing this radio thingy. On the computer.'

'A podcast?'

'Aye, something like that.'

'And it was about Atreus?'

'Jim Sanderson, aye.'

The podcast Karen was supposed to be looking into.

Vicky got out her phone and checked for messages. Nothing. So she either hadn't got round to it, or overnight she'd become as useless as Considine. 'When was this?'

'Almost three years back. Someone had written another book about the case and the lad tore me apart. My whole career. Everything. These people, journalists, writers, they're scum.'

'Who wrote it?'

'William Porteous.'

'He signed a copy of his book to Louise.'

'He's a piece of work. Lives up north somewhere, so I ventured up there one morning and made it clear that he's not to include any of that in any books he's writing.'

'And did he?'

'As far as I know. Removed half of it from the paperback. Made me seem better. And this woman, she... She wanted me to go over it all again, said it would offer closure, a chance for me to get my side across, but it was a disaster.'

'A disaster how?'

'She was interviewing me about it, just asking all these silly questions, but she started digging into stuff she shouldn't have known about.'

'What kind of stuff?'

'The knife going missing. The blame on me. Part of the deal was nobody would know about it. That I'd get away with it, even though I hadn't done anything.'

'Was this in the book?'

'No, even that arsehole hadn't been that brave. But she had.'

'You should've told me.'

'Why?'

'I could've helped.'

'Vicky, I did my time in Forfar. That's like being sent to Siberia when you're a DI in Dundee CID.'

'Did it ever go out?'

'I've no idea.'

'What do you mean? You didn't check?'

'I didn't know how to. After I'd stewed on it for a few days, I called her but she didn't answer.' He pointed out of the window along the road towards the Craigen home overlooking them. 'But she lives in that big fancy house up there. Went round there and persuaded her not to use it. Why are you asking, anyway?'

As much as Vicky wanted to, she couldn't tell him the truth. Could she?

She opened the podcast app on her phone and searched. The *See No Evil* podcast had ten episodes, between twenty and thirty minutes each, though only the first had any reviews. Vicky figured it was Louise trying to jump on the *Serial* bandwagon when everyone in the world seemed to listen to that show and true-crime podcasts were huge for about five minutes. Still might be, she didn't know. Maybe she thought she was using her old journalism skills for something useful, or at least exorcising some personal demons. Growing up with those Atreus murders on your doorstep seemed to traumatise enough people.

But there was no mention of DI George Dodds in any of the episode listings, so maybe Louise had heeded his warning. Only way to be sure was to listen through them all.

'You want to tell me what you're looking at, Victoria?'

She took a long, hard breath, weighing up the pros and cons, then just decided, fuck it. 'Okay. The reason I'm asking is because the body we found, the one who died on Saturday night, it's her husband. Soon to be ex.'

'Ah, crap.' Dad slumped back in his office chair, but it was more like relief than tension building up. 'You thinking she copied Sanderson?'

'It's possible.' Vicky sat on the dining chair next to his desk. 'She might have a good motive, namely inheriting her husband's homes and business, and probably getting a big life insurance payout.' She shrugged. 'And even if all that comes to nothing, it could just be plain revenge. Her husband left her for a younger woman.'

'Well, that makes sense. Hiding her simple motive under a complex MO? Wouldn't be the first time someone's pulled that trick.'

'But?'

'I don't quite know why, but it doesn't feel right to me.'

'Go on?'

'I didn't like the woman, but I just don't see her as a killer. What you and David showed me, that was brutal.'

'What, like a woman couldn't do that to a man?'

'I'm not saying that.'

'What are you saying, then?'

'I'm saying that, having sat with Louise Craigen for four hours, I don't think *that* woman could do that.'

Vicky had only spent a few minutes in her company and in truth didn't have the measure of her. Then again, the number of times she'd seen someone spill their guts and still have no idea of the rage burning inside them. 'Even to her husband who'd made her and her kids virtually destitute?'

'Who knows what that could do to someone? And I know you. You're going to speak to her, aren't you?'

'Of course I am. I don't have a choice.'

'Be very careful. If she's—'

'I know, Dad.'

'All I'll say is, have you considered how far advanced the divorce is?'

19

Considine got out onto the street first. 'Thanks for letting me drive this bad boy.' He caressed the Subaru's bonnet like he would a lover.

Actually, she didn't want to think about Considine with a lover.

'Just don't crash this one.' Vicky set off along the high street, but at least the haar was starting to burn away.

The Chinese takeaway on the corner was where she'd worked for a horrible year dealing with drunks and drug fiends, but the worst of the abuse was reserved for her boss and his lovely wife. And they'd just smiled through it all.

Vicky crossed the road. The war memorial was still lit up despite it being almost nine in the middle of July.

Considine stopped outside what used to be the Carnoustie branch of the Royal Bank of Scotland. Where Vicky had opened her first bank account as a kid and got her first mortgage as an adult. They shut it the previous year, cue constant moaning from her mother, despite having no need for any of their banking services.

The door now led into the Costa branch that filled the downstairs. On the left, a sign advertised properties for sale and rent, under ornate lettering reading "Gray and Leech, Solicitors".

Which made Vicky groan. 'You didn't tell me it was *them*.'

'Should I? Why?'

'Stephen, I wish you'd remember things. It's kind of your job.'

'I spoke to her on the phone, but she wouldn't help.'

'Stephen, you need to be on top of your game. We constantly come across lawyers who have grievances against us for just doing our jobs. You need to overcome it without coming running to Mummy or Daddy.'

'Mummy or Daddy?'

'Me and DS MacDonald.'

'So you *are* shagging?'

'No. God no.' Vicky shut her eyes. 'I'm just saying that you need to be more resourceful.'

Considine blew air up his face. 'O-kay.'

Vicky pushed through the door and started climbing the stairs, but Considine raced up ahead of her. She caught the swinging door at the top and pushed into the office. It smelled like a bank, that weird paper and ink tang hanging heavy in the air.

A smallish woman took one look at Vicky and glowered. Polly Muirhead. She had the face of a middle-aged woman but the body of a teenage girl. 'You've got some cheek.'

'We need a word somewhere private?'

'Through here.' Polly led through a heavy oak door into a tiny meeting room, out of step with the rest of the place. A small desk with two chairs on either side, all bolted in. Just like a police interview room.

Considine took the first seat facing the door.

Vicky stayed standing. She didn't doubt they had plush offices here for property clients, and they probably didn't get too many criminal defence cases down here in Carnoustie. 'We're investigating the death of one Derek Craigen.'

Polly didn't sit either, just stayed by the door like she was going to make a run for it. She couldn't bring herself to make eye contact. 'And you just expect me to help you?'

'You are his solicitor.'

'For my sins.'

'And it seems like you're expecting me to apologise.'

Polly laughed, wide-eyed. 'I don't see how you can expect me to help you with this after what you did to me and my husband.'

'What exactly did I do?'

Polly took the seat next to Considine. 'I liked my life. I loved my husband.'

'Oh?'

'He left me.'

'*He* left *you*?'

'I wasn't enough for him. When you shone a spotlight on our existence, it made him question my commitment to him.'

'Look, I'm sorry but you gave a false alibi in a murder inquiry. We weren't trying to kink-shame you, but you were persons of interest in a serious case and acting like you were involved. And you're lucky you kept your job.'

'Lucky?' Polly's glare just deepened. 'Because of you probing into my private life, you made me the embarrassment of this firm. I had to move to bloody Carnoustie to work in this godforsaken office. I liked working in Dundee.'

'I can sympathise, but I'm not going to apologise for doing my job.'

'Then I won't for doing mine. As much as I'd love to help you, I'm the duty solicitor and I have to go and assist a client in dire need of protection from the police.'

'We just need to understand the state of Mr Craigen's divorce proceedings, then we're out of here.'

Polly stared at her for a few seconds, then tossed a document onto the desk. 'There you go.'

Vicky took the pages, still warm from the printer, and started flicking through them. 'Can you summarise?'

'I didn't draft it.'

'No, but you spoke to my colleague here and you managed to produce this copy pretty quickly, so I assume you've got some idea what's in it.'

'Well, we were close to a settlement.'

'Go on?'

'Louise was going to inherit the flat.'

'And the house?'

'To go to Mr Craigen.'

'What about the business?'

'She relinquished her claim on that. Against my advice, I hasten to add.'

'Do you know why?'

'I'm afraid not.'

'When was it going to settle?'

'We had our date in court on Friday. Obviously that won't happen now.'

'And Mrs Craigen will inherit his entire estate?'

'Correct. And I know what you're thinking but there's nothing else I can shed on the matter.'

Vicky tried to find anything to disagree with, but it was all pointing in one direction. Louise Craigen benefited most from her husband's death. Vicky got to her feet. 'Thanks for your help with this.' She held Polly's gaze. 'And I mean it.'

IT WAS MUCH EASIER to park outside the flat than the previous day. No heavy foot traffic, just a ton of litter the council hadn't cleared yet, though hopefully the Open's organisers were paying for it.

MacDonald was standing outside, mirror shades on and those Apple headphones in, the stupid little sticks without cables.

Vicky got out of her car and walked over. He didn't seem to be aware of her presence, so she waved a hand in front of his face.

He jolted, but soon recovered his composure, easing out his earbuds and placing them in a case like his heart wasn't thundering hard. 'Didn't see you there.'

'You listening to *The Best of Climie Fisher*?'

MacDonald laughed. 'Don't knock them.'

'They had, what, one single?'

'Oh, Victoria Dodds, you have much to learn.' MacDonald

pocketed the box. 'No, I was listening to that podcast. *See No Evil?* Good find, by the way.'

'Wish I could take credit. You get anything?'

'Not yet. I've asked Karen Woods to go through it.'

'As have I.'

'Well, she's got anger issues, that kid.'

'Kid? She's older than you.'

All she got was a shrug. 'Your old man definitely spoke to Louise?'

'For four hours, he reckons.'

'Christ. Worth getting Karen to transcribe that file?'

'I doubt it.'

'Agreed. She's not exactly setting the heather alight, is she?'

Vicky held his gaze. 'What do you mean by that?'

'Wait, you think there's no— Okay. Right.'

No point arguing with the creepy bastard. 'Are you getting anywhere with the guest list?'

'No. And that's what I'm talking about. Karen Woods is so slow she might as well carry her house on her back.'

'What?'

'She's like a snail. I need to have that chat again with Forrester about getting some better resource in. Hate not getting my way, I tell you.'

Vicky didn't want to get into it here.

'Thought you had Considine with you?'

'I did.' Vicky walked over to the flat and hit the buzzer. 'Got him chasing up their bank statements.'

'Good idea.'

Even when MacDonald was complimenting her, Vicky still wanted to strangle him. She looked him in the eye. 'I bumped into Zoey at Craigen's flat.'

MacDonald just stood there, running a tongue over his lips.

Still no response on the buzzer.

So Vicky pressed the next-door neighbour's buzzer.

'Hello?'

'Police, sir. Need access to the stairwell.'

'Rightio.'

The door buzzed and clicked open.

MacDonald gestured for her to go first.

So she trotted up the stairs, past the potted plants on the first floor, then the next flight.

A tall old man was standing in the doorway opposite Louise Craigen's flat, hunched over and with extremely thick specs. 'Mind if I see your warrant card?'

Not that he'd be able to read anything on it. But Vicky held hers out. 'Here you go. DS Dodds and this is DS MacDonald.'

'So they're sending two sergeants to report a break-in these days?'

'A what?'

He gestured over the hallway. The flat door hung open. 'Just seems a bit fishy to me, but what would I know. Ex-job myself. Been retired fifteen years. Still don't miss it.'

'Thanks, sir. Now if you can return to your home.' Vicky stepped over and snapped out her baton. 'Shall we?'

'I'll call it in, you—'

A scream tore out from inside.

'Sod it.' Vicky nudged the door with her baton and stepped through the doorway.

Another scream, but longer and quieter. Came from a door on the right.

The first one hung open, showing a tidy bathroom stuffed with bottles of products. As Vicky approached the second, her nose was tickled by the aroma of bleach. She stopped outside the door and peered in.

A bedroom. Teri Craigen, Louise's daughter, knelt in front of the bed, crying hard.

Behind her, Louise Craigen lay on the bed, her lidless eyes staring right at Vicky. Jordan Russell lay next to her. Both dead.

20

Vicky stood in the car park, hanging below the penthouse apartment with the two bodies inside. The haar was close to clearing now.

She leaned against the SOCO van and looked up. Jenny Morgan and her team were inside, but the only sign of their presence was brief camera flashes.

What the hell was going on? Vicky had no idea, but she needed to get one and soon.

Louise Craigen could be scratched from their suspects list. Vicky shut her eyes, but just got flashes of Louise's lidless gaze staring right at her.

Back in the here and now, Teri grabbed her shoulders, wrapping herself tight. Finding your mother's dead body like that would scar her for life.

MacDonald was consoling her, head tilted to the side. 'Look, I know how hard it must be discovering—'

'My mum and *him*?' But it didn't seem to be the most upsetting part of the discovery... 'My *dad* worked with him and...' She shook her head, half laughing, half crying. 'How long was *that* going on?'

'Teri, we're going to find out, okay? Whatever you need, we're going to do it. Okay?'

'Will you find out who killed them?'

'I can't promise that, Teri, but I've been doing this twelve years. Every case I've worked, we caught the perpetrator.'

She looked at him with her mother's intense eyes, but didn't say anything, just ran a hand through her long hair, fanning it out.

'Teri, can I get you anything? Cup of tea? Can of Coke?'

'I've lost both my fucking parents! The last thing I want is a can of fucking Coke!'

'I understand.'

'Do you?'

'I do. When I was younger than you, I found my dad's body. I know how hard it is. Trust me.'

Teri looked away, nodding.

'Sure I can't get you anything?'

'A Pepsi would be good.'

He gave a smile. 'I've only got Coke.'

And she smiled back. 'That'll do.'

'Come on.' He led her over to his car. 'I've got a cool box in the boot. Hate it when my cans get warm.'

Vicky followed them, easing past the lumbering uniforms guarding the entrance, but she kept her distance, letting MacDonald work his wonders. The number of times she'd done this, she was numbed to it.

'The man in there?' Teri took a sip of Coke and stared at the can like it was responsible for their deaths. 'Uncle Jordan.' Naming him made her gasp. 'He worked with my dad for years. I've known him all my life. There are, like, photos of me in hospital, with Mum and Dad, and he's there in the background. Him and Dad did everything together.'

Vicky wondered how long it'd been going on. If Jordan Russell had been sharing more than just lust, if he'd been involved in Teri's conception. But it was so easy for thoughts like that to telescope, to grow and spread, and she had no evidence. As far as Teri knew, Jordan Russell was just Uncle Jordan. Nothing more, nothing less.

Would a DNA test help?

No, what they seemed to be facing was someone who was targeting people for adultery, just like at the lighthouse. Both parties in a marriage were now dead, along with their new partners.

Just like Atreus.

She couldn't help but think that MacDonald was doing a superb job of it. Then again, it was the flipside of his sleaziness. The sexual predator is an expert at human psychology, at exploiting weaknesses in their victims to their own ends. Teri wasn't so different from a girl in a bar or on Tinder, and he could use the same techniques in both places. Seem like their friend, like he was on their side.

Vicky walked over to them and smiled at Teri, then waited for her to stare back. 'Your dad and Uncle Jordan, did they ever argue or fight?'

'Sure.' Teri finished her drink and crushed her can. 'I mean, all the time. But it never meant anything. They were like brothers.'

A red Fiesta pulled up in the middle of the road and a woman got out, then rushed over to the pair of uniforms guarding the entrance to the car park. 'Let me in or so help me God I will sue you to oblivion!'

The taller uniform stood firm, despite the threat of violence in her raised fists. 'Ma'am, we can't let you in.'

Vicky walked over, leaving Teri to MacDonald. 'Can I help?'

The woman was mid-twenties, her dark hair shaved up the side and her fringe cut into a wedge, lined with orange highlights. She had the most intense stare Vicky had seen this side of a prison. Definitely a Craigen. 'Where's Teri?'

Vicky smiled at her. 'You're her sister?'

'That's right. I'm Pamela.' She frowned. 'And you are?'

'Vicky Dodds. I'm a detective based in Dundee.' She held out her warrant card. 'Your sister's over here.' She led her across the fresh asphalt.

Teri was now sitting on the Subaru's boot.

'This cop came to my door and broke the news, and I tried calling Teri but she's not answering her phone.' She gritted her teeth and reset her fringe over her eye. 'I want to help. Is she okay?'

'She's speaking to a colleague. She... found their bodies.'

'Christ.' Pamela slapped a hand to her forehead. Then frowned at Vicky. 'Did you say bodies?'

'I did.'

'That cop...' Pamela nibbled at her top lip. 'Buchanan I think his name was, he said there was a man with Mum. Was it Jordan?'

'You knew about them?'

'Mum was definitely involved with him. I came back one day, here, and they were both in. Not doing anything, but... She didn't want to come out about it, because it'd be hypocritical of her after her nuclear reaction to catching Dad with some young tart in our sun lounge.'

And that explained why Louise wouldn't want to live there, wouldn't even want to talk about it.

She looked across the car park to MacDonald and her sister. 'Look, can I speak to Teri?'

'In a minute. Your parents were divorcing, right?'

'That's true. Their marriage had been a sham for years. Since I went to uni, really. Mum said they were just waiting until Teri left. Then she found Dad with her like a year ago. Our lives were in a bit of turmoil because of it. I mean, that sack of shit kicked Mum and Teri out. I was okay. Got a flat in Dundee. And Audrey is through in Edinburgh. Dad paid her accommodation in advance. But...' She tailed off, shaking her head.

'You know her?'

'Nope.' She looked up at the flat and seemed to shiver. 'Dad put her up here. I mean, talk about a cliché. Getting a flat for your young mistress.'

'Did you still talk to him after that?'

She exhaled slowly. 'My dad was a man you had to play. Everything was transactional with him. Because he was rich, I relied on him for funding for my PhD. So I had to butter him up.'

'He never introduced you to his new partner?'

'No, and he'd deny he was seeing anyone. Total bullshit, but there was always a point where you had to just let him get what he wanted, make him feel like an honourable father, just to get some cash off him.'

'How old are you?'

'Twenty-four. Why?'

'You just said your father's mistress was the same age as you.'

'So?'

'We still don't have an ID for her.'

Pamela let out a hefty sigh. 'Don't look at me.'

But Vicky was. Cogs were whirring, pins were slotting into place. The more she thought about it, the more connections she could form.

Growing up in a house full of books about serial killers, particularly Atreus, with a mother so obsessed that she recorded a podcast about it. That was the kind of thing that would warp your mind, wasn't it?

But then again, that was the same with people obsessed with JFK's assassination or 9/11 being an inside job. Connections seemed to be everywhere.

'In your father's house, we found a load of books.'

Pamela sighed. 'Mum was really into Atreus, like some people are into Madeline McCann or whatever.'

'The serial killer?'

'If you ask me, part of why their marriage went so badly wrong was she had this big giant brain and he expected her to just be a housewife. I'm not saying that's a bad thing, but it wasn't for her.'

'You didn't feel like she wanted you?'

'I'm not saying that. She loved us girls. But she felt frustrated. So that's why she started that podcast. She was a huge fan of *Serial*, listened to it over and over again, found tons just like it. So she did one about Atreus, but it never really took off.'

'You ever ask her why she was so obsessed with that case?'

'Because it was local and because it happened when she was

young, back in the nineties. The male victim in the Ferry case was in her year at school. It totally freaked Mum out.' Pamela frowned. 'Wait a sec. Your surname... You're not George Dodds's daughter, are you?'

Vicky gave a reluctant nod. 'For my sins.'

'She talked about him a lot. He was generous with his time.'

'Did the episode with my dad go out?'

Pamela shook her head. 'Not that I know of.' She grimaced. 'Can I see the bodies?'

'That's not to be advised.'

'But you need someone to identify her, right?'

Vicky looked over at Teri. 'Your sister found them.'

'My God.' Pamela shut her eyes. 'I need to be there for her.'

'That's fine. We're done now. Give me a second.' Vicky left her and crossed the car park.

MacDonald was nodding slowly, his face tight and focused on Teri. He glanced round at Vicky.

She leaned in to whisper, 'You done?'

'Just about.'

Vicky beckoned Pamela over and handed her a business card. 'We might need to speak to you again, but if you need anything from us, call me. Day or night.'

'Thanks.' Pamela gave her another intense look. 'Catch the bastard who did this.'

'We'll do our best.'

Pamela wrapped her sister in a deep hug. They didn't look that similar, with Pamela about a foot taller.

Vicky led MacDonald away from them. 'You get anything?'

'Just a daft lassie.'

The two uniforms separated to let Prof Arbuthnott through, lugging her medical bag over to the flat entrance, and another uniform. Jenny Morgan stepped out, clocked Vicky and turned around to go back inside.

Vicky didn't know what that was all about. She needed to focus on other things, things she could control. Like suspects. 'You don't think Teri knows anything?'

'Never seen her dad's girlfriend. Far as I can tell, anyway.'

'Same with Pamela. She mention any likely names?'

'Nope. Like I say, she's a daft lassie. Too young to know what's going on. What about your one?'

'My one?' Vicky took a deep breath. 'I'd say there's a slight possibility that she's done this.'

'Even though she's female?'

'Christ, Euan, where do you get off?'

'Wherever anyone lets me.'

'Seriously. "My one. Daft lassie. Even though she's female." Really?'

'Look, I've worked much bigger cases than you. More of them, too. Not a woman doing this. Big guy, I'd say. Strong too.'

'So you're a criminal profiler now?'

'Just giving my expert opinion.'

'Is there more of this expertise?'

He nodded. 'Could be.'

Vicky folded her arms. Time to let him take enough rope to hang himself. 'Go on, then. Let's hear it.'

'Assuming it's a male perpetrator, then his motive is partially sexual.'

'Partially?'

'Not like he's raping people, but he's punishing people having affairs. First Derek Craigen and his mystery younger woman, and now Craigen's wife and the guy who built the company with him.' His eyes narrowed. 'Were they having an affair?'

'Pamela thinks so.'

'Just like Atreus, then.'

Vicky looked over at the two daughters, hugging each other tight. 'Or, one of them did it.'

'You can't think that.'

'Because they're women?' Vicky held his gaze until he looked away. 'Euan, if someone's copied Atreus, then being exposed to that MO your entire life, well...'

'Christ.' MacDonald shook his head. 'See your point. If they were having an affair, then it matches either theory. Need to prove it one way or another, don't we?'

'We do. Look, can you stay here and keep on top of things? I've got an idea of someone who might know if there was something going on.'

21

'Jordan and Louise?' Brian Ogg leaned back against the thick glass, silhouetted by the sun eating away the mist over the sea. He untucked his tie and tugged it out of his collar with a zipping sound, then bunched it around his fist. 'I mean...' The air just puffed out of him. 'Really?'

'That's the case, yes.' Vicky walked over. 'You okay, sir?'

'Am I okay? Am I fucking okay? You come in here and you tell me that I've lost a second friend in a day and you ask me if I'm fucking okay?' Ogg tossed the bunched-up tie onto the table by the window. 'No, I'm not fucking okay!'

'We can come back later.'

Ogg stood there, his eyes narrowing. 'No. I'm sorry, I shouldn't have said that.'

'I've been on the receiving end of much worse, sir.'

Ogg actually laughed. He locked eyes with Vicky, then swallowed hard. 'So what do you want?'

'We need to speak to anyone who knows Mr Russell.'

'Next of kin?' Ogg walked over to his desk and eased himself into his seat. He clattered at his keyboard, which sounded like an old typewriter. 'Okay. Well, we've technically not got a next of kin for Jordan.'

'Oh?'

'It was Derek Craigen.'

'That can't be right.'

'Jordie never married. Both his parents are dead and he was an only child. Him and Derek were tight since school. Lived a playboy lifestyle, never saw anyone longer than three months.'

'What about Louise?'

'Well, I've no idea how long that's been going on. Listen, that stuff I told you about Dubai? Jordan was mental for that lifestyle. Used to fly off every couple of weeks, car down to Edinburgh or Glasgow, sometimes Newcastle or Aberdeen, and he'd work on the way so he'd expense it. And he'd fly to Florida, Dubai, Greece, Monaco, Nice, you name it. Mad bastard went to Hong Kong for a weekend last year.'

'And you had no inkling about him and Mrs Craigen?'

'No, I mean, I don't know. Maybe.'

'We believe this might've been going on for a while.'

'I've seen them talking, but I didn't think they were... Whatever bedroom hopping's been going on, they kept it to themselves. I mean...' Ogg leaned across the desk and lowered his voice. 'All that playboy shite with Jordie, some of the lads here thought he was gay. All that "methinks the lady doth protest too much" kind of thing. He was really homophobic, like, frogmarched this boy out who'd come out. Sacked him for stealing paperclips or something.'

'Paperclips?'

'No. Him and a few lads swiped a load of metal from the yard on the night of our Christmas party. Jordie was a lucky bastard, otherwise he'd have been taken to the cleaners. Honestly, you can't say that kind of shite these days. Calling him a nancy boy and all that "ooh ducky" shite.'

'Okay, so do you think this man might have a serious grievance against him?'

'Not likely. He's in the jail. Five years, not even served one so far.'

'For stealing scrap metal?'

'God no. He was up to all sorts with some Albanian boys down south.'

~

No sign of MacDonald, but Forrester had finally bothered to show up, slurping from a Costa coffee cup as he jabbed his finger at Jenny Morgan. 'I'm just asking if you bloody found anything! There's no need to go tonto at me!'

Here we bloody go. Vicky left the car and charged over to the entrance.

'This is just the straw that broke the camel's back, David.' Jenny was keeping a distance from him, arms folded. 'It's *always* like this. You push and you push, always expecting answers way before I can give you anything. It's far too early to tell.'

'But you always have something.'

'Aye, but every single time I tell you something ahead of schedule, you'll go off on some random tangent, trying to pin it on someone. And then you'll blame me when it's not them. "Oh, it's not my fault. Jenny Morgan fed me a pack of lies." Well, I'm sick to the back teeth of it.'

'I'm just asking you to do your bloody job.'

'Calm. Down.' Vicky got between them, switching her gaze between them. 'You're acting like a pair of children!'

'She started it.'

'David!'

Forrester ran a hand down his face, then slurped some coffee through the lid.

Vicky thumbed over at the car. 'Is MacDonald about?'

'That reminds me.' Forrester toddled off towards the flat.

Vicky shook her head. 'I'd apologise but it looked like you were just as bad as him.'

'Me?' Jenny's pencil eyebrows almost touched her hairline. 'This is his—'

'Jenny, you're the one not playing ball.'

'But he—'

'I know. He's a dick. But you're the one who looks like they're withholding information.'

'Right.' Jenny was acting all ice queen again. 'Look, the reason I'm not sharing anything is because there's nothing to share. It's the same story as the lighthouse.'

'Bleach, so no forensics?'

'I mean, you might want to search for people with access to gallons of bleach.'

Vicky winced. 'Like a plumber?'

'Hell yeah.' Jenny was nodding. Back on it now. 'Those plastic bottles we got at the lighthouse are generic, so it's not like you can just pop into the Asda and get a couple. They're strictly commercial.'

'That could actually be useful. You think it's the same killer?'

'I don't think it's not the same.'

That mangled Vicky's head. 'Okay, so it could be?'

'The reason we've got nothing so far is that our killer is covering his or her tracks and bleaching the crime scenes. The lighthouse was forensically dead. The rain washed away anything from the bunker. But the female victim... Whoever attacked her, they didn't leave a trace. She wasn't sexually assaulted, so no pubes or spunk or—'

'Jenny...'

'Come on, Vicky, now's not the time to get squeamish.'

'Pubes or spunk?' Forrester was over with them now, sneering at them. 'You can't use language like that.'

Vicky tugged at Jenny's arm. 'Listen, I asked you to look back at the records for the Atreus case.'

'And I have. He was the same; most of the crime scenes were forensically dead. This was before DNA was a thing too, but he was ultra careful. Maybe he's a germaphobe.' She shrugged. 'The only evidence they found in the Broughty Ferry case was a knife, which—'

'Less said about that, the better.' Forrester glowered at her.

'Come on, David.' Jenny fixed him with *that* stare, thin eyebrow arched and a coquettish look on her face. 'While it wasn't her dad's fault, David, he did lose the knife. And now four people in Carnoustie are dead.'

'Jenny, this isn't Jim Sanderson.' Forrester glared at her. 'For starters, it doesn't match the MO.'

'Of course it does. I've seen the photos of the old case and—'

'Aye, photos are photos.' Forrester stabbed a finger off his chest. 'I might've been a uniform, but old Syd Ramsay took us all to the crime scene in the Ferry. Made us take it all in, made us know what we were searching for.'

'David, you need to be open to the possibility that you didn't catch Atreus back—'

'No.'

'What?'

'I said no. We caught Atreus and these are different cases.'

Vicky shot Jenny *her* look back at her and, for once, it made her shut up. 'David, can you explain?'

'For starters, he had a nine-month cooling-off period. Eight months minimum, ten max. These murders are a day apart. That's a spree killer, not a serial killer.'

'Thanks. I've watched *Mindhunter* too.'

Vicky got hold of her and tried to push her away, but she seemed insistent on goading Forrester. 'Jenny, I swear if you don't—'

'Enough!' MacDonald's shout echoed around the car park. 'Christ, you two are like my niece and nephew. Whatever's going on here, this stupid argument isn't finding the killer.'

Forrester and Jenny couldn't bring themselves to look at each other. Just like Bella and Jamie after a particularly bad ding-dong and a strong roasting from Rob in his Bad Cop role.

MacDonald narrowed his eyes at Jenny. 'Current theory is that this is a copycat. You suggesting we didn't catch the original killer? If so, we need to know everything you've got.'

Jenny snarled at him, her small tongue darting across her teeth like a lizard running across rocks, then she stepped away, forehead creased. 'Okay, so... Look, this needs to be validated by Shirley Arbuthnott, but as far as I can see, your killer has copied the

Atreus MO exactly. And I mean *exactly*. The bleach, cutting the eyelids, doing it in pairs, you name it.'

'And what about David's point about it being a spree killing rather than serial?'

'Not my wheelhouse, daddio. I'm just checking the evidence.'

MacDonald smirked. 'Okay, but it's possible this could be a copycat, right?'

'Well, yes.' Jenny was nodding. 'A very good one who knew precisely what Sanderson was doing.'

'That's not true.' Forrester folded his arms. 'These victims, the lassies weren't raped.'

Vicky frowned at him. '*Raped*?'

Forrester nodded. 'The old "hold back evidence" trick. It would've come up in the court case, but well. It never got to court, did it?'

'The victims were raped?'

'The female ones, aye.' Forrester ran a hand over his neck and winced at the pain. 'We deliberately held it back so we could snare Sanderson in court.'

'The victim we found in the bunker wasn't raped, though. But our working hypothesis is she got away. Probably before she was... raped.'

'Was Louise Craigen?'

Forrester looked up at the apartment. 'One for Arbuthnott.'

Jenny shrugged like this was nothing really. 'So it's still possible that you didn't catch him back in the day?'

Forrester looked away.

But it still felt to Vicky like he was holding back something. 'Was there ever any DNA from these rapes?'

'Why do you think we were so confident Sanderson did it?' Forrester scratched at his chin. 'We found semen inside the Ferry victim. Ran the DNA on it and it matched the other four cases. And it matched Sanderson. It was seriously cutting edge at the time, not quite admissible.'

'But there could be something in what Jenny's saying.' MacDonald looked over at Vicky then Forrester, then back at her.

'Okay, Jenny, I know you've been going through the old cases, but I need you to work with Arbuthnott and compare the knife wounds. All that shit like angles, handedness, matching blades, aye?'

'Seriously?'

'Seriously.'

'You know that'll cost a ton.'

'Do it.' Forrester cleared his throat. 'Whatever the cost.'

And that was as likely as MacDonald running away from an attractive widow at a crime scene.

So Vicky eased Forrester away from them. 'You not worrying about cost. What's going on?'

'Eh? Oh.' Forrester swallowed hard. 'I'm getting a piledriver of pressure on my bonce from Raven. He needs this cleared up.'

'So what else is new. You say that like it's never happened before.'

Forrester glanced at her.

'Come on, you know more than you're letting on.'

Forrester focused on Jenny, standing with MacDonald. 'Look, when you two arrived, Jenny was bringing up all this shite about us not catching the right guy. But George lost that knife.' He stared at Vicky. 'The bugger of a thing is that all the paperwork should still be there. But it's gone walkies.'

'Who took it?'

'Well, it's just as likely that some idiot in Jenny's department lost the knife, not your old man.'

'Meaning Dad got the blame for something he didn't do?'

'Your old man's an honourable sod. He took the blame, aye, but it's possible someone made him the fall guy.'

'And you think whoever did it is killing again?'

Forrester looked away. 'That's what I'm worried about.'

_____

22

Dad was still in his office, but he'd progressed from hunkering behind the screen to standing by the door, connecting prints together with bits of string. He looked round at them with the mad eyes of a conspiracy nut. All he was missing was the tinfoil hat and a bunker in the back garden. 'What now?'

'We need another word.' Vicky joined him by his wall of insanity, while Forrester took the office chair. She scanned around the pages, trying to spot anything useful or pertinent to their case. Prints of the murders in Dundee. Jim Sanderson's face gurning at the camera. His solicitor's campaign for justice.

And it was all just bullshit.

Dad was holding a print like he was trying to slot it precisely into a timeline.

Vicky snatched it from him.

A print of an article about Louise Craigen from the *Courier*. "Local Woman Taps Into Podcast Craze!" She was photographed outside the Broughty Ferry crime scene with a stern look on her face, holding up a smartphone showing her podcast's logo, and a pair of white earbuds stuffed in.

Vicky rested it back on the desk. 'Dad, you need to hear this.'

He picked up the page again. 'I'm listening.' He pressed a drawing pin in on the far right of the wall, then held it in place with another.

'Can you stop doing that and take us through the details of the original cases, please?'

'Why?'

'Because.'

'It's always just "because" with you, isn't it?'

'Dad, I went round to Louise's home. I found her dead body. She'd been attacked by someone, her and her apparent lover. Their eyelids were cut off, Dad.'

'Christ.' He pinched his nose and stood there, but didn't look round at her. 'She was... nice enough. Sounds like she had a good life, raising three kids. Not many people get that.'

The futon crunched as Forrester leaned forward. 'George, it appears she was having an affair. We found both their bodies, same MO as her husband.'

Dad just sighed.

Vicky caressed his arm, but it made him flinch. 'We need you to take us through it all.' She tapped on the Broughty Ferry photo. The murder scene flat was now a fancy upstairs restaurant. 'You were both in the room where they were killed, but you were there when the bodies were still in situ. We need to know what wasn't in the papers, what's not in the books or on her podcast. What only Atreus knew.'

Dad took a long look at her, but didn't say anything.

'Look, whoever did this has copied the MO to a T. Cutting eyelids, stabbing them through the heart, bleaching the bodies and the crime scene.'

Still no response.

'Dad, all we've got is case files and photos. If we can understand everything, then maybe we can trace it to someone who couldn't know any of this. You were there, so can you—'

'So was he.'

Forrester shook his head. 'I wasn't, not really. I was walking the beat, asking questions, checking bus timetables and gas meter readings and phone calls. You were in that flat several times, George. You saw the bodies on the slab during the post mortem. You worked with the forensics guys.'

'Dad, if this is a copycat, and I mean someone unrelated taking up the MO, then they'd have to know every single detail. Like the fact the female victims were raped.'

That got him. His head sunk until his chin touched his chest. 'You told them?'

'George, it came out. They think Sanderson didn't do it all.'

'You're clutching at straws.' Dad walked back over to his wall, but he just stood there, scowling at his documents. 'Sanderson was stabbed in jail in West Bell Street nick. Vicky, I know you want to help me, but—'

'No, they've killed four people in forty-eight hours. That's technically spree killing but I need to catch them before they do it again.'

He tilted his head to the side. 'Right.'

Forrester joined them at the wall. 'George, we don't have any proof that it's the exact same MO. Jenny Morgan's going through it all with the pathologist, but it'd be really helpful if you could give us the gen.'

Vicky felt a jolt of fear in her neck. She was losing control here. Almost had him, and now he was off down another track.

Forrester was pointing at the new items on Dad's timeline, the stories from that morning's *Argus*. 'Derek Craigen, the first victim, he had this deal going through where he was buying an English company. Then his number two turns up dead. I mean, Vicky is thinking it's because he was sleeping with Craigen's ex, who'll inherit the business as far as we can tell. But it could be related to this takeover.'

Dad looking like that was a straw he was clutching to, that he'd cling to like a mast on a ship. 'You're thinking that whoever's doing this used the Atreus MO to throw you off the scent?'

'Something like that.'

Dad nodded.

'Or it's one of the kids looking to pad their inheritance. Follow the money, who stands to profit? Louise stood to inherit, but now that she's gone, well. Pamela, Audrey and Teri all come into focus.'

And Vicky had lost all control now. She got between her father and his murder board. 'Dad, there's no evidence to support that. His wife was our suspect and she's dead now.'

Neither Forrester nor her father looked like they wanted to let the facts get in the way.

'Dad, I want us to assume it's a copycat, then we can dig into the old case and either prove or disprove it. We see where the copycat's MO differs from the original MO. Might be something we can use to catch them. And the podcast might be related to it. But it might be that it's only superficially related.'

Dad stared at the wall, smoothing a hand across his stubble. His eyes seemed to scan every single document, trace down every single perceived connection.

Vicky walked over to the window and looked along Bruce Drive, the same view she'd seen at least twice a day when she was growing up. Listening to the radio while doing her homework, when she was getting ready for school, when she was waiting for her boyfriend to pick her up in his car. She leaned against the window sill and looked back into the room. 'The other possibility is that you caught the wrong guy back in the day. That Jim Sanderson was innocent.'

Forrester couldn't look up at his old boss, just sat there, hands on his lap like a little schoolboy. 'We're looking at the possibility that he wasn't Atreus.'

'For fuck's sake!' Dad was shaking with rage. 'Of course he was!' He collapsed into his office chair. 'Vicky, if this is you going over my failure, about the fact I lost the knife, that...' He slumped back in his chair, like the gravity of the situation had just hit him and pinned him down.

Vicky felt terrible for doing it, but she needed to get through to him. 'Dad, could you have got the wrong person?'

'Absolutely not.'

'So why can't Jenny Morgan find the paperwork about that knife?'

'What?'

'The paperwork is missing.'

Dad looked round at her with narrowed eyes, but didn't say anything. He threw his hands up in the air. 'This is bollocks.'

'So there's not even the slightest possibility that Jim Sanderson didn't do the original murders?'

Dad shut his eyes.

'If I'm so wrong, prove it to me.'

'These were different times, Vicky.'

'You still had chain of evidence, though.'

'Not like you have now. And in those days people actually respected the police.'

'So why isn't the knife catalogued?'

'I don't know.'

'So, what, this was all just some admin blunder and that's it? End of?'

'Vicky, I was hauled over the coals for this. It could've been my fault, it could've been the clowns in the lab. The important thing is we lost the knife. This is why I lost everything. Why I don't want to even think about it.' He exhaled slowly. 'And you're accusing me of catching the wrong guy?'

'Dad, who could've taken the knife?'

'Vicky, I know what you're trying to do here. You can't change the past. What happened, happened. My career, this case, it's done. Over. Finito.'

'I'm not trying to change the past. I'm trying to solve a case in the present. If someone on the inside took the knife, that means you caught the wrong guy. Or you caught the right guy but he had help. That means whoever killed those people is out there doing it again.'

Dad and Forrester shared a look that was hard to read.

'Who would've done it, Dad? Who would've benefited from it?'

Forrester raised a hand in warning. 'Vicky, can you give us a minute?'

23

Vicky stepped through the hallway and got a blast of Mum's lavender perfume. Obviously heading out somewhere, and she'd happily ignored the shouting coming from Dad's study. But Vicky couldn't handle her hectoring today, so she walked out the front door.

'Hey.' Andrew was sitting on the bench outside Dad's office, staring into his iPad. 'I take it you won that barney?'

'A barney? Are you fifteen?'

'I'm not the one fighting with him like I'm still a teenager.'

Vicky collapsed onto the bench next to him. Looked like he was playing some complex game. 'Says the man who still lives with his parents and is hooked on computer games.'

'Even for you, Vicky...'

She slouched back on the bench, feeling like utter shit. 'You're right, I'm sorry. I shouldn't have said that.'

'I'd ask you what that was all about, but half the street could hear it through the window. It sounds like you're being too hard on our old man.'

'I'm being just as hard as he ever was on us.'

'Ha, this is nothing.' Andrew locked his iPad and hugged it

tight. 'Look, Dad went to hell and back over that case. But he got over it. And now this? After you went this morning, Mum spent like an hour trying to calm him down, and he flew off the handle at her. Now you and that old crony of his are just making things worse.'

'That old crony is my boss.'

'I remember. He kept busting my balls over that Airwave scanner. Don't even use those pieces of shit any more.'

The door opened and Mum stepped out, her keys jangling. 'Andrew, are you—' She frowned, dressed up like it was midwinter and not a baking July morning. 'Victoria? What are you doing here?'

'Seeing Dad.'

'Ah, that explains the shouting. Well, I'm glad that me and your brother won't be dealing with the aftermath today.' She reached out a hand and helped Andrew to his feet. 'Come on, son.'

'See you later, Vicks.' He ambled over to Mum's car with all the energy of an elderly man.

Vicky stayed where she was, but spoke in a low voice. 'What's up with him?'

'Same old. He keeps trying to go back to work too soon. And when he's not at work, he's up all night playing computer games or talking to people on Schoolbook.'

'Do you want me to have a word with him?'

'Vicky, I see what you having a word with male Doddses does to them.' She sighed. 'But Morag's daughter has ME too. Chronic Fatigue Syndrome. Poor thing was always in her bed, but she turned the corner. Got a flat, got a job. Morag gave me the name of a doctor in Glasgow. So, we're going through there to see this chap. Maybe it'll fix him, but I doubt it.'

'Well, good luck.'

'Thanks.' Mum leaned over to kiss her cheek, giving her a taste of perfume, then tottered off down the slab path to the car and took an age of man getting in. The car drove off at the usual ludicrous speed, clearing forty and barely slowing as she left Bruce Drive.

Vicky sat on the bench, basking in the warm sun. Now the haar had burnt off, it was a nice day. Blue skies with a few wisps of cloud. And the distant clanking of someone hammering something, and two lawnmowers giving a stereo image just out of sync with each other.

At the far end of the street, two kids were outside playing kerby, bouncing a football off the opposing kerbs, just like she'd done in the ancient past with Andrew. One got a bounce and ran into the middle of the road and caught the ball. A car approached from the other side and honked its horn.

Vicky got out her phone and called Rob. He'd answered it by the time she put it to her ear. Music thumped and kids screamed.

'Hey.'

'Hey. Where are you?'

'I'm up in Dundee with the kids. They're having a great time.'

Despite everything, she felt herself smiling. 'And you?'

'Well. Let's just say I'm looking forward to them being shattered later on.'

'Good plan. I wish I was with you.'

'Me too. But we've got Crete coming up.'

'Seems like such a long time away.'

'You free for lunch?'

Vicky got a stab of regret deep in her gut. 'I'm stuck in Carnoustie.'

'Oh.'

'Aye, oh.'

A long pause, filled with the sound of a thousand kids begging their parents. 'Was that Alan this morning?'

'God no. It was Euan. Euan MacDonald.'

'Should I be worried about that?'

Vicky couldn't help but grin. 'No way. Even if he was the last man on earth. He's such a dickhead.'

'So am I, though.'

She laughed. 'You're the good sort of dickhead, Rob.' Then her phone rang, warning her Karen was calling her. 'Look, I'd better go. Give them both a big cuddle from me. Love you.'

'Love you too.'

Vicky let herself breathe, trying to shift from wistful mother to Detective Sergeant, then she switched calls. 'Hey, Karen.'

'This is the worst piece of shite you've ever given me.'

'What is?'

'The podcast! It sounds like she's in a broom cupboard and it's all just a load of shite. And there are *hours* of it!'

'You know you can listen to it on double speed, right? Triple even.'

'Eh?'

'Have a look for Overcast on the App Store. It boosts voices too. Think there's also another one that does it.'

'Wish you'd told me that earlier.'

'Officially, it was MacDonald who got you to do this, not me.'

'Still blame you, though.'

'You getting anything from it?'

'Not really.' Karen paused. 'She's not got much first-hand stuff. And she's taking an episode per victim pair. I'm just about to start listening to the Inverness one.'

'Well, let me know if there's anything I should focus on.'

'Mm.'

The door opened again and Forrester barrelled out, heading towards the pool Subaru.

'Got to go, Kaz.' Vicky ended the call and followed him over. 'Did you get anywhere?'

Forrester opened his door but didn't get in, instead looking over the car to her. 'For George's sake, we need to put this nonsense to bed.'

'You don't think it's the same guy, do you?'

'No, I don't.' Forrester got behind the wheel and had started the ignition by the time Vicky was in the passenger seat. 'And it's tearing your old man apart.'

'Did you get anything out of him? Anything at all?'

'He's... He's starting to come round to our way of thinking, but this isn't easy on him, Vicky.'

'I know.' She looked back at the house. Through the blinds in her old window, she could just about make out Dad standing by his madman's murder board. 'If that knife went missing for nefarious reasons, then—'

'Nefarious?'

'You know what I mean. If it went missing for nefarious reasons, it was either because someone on the case was involved with the killer, or the killer was on the case.'

But Forrester hadn't driven off yet. 'Come on, *seriously*?'

'Try and persuade me otherwise.'

'But who on the case benefited from what happened?'

'You did.'

His head jerked round. 'What?'

Vicky shouldn't have said that, no matter how true it was. But was his reaction anger or guilt? 'I'm just saying, David. You are where you are now because of that case.'

'Be careful what you're saying here.'

'You were made a detective and have been promoted a couple of times since then.'

'Come on, Vicky. That's complete bollocks.' Forrester killed the engine and slumped back in the seat. 'If someone was paying me off by promotions, then they could've done a better job of it.'

'Or you're just cheap.'

He laughed. 'You don't believe that, do you?'

'No, but I think we should speak to anyone who worked the case back in the day. We still don't know if our guy is copying every detail. If there's something that wasn't public knowledge, then...'

'Then what?'

'I don't know.'

'I've been trying to get in touch with the old team since last night. It's been a struggle. They're all dead or senile. Your old man's one of the few who can still track down their marbles. At a push.'

'So we need to speak to everyone who's lost their marbles then too.'

'That's what I was up to in there. Your dad's still in touch with his old boss. Syd Ramsay. He was the SIO on the case. Eventually became Chief of Tayside Police for his work on the Atreus case.'

'You know where he lives?'

24

Rob's house was barely three hundred metres away.

Not a house, a home. And not his, theirs. She could see her next-door neighbour but one, Karen Woods' home. Never felt that claustrophobic, but looking at it, maybe it should. A back road led up to those new houses on the ancient cliffs that overlooked Carnoustie and ran all the way to Arbroath.

Forrester got out of the Subaru and met Vicky outside the house. 'Old Syd's done well for himself.'

And he had. Syd Ramsay's house wasn't far from the local parish church, meaning it was probably the local manse, but there were a few contenders for it, other big Victorian mansions. His was a sprawling thing set back from the main road between Carnoustie and Dundee, the low road that was long since bypassed. Vicky could still remember a million teenaged bus trips into town and all the promise shopping in Dundee offered back then.

'Ladies first.' Forrester scraped back the gate to let Vicky go up the short path.

The house was made from that brown stone so typical of Tayside, seen everywhere from Arbroath to Perth. And it was hidden from the main road by a row of copper beech trees, turning the front garden into a dark little hovel. The back wouldn't be much better, trapped between the house and the hill.

Vicky tried the bell and stepped away.

Lights on inside, though, and *The Archers* theme blasting out from somewhere, its jaunty English musicality out of place in provincial Scotland. The door clattered open and a middle-aged woman stood there. Well-dressed, with a hairdo that looked like it cost a fortune. 'Can I help you?' A local accent, but twisted by years living somewhere else, somewhere hard to place.

Vicky held out her warrant card. 'DS Dodds, ma'am. Looking for a Syd Ramsay.'

'Oh.'

That wasn't good. 'He does live here?'

'Right.' The woman stepped outside. 'Listen, I'm Syd's sister, Irene. Irene Schneider. You know Syd?'

'DI David Forrester.' He held out his hand. 'Worked together for a few years. Had a good few meetings with the old rascal. That body found in the sewers under Dura Street? He took an active role in that one. One of the last cases he worked, I think.'

'Yeah, Syd and Janice had a good retirement.' She snorted. 'What's this about?'

'Just need a word.'

'Join the line, honey.'

'Excuse me?'

'You ain't the first to "just need a word" today.' Her accent was slipping to an American drawl, real New York attitude. 'Had a ton of folks here, asking about it.'

A clusterfuck of journalists, no doubt. 'I'm sorry about that.'

'Well, I don't begrudge anyone trying to make a crust in this world. Can I see some ID?'

'Okay...' Forrester unfolded his warrant card and let her inspect it. 'That do you?'

Her lips twitched and she twisted round to look at Vicky. 'And you.'

She complied. 'Were they reporters?'

'Yes. Now, why are two cops turning up here?'

Forrester gave her his best professional smile. 'Irene, the reason all those journalists are snooping around, pestering you...' He sighed. 'Well, there's a serial killer copying Atreus.'

'Oh my God.' She stared down at her feet. Bright-red toenails in fancy sandals. And a deep mahogany tan. 'I remember that case.'

'Right. I worked it as a young cop. Vicky's old man was Syd's deputy.'

'George Dodds?'

'Right.' Vicky glanced at Forrester but he was just standing back and letting her make a royal arse of this. 'Listen, we need to speak to your brother.'

Irene raised her eyebrows.

Forrester flashed her a grin. 'We can go, if you want.'

Irene snarled at him. 'With the implication that there's a serial killer out there and I've stopped you catching him? Get real. Trouble is, he's not here.'

'You know where he is?'

$\sim$

'OVER HERE, SIR, MADAM.' The golf club manager led them across the restaurant area, but only four of the twenty or so tables were occupied. And just cups of tea by the looks of it. Usually golf clubs would be more like pubs than even pubs were.

Vicky matched the manager's stride as they walked across what looked like it had once been a ballroom. 'The new drink-driving limit hitting you at all?'

'Correct.' He rolled his eyes at her. 'We're struggling to break even these days. Putting on taxis and coaches to shuttle them in. Laying on high teas, quiz nights, steak dinners, you name it. But this... LA Golf, I'm afraid it'll be the final straw.'

'Isn't it more expensive?'

'Well, yes, but...' He stopped by a table. 'Here you go.'

Just one man at the table, chewing slowly. But two plates, both halfway through fish and chips; the fish might've been shark it was that big.

'Sir, is Mr Ramsay unwell?'

'In a manner of speaking.' The man was mid-sixties and spoke with a similar New York drawl to Irene. He held out a hand to Vicky and Forrester, even though neither had been introduced, and smiled with a perfect gleam. 'Buddy Schneider. Pleased to meet you.'

Vicky looked across the lush garden towards the golf course. A few outside waiting to tee off. In the nearby rose garden, butterflies and bees seemed to be thriving. 'We're looking for Syd Ramsay.'

'He's just gone to the bathroom, ma'am.' Buddy frowned. 'He's got troubles with...' He pointed down at his nether regions.

'Okay, we can wait.'

'Well, we're kinda in the middle of fish and chips here.' The words ran together—fishanchipz—like it was a German speciality rather than British. 'You give me your number, I'll call you.'

'It's important that we speak to him now.' Forrester smiled at him.

Buddy's lips twisted up. 'You want me to have a look at your teeth?'

'Excuse me?'

'I own a dental surgery in upstate New York. You need a lot of work.'

'There's nothing wrong with my teeth.'

Vicky cut in, taking the empty seat next to him. 'Is Buddy short for something?'

'Donald.'

'Donald? Seriously?' But she was getting lost in this. 'Never knew that.'

Buddy leaned in close to her. 'You know he's dying of cancer, right?'

It seemed to hit Forrester in the balls. 'Dying?'

'Irene wanted to come over to see her brother one last time.' Buddy pursed his lips. 'And I could watch the golf. We're at the Carnoustie Hotel. Costing a bomb, but hey, it's a once in a lifetime thing. And I work my ass off.' He looked at Forrester again. 'You look like you got the sun there?'

'Still paying for it.' Forrester took the other free seat. 'How bad is he?'

'It's bad, really. Irene is so angry with him.' His cool bluster was torn apart by a snarl. 'If Janice was still here, she'd have made him go to the doctor's for his prostate exam every year. Instead, it's—'

'Janice was a good woman.' Syd Ramsay had that giant frame that old cops like her dad all seemed to have, like anyone over six foot was automatically siphoned off into the police force. A long golf hat hung over his head. But he appeared to be a beacon of good health. Tanned and lean, strong arms and a polo shirt that fit his toned frame. He stared at them with the look of a long-serving police officer. 'Davie?' A glint in his eyes. 'What are you doing here?'

'Come to see you, you old bugger.' Forrester got up and clapped his arm. 'How you doing?'

'How does it look?'

'Well, a bit surprising. You look well.'

Syd sighed, then scowled at Buddy. 'You daft sod. Big mouth strikes again.'

'Come on, Syd. You have cancer.'

'Aye, but I'm not dying.' Syd took off his hat and flopped it on the table. He was completely bald, even his eyebrows gone. 'Six sessions of chemo and it's under control.'

'But this lousy country, man. You're not—'

'Buddy, if you weren't Irene's...' Syd smiled. 'You mind giving us a minute?'

Buddy looked hard at him, then smiled. 'Sure.' He grabbed his plate and moved to an empty table.

Syd took his chair and picked up a chip. 'Christ, eating with that guy is worse than having cancer.'

'You didn't think to tell me?'

'I'm fine, Davie. Almost in remission.'

'Not the way he tells it.'

'Listen, that guy's a tube, don't listen to him.' Syd glanced at the next table, where Buddy was tucking in with some music playing from his phone speaker. 'Seriously, if you could cover up me murdering him...?'

Forrester laughed. 'Prick was asking me if I wanted dental work.'

'All that shite you've been eating, David.' Syd coughed out a laugh. 'But I know you. This isn't a social visit, and you wouldn't bring your daughter with you, if it was.'

Vicky raised her eyebrows. 'I'm not his kid, Christ.'

'You must be twenty-five at most.'

'Flattery will get you everywhere. George Dodds is my father.'

'Old Dode Dodds.' Syd smiled. 'One of the best, him. Took me to my chemo last week.'

Forrester shook his head. 'And neither of you told me?'

'When he turned up, Irene wasn't going to let him in.' Syd's laugh was a wet rattle. 'She's a nightmare. Thank Christ they're heading to Edinburgh tonight. Cramping my style, I tell you.' He winked at Forrester. 'You're here about Atreus, right?'

Forrester raised his eyebrows. 'How did you know that?'

'Davie, I might be on the way out but my mind's still working.' Syd tapped a bony finger against his temple. 'And so much of police work is reading between the lines. At least as much as actually reading the lines. Saw this morning's paper, had a piece about how you've got a lad with his eyelids cut off. And a lassie who might've escaped. Doesn't take much to put two and two together, does it?'

'We found another two this morning.'

'Related?'

'Wife of the first victim.'

'I meant... Wait, so the second set of victims, it's the wife of one of the first?'

'Looks like adultery on both sides.'

'Which would match our old friend's pattern.' Syd shook his head, his face screwed up tight. He locked eyes with Vicky. 'Atreus comes from Greek mythology. He was a—'

'I know where it comes from.' Vicky folded her arms. 'The

reason we're here is we need to know whether this is a copycat, or the original killer.'

Syd stared at her for a few seconds. 'But he's—' He started coughing, loud rasps that boomed through the room. 'Atreus is dead.'

'*Jim Sanderson* is dead.' Vicky left a pause, watching his reaction. 'But what if it wasn't him?'

If Syd knew anything, he wasn't giving it away. 'Davie, what the hell is she on about?'

'You need to be straight with us, Syd. Is it possible we caught the wrong guy?'

'Absolutely no way.'

'Sure about that?'

'What else does "absolutely" mean?' Syd swivelled round to stare at Vicky. 'George is a good guy, but he made a massive cock-up.' He shrugged. 'Fail to see the problem. Man loses knife, man pays for losing knife. Roll credits.'

'You're *adamant* it was his fault that knife went missing?'

'Christ, you'd think I was on trial here. Yes, it was his fault. Much as it pains me to admit it, it was Dode's mess. We found a knife in the bin downstairs. Covered in blood. And then we didn't. I was grooming your old man as my deputy. Made him Acting DI but he was on a fast track. I fucking trusted him to get that to the lab. It just never showed up.'

'So you busted him for it.'

'I had no choice.' Syd rested his head back against the chair and folded his arms. 'Look, I know you *think* you're helping here, trying to show that it wasn't your dad's fault the knife went missing, but it was. He screwed up, big time. And I tried to keep him on, but... Well. I had no choice but to put him back into uniform. I'm not saying being a detective is better than a uniform, but he needed a fresh start and to be kept away from murder cases. Besides, Forfar was an easier commute for him, so he could see his kids more. And nothing happens in Forfar.'

Vicky stared out of the window. She could see the church spire, not too far from her home. A couple of miles to Dad's home.

And Syd was right. She was digging up the past to try and save her father. Maybe even at the expense of solving the current case. And Dad was big enough and ugly enough to fight his own battles, so maybe it was time to let this go.

But she just couldn't. 'You did well out of the whole mess. You were a DCI at the time. You became the Chief of Tayside Police.'

Forrester shot her a glare. 'Come on, Doddsy, that's enough.'

'No. My dad lost out, but Syd here benefited.'

'Listen to me, missy. We could've caught Sanderson, but your dad fucked it right up. You might not like to hear it, but it's the God's honest truth.' He held out his palms. 'We caught him but we didn't have a case because that knife went missing. We were *lucky* he took his own life.'

Vicky wanted to jump in again, wanted to tear and claw away. But she was just tormenting an old man.

Not that Syd was giving up. He popped a chip in his mouth but kept on. 'That Atreus case was hell. I was up to my nuts in shite for *months* until we caught Sanderson. And on our fucking doorstep too.'

'But he died on remand.'

'Aye, and everything we did was pored over by that prick. What was his name?' He clicked his fingers a few times. 'Big fancy Edinburgh lawyer, always soaking up the attention, when he should've been keeping Sanderson in prison where he deserved to be.' More clicking. 'Campbell McLintock, that's it. Total fanny. Had it in for the cops. Threw money at that case, which meant a ton of resource, just to make us look like clowns. Kept on insisting that Sanderson was innocent and or that we'd had him killed or whatever he wanted to suggest. Heard the prick died recently, but I tell you, I wish he'd died a long time ago. Maybe I'll meet him in hell.'

'Come on, Syd, you're not going to hell.'

'I'd settle for an eternity in limbo.'

It seemed to stack up enough for Vicky. She'd heard of Campbell McLintock. An old flame of hers from the deep distant past had enough run-ins with him over the years to know how bad he was. But he was thorough and taking appeals through the court system would have brought any discrepancies to light.

'And then that woman did that radio thing. What do they call them...?'

'A podcast.'

Syd scowled at her. 'A what?'

'It's... Never mind. Did you speak to her?'

'I did. Carnoustie lassie. Louise something. And you know something? It was actually quite cathartic for your father too. I went for a pint with him afterwards. He said he could see the whole story, see how little of it was his fault. See how I'd backed him to the hilt.'

'So what exactly happened? At the crime scene, you gave the knife to my dad?'

Syd's glare cut right through her. 'No, he had it. Took it in his pool car, all wrapped up. He was supposed to give it to this lab tech in Dundee, but that's where the story ends.'

'You don't think he got rid of it?'

'Of course not.' Syd sprinkled salt over his food and crunched into the fish. 'Christ, that's salty.' He sipped at water, then dabbed at his lips. 'Whatever you think you can achieve here, your old man isn't the real victim. The Sanderson family were.'

It hit Vicky like a truck. 'He had a family?'

'Wife and a son.'

'Christ. I didn't know.'

'That's kind of my point. You're obsessed with proving how your old man was innocent. They went through hell. Imagine finding that the man you loved, or your father, was a serial killer? I spent so much of my time supporting them through the prosecution.'

And he was right. Vicky was focusing too much on the there and then versus the here and now. But surely that's where she needed to focus her attention on a case like this. Right?

Forrester was on his feet, hands in pockets. 'Syd, you think it'd be worth us speaking to them?'

'Why?'

Vicky caught a look from Forrester that mirrored her thoughts. 'You're thinking his son could be the copycat?'

'Stranger things have happened, Doddsy. Like Syd told us, imagine finding out your old boy was a serial killer? What would that do to someone?'

25

Broughty Ferry bustled around her in the sunshine. The posh bit of Dundee and way snootier than Carnoustie. Definitely an upmarket cousin, separated by Monifieth and Barry, and full of galleries and cafes.

Vicky sat back in her car seat, chewing on a lardy supermarket sandwich from the Ashworth's round the corner, and flicking through her notebook. There was a door there, a strand on the case, that she could knock out pretty quickly.

But it meant opening up a wound that she thought was long healed and just wasn't.

Bugger it.

She found his number and hit dial, then put her phone against her ear.

And it was ringing. 'Cullen.' Sounded like he was in an office somewhere.

'Scott, it's Vicky.'

'Can you narrow— Wait, Vicky Dodds?'

'The one and the same.'

His sigh wasn't exactly welcoming or encouraging. 'What can I do you for?'

'Campbell McLintock. You've dealt with him a few times, right?'

'Sadly. You know he's dead, right?'

'Seriously?'

'Yeah. Murdered last year. Sorry, Vicky. Look, I've got to go.'

'So that's it, Scott? McLintock was murdered?'

'I don't know what you want me to say, Vicky. It was all over the papers last year. We know who did it.'

'You catch them?'

He paused. 'Ish.'

'How was he killed?'

'Vicky, that's a story and a half and right now I don't have the time or inclination to delve into that for you.' He sighed. 'Look, Elvis is acting up so I'd better go.'

Before Vicky could ask who the hell Elvis was, he'd hung up. Superb.

Well, that was a closed door at least. Two, more like. Still, it felt like someone had punched her in the throat.

Vicky finished her lunch with a glug of lukewarm cola and tried Rob's number, but just hit his voicemail. She had visions of him stuck in traffic up on the Kingsway with Jamie and Bella screaming at each other, not being able to rely on Vicky's police officer's glare to stop their malarkey.

A text pinged. Forrester:

"Still with Syd. Nothing to report. Lemmeno how it goes."

She pocketed her phone. Over the road, Karen was making a royal mess of a reverse park. Vicky got out and jogged across in time to weather Karen's frosty glare as she got out. 'What have I done now?'

'That bloody podcast.' Karen was shaking her head. 'I mean, if it wasn't for the fact the woman was already dead, I'd want to kill her.'

Vicky laughed at that. 'Take it you've got nothing?'

'Well.' Karen pointed at a flat above a pub. 'I listened to one with the family.'

'Louise spoke to them?'

'Right. I mean, when Forrester announces that this podcaster is a victim, it's going to explode, right?'

'Which is why he's keeping it under wraps for now.' Vicky tried to play it through. Louise Craigen was kicking up a hornets' nest. Gave them a connection between suspects. 'On that podcast, how did they seem?'

'Hard to tell. Mum and son were on at the same time, so I don't think she got the full story out of each of them.'

'Only way they'd speak on the record is with support. Figures. Did she speak to the defence lawyer?'

Karen nodded. 'Not that he said much. Just a lot of fluff about justice and all that. Tried calling his office, but it's shut?'

'Syd said the lawyer died. Confirmed it with someone who worked the case.'

Karen raised her eyebrows. 'Oh, that old flame of yours from Edinburgh?'

'Old flame? How old are you? Going to dance the Charleston next?'

'You know what I mean.'

'He's not an old flame. Christ.' Vicky walked over to the door between a gallery and a café, and pressed the buzzer. 'But it's not connected, no.'

'Hello?' A woman's voice, heavily distorted by the intercom.

'Mrs Sanderson?'

'Speaking?'

'It's the police, ma'am. Need a word.'

'Right.' The door buzzed open.

Karen entered first. 'But it is that Edinburgh cop you were shagging, right?'

'No, Karen, it's not.'

Karen was raising her eyebrows. 'You did shag him, though. In London.'

'Fine. Once. But it was ages ago.' Vicky barged past and climbed the steps. 'Ancient history.' She broke out onto a landing.

Just two doors and a load of pot plants basking in sunshine from the large windows overlooking a garden. The door on the right was open and a woman stood there, hands on hips and wearing an apron covered in flour, shrouded in the smell of baking scones and the sound of Northern Soul. Silver hair cut short into a bob and barely five foot, but her fervent gaze made her look like she wouldn't take any nonsense. 'Can I see your credentials, ladies?'

'I'm Vicky Dodds.' She unfolded her warrant card. 'This is Karen Woods. We'd like to—'

'And Karen Woods won't mind if I see her ID card?'

Karen frowned. 'Why?'

'Well, it wouldn't be the first time a police officer showed up here with a journalist, pretending to be a cop.' She took Karen's ID and checked it. 'Right, what do you want?'

Vicky tried a smile. 'It's probably best if we do this inside.'

'Fine.' She led them inside to a long hallway. A couple of open doors with the din of a TV coming from a closed one. Stairs up, meaning it was a maisonette rather than a flat. She led into the kitchen and opened the oven. With the heat outside, she was baking cakes. Unreal. And she pulled a tray of scones out of the oven with her bare fingers. Crazy. 'You can call me Ann, if you wish.' She gestured at a pair of stools at the breakfast bar. 'Can I get you a coffee or tea?'

'Tea, thanks.' Karen perched on a stool. 'Just milk.'

'Okay.' Ann filled the kettle and set it to boil. 'So, what do you want to know about my husband?'

'We didn't say it was about him.'

'It's not going to be about anything other than Broughty Ferry's serial killer, is it?' And there it was. Years and years of confusion, frustration, denial, rage and acceptance. 'My husband, Jim Sanderson, killed ten people. That we know of. I've accepted who my husband was, what he did and what the world thinks of me. I'm in my sixties now and he's dead.' The kettle boiled but she didn't move. 'So I take it you're here because of what's in the papers today?'

'More or less.'

'I've told this story so many times that it feels like it

happened to someone else.' She stared up at the ceiling, arms folded. 'I used to be in denial about it, about what he did. We had this big house up on the hill in West Ferry. Six bedrooms. Huge garden. Had to sell it to pay for his criminal defence. Big fancy firm from Edinburgh.' She walked over to the cupboard and tipped a scoop of leaf tea into a metal pot. 'Not that it was worth it.'

'So you were well off?'

'Ish. Jim worked in oil. He wasn't an exec or anything, but he was based up in Aberdeen and earned good money during the boom. We were both from the Ferry. I didn't want to move and he didn't mind the drive. Back then, he had a carphone so he could keep up with work on the way up there. And he used to go to conferences a lot all across the country.' She poured water into the kettle, shaking her head. 'It's how they think he picked his victims. He used to see a lot of people at these functions in the bars, sleeping around.'

'Any idea why he didn't approve?'

'Jim *hated* adultery. Couldn't abide it. His father was a minister, a hardcore Calvinist full of fire and brimstone and all that, and he drilled it into him. We met through the kirk. My brother had an affair and Jim disowned him.'

'But he didn't kill him?'

'What do you mean?'

'Well, he killed all these people across the country but not your brother.'

'No.'

The TV noise swelled and footsteps thundered along the hall-way. A man appeared in the doorway. Tall, bearded, with a distant look in his eyes, and a dog collar on his maroon jumper. He held a phone to his ear. 'Yes, the Dundee to Aberdeen train. I presume both tonight and tomorrow are at the same time?'

Ann smiled at him. 'You want a cup of tea, Francis?'

'That'd be smashing.' Whoever he was, Francis was mid-thirties if a day. A new husband seemed stretching it a bit so he must be the son. 'And that stops at Broughty Ferry? Just Arbroath?

Excellent. Okay, well thank you.' He ended his call and looked right at Vicky. 'Francis. Nice to meet you.'

'Vicky, sir.' Mindful of Ann's doorstep inspection, she flipped out her warrant card. 'I'm a detective sergeant. Can I take your full name?'

He was transfixed by her card. 'Francis Sanderson.' He held out a hand for her to shake.

She took it, and he was gripping it tight, so she responded in kind, exactly like she'd been trained by her old man. 'Which faith are you?'

'Church of Scotland. I'm the minister in Carnoustie.' Where Vicky's mum used to go until she just stopped attending one day. 'Just like my grandfather.'

Vicky frowned, confused. As far as she knew, Ann and Jim only had one son, James Jr. 'Right. So you're Ann's son?'

'Correct.' He grimaced. 'James Francis Sanderson, the fifth. I'm sure you can understand why I might not wish to take my father's name.' A statement, not a question.

'I get that.'

'I hated him for what he did.' Francis stood in the doorway, eyes shut. 'He got what he deserved. Dying in prison like that.' He opened his eyes again, full of the fire and brimstone he'd been raised to believe in. 'No, he deserved worse. They caught him when I was nine. Have you any idea what that was like growing up? At high school, I...'

'I understand.'

'Do you?' He laughed. 'Nobody can know what it's like to grow up as the son of a serial killer.'

'I grew up the daughter of a cop.'

'Well. Look at us, two sides of the same coin. The Lord works in mysterious ways. The daughter of George Dodds interviewing the son of James Sanderson.'

Vicky got that creepy feeling in her neck. They were looking for a copycat, someone taking on the mantle. What better way to prepare for that than being the son of the original? Who knew how he'd suffered, what he'd learnt from his old man, how it had all twisted up inside that head? 'Can I ask you for your movements on Saturday night?'

'This is about that killing near Carnoustie?'

The creepy feeling just got worse. Vicky held his gaze, matching his fire with ice. 'Let's start with four o'clock until midnight, shall we?'

'You can't honestly expect that I know anything about it.'

'Just give me your movements and we'll be out of your hair.'

'So let me get this straight. You believe that, because my father was a murderer and I'm his son, that I'm also a murderer? Despite my upbringing, my distaste for what he did, my revulsion at what he represented and my abject horror for those involved? You really think that, because I share half my DNA with him, I should fall down the same wretched path?'

'That's not—'

'No? Is your past so pure and clean that you can come in here and accuse me like this? Perhaps your DNA makes you as inept as your father.'

'Sir, I'm serious. If you don't give us your movements, then I'll have no option but to take you to a police station for questioning.'

'Francis, for goodness sake! Just tell her!'

But he stepped out into the hallway with a disappointed look on his face. 'I'll fetch my jacket, while you reflect.'

26

It would've looked a lot cooler to have taken Francis Sanderson up to Dundee, and certainly would've been nice to have him stew in the back of her car for fifteen minutes. But Broughty Ferry's police station was just two blocks along Brook Street.

A quaint police lantern, more decorative than functional these days, sat outside a squat Victorian building, almost hidden between a much larger place, probably an old hotel from when this town was a resort, and next to the Ashworth's supermarket. Vicky remembered it being a Safeway before they went bust, and it might've been something in the interim. Needless to say, her mother spent a lot of time and money in there.

And just one cheeky civilian bugger in the police spaces outside, so Vicky pulled up and killed the engine, looking at Karen. 'Can you get us a room?'

'Sure thing.' She got out and entered the building with a swipe of her ID.

Vicky sat and looked at Sanderson in her rear-view. Not the first time she'd had a church minister in the back of a car awaiting interview, but certainly the creepiest.

He was just sitting there, eyes shut, like he was praying.

But it was his preying she was interested in. Was he really a serial killer? And what did a serial killer look like? Anything from Ed Kemper's six foot nine down to Charles Manson's five-seven or five-two, depending on who you believed. Fred West to Harold Shipman.

It was what was inside that counted.

The station door opened. Karen appeared, accompanied by a pair of uniforms, and beckoned them inside with a grim expression on her face.

$\sim$

THE INTERVIEW ROOM WAS PERFECT, with some historic renovation making the space feel even smaller and more like a holding cell.

But Francis Sanderson wasn't responding to it. He just sat there, eyes focused on Karen.

She held his gaze. 'Sure you don't want us to get you a lawyer?'

'I can handle you all by myself.' Sanderson rasped out a sigh. 'Do you know what my poor mother has endured over the years?'

'I have a good idea. But the person doing anything to her is you. Not me. If you'd just give us an alibi for Saturday and for—'

'I'd be happy to, Victoria.'

Now she had it, Vicky held his gaze for a few seconds. 'Go on.'

'But I shouldn't have to. I'm a man of the cloth.'

'Who also happens to be the son of a serial killer. Surprised they let you join.'

'I paid for the sins of my father many times over.' He took a deep breath. 'And what does your father do? Oh yes, he was a cop. And it doesn't appear to be okay for me to tar you with the same brush as him, does it?'

'Most people do.'

'Do you always try to brush everything off like that?'

'A lot of the time it works.'

'I'll let you know when it starts to, Victoria, I am a patient man.' Sanderson sat back and rested his hands behind his head. He sat there, just looking at her.

Vicky wanted to jump in, but all her training and experience screamed out that that was the wrong thing to do. She needed to let it play out, let Sanderson fester in here, let him crave freedom.

Karen flipped over the page in her notebook. 'I don't understand something.'

That made Sanderson frown.

'If you didn't do it, you should just say so and stop wasting time so you can be eliminated from our investigation and we can move on to a more suitable suspect. Unless of course you did it.'

'Because I don't have to prove anything. You do.'

'Another thing. If I was the child of a serial killer and the cops had brought me in to question me about copying his MO, then I'd do everything I could to disabuse them of that notion.'

It seemed to be getting at least some of the way through his defences.

'Doesn't us accusing you of copying your father *disgust* you?'

'Of course it does.'

'But you're still not going to tell us where you were?'

'It disgusts me at how absolutely inept the pair of you are.'

Vicky nudged Karen's knee with her own, indicating she was taking over. 'Mr Sanderson, I need to understand something.'

He switched his gaze to her, like a raptor surveying a field for mice. 'Okay.'

'Do you believe your father killed those people?'

Sanderson jerked forward in his seat. 'Excuse me?'

'In your heart of hearts, do you believe your father was the serial killer known as Atreus.'

He didn't speak.

'Do you believe he murdered ten people?'

Sanderson rested his elbows on the table, running his hands through his hair. 'You just told me your father is a cop. I presume during your career that you learnt things about him?'

Vicky gave him a shrug. 'Maybe.'

'Well, can you imagine what it must be like, then, from the age of ten to hear everywhere you go, to school, to church, to Boys

Brigade, everywhere, that your father is the living embodiment of true evil? Can you imagine what that feels like?'

'I sympathise with your situation, Mr Sanderson.'

'Anyone can sympathise, Victoria, but perhaps you can empathise?'

'It can't have been easy at all. Especially when your father denied it all.'

'Right.' He sat back and shut his eyes. 'The hardest thing I've had to do in my life is to accept that I might be descended from that.'

Vicky waited for him to open his eyes and look at her. She felt him reaching out to connect with her, meeting her and readying himself to open up. 'I can only imagine.'

'You ask what I believe, well, I don't know what I believe, if you can imagine a man of faith without any. It's been—'

The door burst open and Forrester appeared, jabbing a finger at Vicky then out into the corridor, then disappeared again.

Perfect bloody timing.

Vicky leaned over the table. 'Interview paused at two forty-three.' She flashed her eyebrows at Karen, then left.

Forrester was pacing around the corridor. He stopped and waited for the door to shut. 'What the hell are you playing at?'

'Interviewing a suspect.'

'A *suspect*? Him?'

'He won't give us an alibi for either murder.'

'For crying out loud. And is he likely to?'

'Don't think so. He's just a smug wanker.'

'Okay.'

'Did you get anything else out of Syd Ramsay?'

'Nothing much.' Forrester's shoulders deflated. 'I just suddenly needed to spend time with the guy.'

'You've been avoiding him?'

'Ever since I heard about the "Big C". Your old boy's been a rock for him. Sees him twice a week. Drives him to his chemo...'

'I didn't know.'

'And after all Syd has done to him.'

'Look, there's a suspect in that room who refuses to give an alibi. If you want to help, you're more than welcome to.'

'Explain your logic.'

'I have. Son of a serial killer, tortured by twenty-five years of knowing his dad's the devil. Thought he could control it by becoming a minister, but he couldn't. Now he's doing the same thing.'

'That's all bollocks, Vicky.'

'Okay. It might be. But let's see if we can eliminate him.'

'Fine.'

So Vicky went back into the room.

Karen was writing, and Sanderson was staring up at the ceiling. Nobody was talking.

Vicky pressed the recorder button and checked the clock on the wall. 'Interview recommenced at two forty-five. DI David Forrester has entered the room.' She took her seat again, still warm.

Sanderson looked down and gave Forrester a brief nod, then went back to staring upwards.

'Nice to meet you, Mr Sanderson.' Forrester stayed by the door and started rolling up his sleeves. 'But I'm a bit dismayed to find out that you're not co-operating with my officers. Anything I can do to help?'

'Well, you can let me go.'

'You know you're here for a reason, right?'

'I'd assume I was, yes.'

'Look, we need to know your movements on Saturday evening and again this morning. You give us them, we'll check them, then you can get on with your day.'

'I know I'm in here because of what my father did. I don't envy the role of a police officer, you know. You're so full of suspicion and darkness. It must be difficult for you to see people as they really are.' He smiled. 'It's not often I quote something other than the good book, but sometimes Nietzsche is all there is to explain this. "Whoever fights with monsters should see to it that he does not become a monster in the process. And when you gaze long into an abyss the abyss also gazes into you." Sound familiar?'

'If you won't give us your movements, we'll have to identify them ourselves. That'll take a lot of manpower. It'll probably mean bringing your poor mother in for questioning.'

But he just shook his head again.

Vicky got his attention. 'Why won't you talk to us?'

'Because I've spent my entire life denying who my father was. All that time, I told people that he wasn't Atreus. But he was.'

'So just tell us, and it'll all be hunky dory.'

'You want to know where I was?' He swallowed hard. 'Are you your father, Victoria?'

This again? She sighed. 'No, I'm not.'

'But what darkness did you inherit from George Dodds?' He sat back and stared at her like he was in the pulpit, channelling the Holy Ghost. 'Are you inept, are you weak, do you hate?'

Sod it. She needed to play him at his own game. 'Of course I do. Everyone does. Your dad did, my dad still does. Did you kill them?'

'Three weeks ago was the anniversary of my father's death. Someone stabbed him in jail while he awaited trial. Just a random act. Maybe targeted. Who knows. But I find it very hard every year. All that stuff about him comes up. Legal fees, losing the family home to pay bills and find some form of income. The strain it put on my mother. And at the heart of it, if my father is evil, then I've got to be too. I'm his flesh and blood, after all. There's no amount of praying will save me.'

'Save you from what?'

'From seeing the world in a certain way.'

'Which is?'

'I'm having a crisis of faith.'

'A crisis of faith?'

'It's taken a lot of time to unravel this, but I don't have what it takes for this.' He tugged at his dog collar. 'I'm not a minister, not in any meaningful way. Not in any way that can service my community. My heart's not in it any more. My soul is more philosophy than religion. And I didn't want to admit it to anyone, least of all my mother, but I don't think I can keep doing this. So on Saturday night, I drove up to Aberdeen to speak to the deacon. I wanted to quit, but he persuaded me to think on it.'

Vicky looked over at Forrester and got a nod. 'Sir, I wish you'd told us that earlier. I've lost an hour.'

'And I've lost twenty-five years of my life.'

'Okay, once we've validated your movements you can go. Next time the police show up, I suggest you be honest, aye?'

'The deacon should be able to provide suitable accountancy of my actions. But you might wish to speak to him, Victoria, since your heart is so dark.'

27

Vicky stepped out in the smoggy heat. Whatever the station had going for it, which wasn't much, it at least had air conditioning. Out here, it just felt so *ugh*. She looked over at Karen. 'Are you able to get on with checking Sanderson's alibi?'

'Sure.' She didn't look pleased at the prospect of a drive up to Aberdeen. 'Maybe I can finish that podcast while I head up to sheep-shagging country.'

Forrester was staring at his phone. 'What podcast?'

'The one our second female victim recorded?'

'Oh, that. Right, aye, good luck.'

Karen shook her head all the way to her car. One last look at Vicky and she got in, then tore off into traffic.

Forrester put his phone away. 'So?'

Vicky leaned back against her car. 'I was convinced it was Sanderson Jr. Still am.'

'Just because you're ashamed of your father doesn't—' He sighed. 'Sorry. That's not funny. This is just bringing up a load of crap in my head.'

'Mine too. You heard him in there. We're both sides of the same coin.'

'And you're not doomed to make the same mistakes as George. You can rise above it.'

'You sound just like him.'

Forrester shrugged. 'You honestly think he's lying to us?'

'What his father did has clearly fucked him up. If he's innocent, then he's got my sympathy. But if he's not, well... we've got our explanation.'

Forrester looked like he was having a hard time processing it. Processing anything. 'Well, Sanderson's staying here until DC Woods gets to the bottom of his Saturday night meeting.'

Vicky's phone rang. Rob calling. 'Better take this.'

'No worries.' Forrester tapped the roof of her car, then winced at the heat. 'Well, I'm heading back to the crime scene in Carnoustie. Catch you later.'

'See you.' Vicky leaned and answered it. 'Hey.'

'Hey.' He was out of breath. Impressive for a PE teacher. 'You okay?'

'Busy. What's up? You okay?'

'Yeah, just back from Dundee. I'm cooking for the kids. I swear, Bella's going to turn into a cookie.'

'Oh, don't tell me—'

'I'm kidding. She just keeps banging on about them. I'm doing homemade pizza.'

'Just try and make it look less like a crime scene than last time.'

'Noted.' He laughed. 'Any idea when you'll be home?'

'Expect me later rather than earlier.'

'Even though this case is in Carnoustie?'

'Even so.'

'Well, love you.'

'Love you too, Rob. Bye.' She killed the call and gave herself a few seconds to smile and just enjoy being in love for once. And in love with someone who—

'Aw, that's so sweet.'

Vicky swung round and had to shield her eyes from the sun.

Alan was leaning against the side wall, his left hand deep in a bag of cheesy tortillas. 'Nice to see you too, Vicks.' He took a bite of an orange chip and chewed, mouth open, lips smacking together. 'Not going to say how well I look, Vicks?'

She stared down at him. 'I need to get on, Alan.'

But he could shift. He went from leaning against a wall to blocking her car door in seconds. 'Having a nice chat with a serial killer's son?'

'What?'

Alan took another chip and chewed slowly. He probably knew how much it grated on her nerves. No, he *definitely* did. The number of arguments they'd had about it way back when. 'I'm covering this story for the paper.' He licked his index finger clear of cheesy dust. 'And now I've found that the cops are investigating how the new serial killer links back to Atreus. You really think it's his son?'

'Alan, I swear I'll—'

'You'll what?'

'How do you know?'

He took another handful of chips.

'Come on. This isn't fair.'

'No? And hiding the fact I have a daughter was *totally* fine?'

'This is different.'

'Doesn't feel like that.' He tipped the crumbs at the bottom of his bag into his mouth then started licking his fingers. 'Feels a lot like you lying to me.'

'I'm not *lying*.'

'No?'

'How do you know?'

'What, the fact you've got a copycat or another two victims?'

Vicky shut her eyes and gritted her teeth. Anything to prevent herself from swinging for him. 'How. Do. You. Know?'

'Can't name my sources, Vicks.' He started folding the bag into a long triangle, then in half again. Just like he always used to. 'It's amazing how you can eat a lardy sandwich like that and still look like that.'

'You've been trailing me, haven't you?'

'You're a cop, Vicks. Thought you of all people would notice being stalked.' He laughed, showing orange-encrusted teeth. 'And by an ex-partner of all people.'

'Christ, the last thing you are was a *partner*.'

'Lover? Fuckbuddy? What was it?'

'Let's just settle on ex with a tiny cock.'

'Vicks, we talked about living together.'

'You talked about it. Last thing I'd want is to share my life with you.'

'I'm actually hurt.'

'Good.'

'I'm not hurt, just so we're clear.'

She gave a sarcastic nod. 'Rightio.'

'And it was, what, six years on and off?'

'No. One drunken handjob and a snog in a pub six years later, followed by a wretched few months of terrible dates and worse sex. That's not on and off. And you chose your job in Edinburgh over me.'

'Least you got a daughter out of it.'

'Alan. Who is your source?'

'I can't tell you. You know that. But you're not denying that you've got two sets of victims.' He moved his hands like he was constructing a billboard. 'God, the public just love a serial killer. This'll be all over the nationals, all mentioning me. The doors this could open for me.'

'Even after all your years of adulation?' She rolled her eyes. 'I never said it was two sets of victims.'

'No, but it is.'

And she got it. A flashback to the hotel car park. Alan speaking to someone. 'I know who your source is.'

Mischief filled his eyes. 'Aye?'

'DC Considine.'

He tilted his head to the side. 'Who?'

Shit, shit, shit.

She'd overplayed her hand. Again. Always came down to that with him.

'So I can speak to this DC Constantine too, can I?'

'As difficult as it is for you, Alan, don't be a dick.'

'How about you give me a little bit about the case and I'll give you a clue.'

Always the tease. She remembered a night where he'd—

And she was blushing. 'Of course I won't give you anything.'

'You always used to give me stuff, Vicky. It's just a case of waiting until you cave in.'

'Go on, then. Why are we talking to Sanderson?'

'You're asking about his old man not being Atreus, right?'

What the hell?

Vicky gave him a warm smile, but kept her mouth shut.

'I know who your female victim is.'

She couldn't keep her mouth shut any more. 'Sure you do.'

He wagged his orange finger. 'Like I said, I don't name my sources. You don't even have her name, do you?'

He was winding her up, she knew it. Sod it, she opened her car door. 'I don't have time for this.'

He caught the door and held it. 'Come on, Vicky, you should be charming me here. Think how this will look for your career?'

'Okay, so who is she?'

'Need a little quid pro quo here, Vicky.'

'What do you want?'

'I just want a little look around the crime scene.'

'Can't your leak get you that?'

'Come on, Vicky, there's no leak on the police side. Not even DC Constantine. I've just been following you. Don't you want to help your baby daddy?'

'You'll never be Bella's father. And you shouldn't be using your own daughter's wellbeing to influence me.'

'Christ. How could you be so cold as to think that?'

'Matches your psychopathy.'

'I'm not a psychopath!'

'Suuuuuure.' She huffed out a sigh. 'Alan, you need to give me this woman's ID, and proof it's her, before I even *consider*—'

'Oh it's definitely her. I was just up in Dundee at our sister paper, digging into their archives and checking some details, when I struck gold.'

She grabbed his wrist and held it tight. 'Out with it.'

'Fine.' He shook her off. 'See, I got a photo of the victim.'

'How the hell did you get that?'

'Vicks. I know who she is, but I can't lose the exclusive. You don't know who she is, but you can give me access to the victim's home. And I'm taking photos.'

28

Vicky drove along the A92. The traffic was early-afternoon light. She checked her rear-view and Alan's car was still following, right up her tail, like he didn't want her to escape.

Horrible little prick.

She pulled off without indicating, winding round the off-ramp towards the road into the top of Carnoustie.

Onto the straight road down and her phone blasted out through the dashboard, set Bella loud. Forrester calling. She turned it down and hit Answer. 'David, I'm—'

'Are you safe to talk?'

'I am, why?'

'Have you gone fucking mental?'

'Excuse me?'

'I got your voicemail. You're trading info with this wanker?'

'I don't see any choice.'

Forrester went silent, making her think she'd lost him as she weaved past the high school. 'We should arrest him for with-holding information.'

'That'll play badly.'

'I know it will, but *Christ.*' Forrester took a slurp of something.

So he was probably back in his office up in Dundee, and not the crime scene. 'I really don't want to let him into that house. Are there any other journalists at his paper who could do it?'

'And let them know he's on to something? I doubt he'd agree.'

'Christ. Okay. But you're in charge there. Don't fuck it up.'

Vicky pulled off the road and trundled along the lane towards the gates guarding Craigen's mansion.

Alan appeared in the rearview and he parked his Mondeo just behind her.

Through the gates, MacDonald was standing by his car, shades on and trying to look badass.

She tried to get out first.

But Alan was already crunching across the pebbles towards MacDonald. 'You must be the next Mr Victoria Dodds?'

MacDonald laughed. 'No way.'

'A past one, then?'

Vicky got between them. The last two men in the world she'd want to fight over her. Not that it was her thing. 'Okay, here's the deal. No photographer, just you and your smartphone. Assuming you've finally got one.'

'Had one for a while now. Can even use it.'

'Okay. So you just want general shots?'

'I'll know what I'm looking for when I find it.' He walked off up the drive.

MacDonald gave Vicky a look over his shoulders, his eyebrows raised above the tops of his shades, then traipsed off after Alan, catching up just outside the house.

Vicky followed slowly, giving them space. Sod it, she was letting MacDonald screw this up. If it was going to be on anyone, it was going to be on him. She stepped through the door and it sounded like they were already upstairs. Like Alan knew exactly where to go.

Vicky raced up and followed the clattering to Louise's old study.

'This is amazing stuff. Gold dust.' Alan was pointing at the Atreus bookcase. 'That. Ten of each shelf, please.'

MacDonald was taking snapshots with Alan's phone.

Vicky got between MacDonald and the shelves. 'Alan, you just came straight up here. Someone's been feeding you information, haven't they?'

'Give me my phone back!'

MacDonald looked at Vicky. 'What do you think?'

'Don't.'

Alan laughed at her. 'You really don't want to know the identity of your victim?'

MacDonald was frowning, but seemed to know enough to play along. 'Come on, you're up to something, aren't you?'

'I'd heard she had a bookcase. That's it. Didn't realise it was like this.' Alan took in the space. 'This is serious stalker shit.'

'Look, Alan, you're in here and you can see everything. I need you to give us the victim's ID.'

'Give me my phone back first.'

MacDonald frowned at Vicky.

But she looked at Alan, instead, shaking her head at him. 'No, because the second you're out of here, that's up on the web and we'll be for it.'

Alan stood there, shifting his gaze between them, but it settled on Vicky. 'I know what you're up to here.' He paced across the study and picked up some folders. 'This is all about your dad, isn't it? Guy never liked me, did he?'

'Does anyone?'

'You sure did.' Alan sniffed. 'All the times you'd screa—'

'Alan, who is she?'

'Was your old man involved in this Atreus case?' He clicked his tongue a few times. 'Because there's a whole ring binder here with his name on it. George, isn't it?'

Vicky didn't feel like she had much of a choice here. Hauling him out of the room without getting the victim's name would feel like a defeat. 'Dad worked the Broughty Ferry case.'

'Really? That's interesting. Forgot he was a cop, but then he took me out for a pint once and gave me that big speech about looking after you. Threatened to kick the shit out of me if I ever mistreated you.'

And that sounded like Dad. Last of the cavaliers. Warning him off like that. Christ. He'd expect to be consulted if Rob ever asked to marry her.

Vicky sighed. 'Give him his phone.'

'Sure?'

'Sure.'

'Many thanks.' Alan took it back and started snapping shots. 'So, her name. You got it?'

Vicky looked at MacDonald and got a shrug. 'Marie.'

'Not particularly impressive for however many cops you've thrown at this, is it?'

'I'm warning you. That phone will go out of the window...'

'I doubt I'll get approval to use them anyway.' Alan tapped his temples. 'It's all stored up here, Vicks. If you want her name, I just want one more thing.'

'What?'

'A meeting with Bella.'

'Christ.'

'Just one. You can be there the whole time.'

Vicky stared at him and saw some human emotion in there. 'Fine.'

'Her name is Marianne Gall. G-A-L-L. Lives on Station Road in Carnoustie.'

29

P rof Arbuthnott looked up at the woman with raised
eyebrows. 'Are you ready?'

Stella Gall was tiny, and seemed to shrink in on
herself. A severe fringe stayed at the eyebrow level and seemed to
keep to the same length all the way up, but was shoulder length at
the back and sides. And all shot through with silver. She stood
there, the room humming, and nodded slowly. 'Okay.'

Arbuthnott pulled back the sheet.

The female victim lay there, ice cold and ice white. Her
wounds had been stitched up, maybe not to mortician standards,
but tidied up enough for this.

Stella covered her mouth with a hand. 'Oh my God.' She
looked up at the ceiling. 'That's her. That's my Marianne.'

Arbuthnott gritted her teeth. 'Do you need a minute with her?'

Stella trained a fierce glare into Vicky's eyes. 'Do you know
who did this to her?'

'We're working on it.' Vicky gestured at the family room door.
'We should do this through here and—'

'Do either of you have kids?'

'I've got three.' Arbuthnott nodded. 'Two girls and a boy.'

She looked at Vicky. 'And you?'

'A girl and a boy.'

She stared at her daughter. 'Oh, Marianne. Why did they do this to you?'

Vicky was stuck in limbo between letting her grieve and needing to open the floodgates wide to gain information. 'Ma'am, can I get you a cup of tea?'

'You don't need to ma'am me.'

'Sorry. We have coffee too.'

Stella looked at her with a puzzled frown. 'You don't remember me, do you?'

'Why don't you enlighten me.' Vicky walked over and opened the family door. 'Tea? Milk? Sugar?'

'Tea, black. Thanks.' And she finally left her daughter's body and brushed past Vicky. She perched on the sofa and hugged a pillow, sobbing quietly.

Vicky caught her sweet perfume and wondered how it'd feel to identify Bella's body. Christ. She needed to stop thinking like that. She gave Arbuthnott a final thank-you nod, but she was already wheeling Marianne's body away, so she walked over to the kettle, freshly filled in preparation, and clicked it on. As it started hissing, she dug out mugs and teabags. Milk seemed to be in short supply, so she'd go without. They had the coffee her mum drank, so she scooped out a couple of measures into her mug.

'You really don't remember me, do you?'

Vicky looked over at her. Remove the lines and the grey and something was tingling in the back of her memory, but it was too many years and too many faces ago. 'Sorry.'

'I was your teacher in Primary Four. Mrs Brewer.'

It didn't come back to her at all. A whole year when she was nine and no recollection.

'Of course, I became Ms Gall. My maiden name.' Her lips tightened to a pout.

The kettle rattled to a boil and Vicky poured water over the bag.

'Quickly!' Stella was like one of their greyhounds across the beach, shooting over and grabbing a teaspoon to flick out her teabag before Vicky was aware anything was going on. 'You can't let it sit.'

'Okay.' Vicky took the teaspoon and stirred her coffee. Didn't smell as nice as her mum's, so maybe she'd picked the wrong brand. 'Can I get you any sugar?'

'I'm fine.' Stella slurped at her scalding-hot tea like it was chilled juice. 'My older daughter Amy was ages with you at the high school.'

But Vicky drew a blank. She tried to do the sums in her head. She was thirty-six now, but was young for her year. This Amy would be thirty-six or thirty-seven now but Marianne Gall was twenty-eight. A big difference, but not huge. But she still couldn't remember her. 'Sorry, I can't think.'

'Good heavens, and they let you be a police officer with a mind like a sieve?'

'It's not that, it's just—'

'I'm kidding. It was all a long time ago. Happens to the best of us. No, Amy obviously wasn't in your class in primary as I wouldn't have taught you.' She frowned. 'But I think you were in the same class in high school. She certainly talked about you a lot.'

Vicky held her mug in front of her face and let the steam mist over her face. 'I need to ask you about Marianne.'

'What's there to tell?' Stella looked over at the door. 'We were close until...' She gasped. 'Marianne moved out of home about a year ago. I never heard from her again.'

'That must be really hard.'

'You don't know the half of it.'

But Vicky had an inkling that she knew a good fraction of it, if not a half. 'Did you have an argument?'

'We didn't, but Marianne... Marianne wasn't the most forthcoming of people. Always kept secrets. Amy was the same. She got involved with this man, a married man, and he got into her head and under her skin and all of the clichés. And Marianne never talked to me about it, oh no, she just kept on seeing him. Just like her bloody father before her.'

'You don't have any other kids?'

'No, but there was a gap between Amy and Marianne. My husband had this idea we could have another child and it might save our marriage. Stupid as I am, I went along with it and lived to regret it.'

And Vicky caught a flash. A pregnant teacher, her belly swelling and growing over the course of a school year, and educating her children about what was going on in her body. 'Was this while you were my teacher?'

Stella frowned. 'You know, it might be. Marianne was born in 1990, just after the World Cup. Thank God it wasn't during, otherwise I wouldn't have seen my husband for love nor money, not that there was a lot of either.'

'We'll need to speak to him.'

'You really don't want to.'

'Be that as it may, I do need to.'

'Well, good luck. The girls' father left not long after Marianne was born. I had to raise both kids myself. Her big sister helped out, but I think she found it all such a strain, like everything.'

'Is there anyone who might know where your husband is?'

'Amy tracked him down, I think. I'm not sure if they kept in touch.'

'Can you give me Amy's address?'

30

Vicky pressed the buzzer and waited.

Dens Road thrummed around her. One of those Dundee back streets that seemed to get more than its fair share of traffic. The address was a flat, the last in a row of stone tenements dotted with satellite dishes that overlooked the bank opposite, the trees shrouding the houses from view. The adjacent plot was a gap between tenements, though the other side was that characterless style of fifties block that seemed everywhere in Dundee. Behind the electricity substation was a building offering "Love For All, Hatred For None". In Dundee. Sure.

'Hello?' A female voice.

Vicky leaned over to the intercom. 'Police. Looking for Amy Gall?'

'This is she.'

The door buzzed and Vicky pushed inside the musty stairwell.

A cat was mewing outside a ground-floor flat. It looked round at Vicky, then up and down like she had the temerity to come into her domain. Then it went back to the door. 'Meow.' It sounded sarcastic.

The door opened and skinny arms reached out to gather up the cat. 'There you are, Catlyn!'

Vicky edged towards her, warrant card out. 'Amy?'

'Honey...' Amy gave an exaggerated eye roll. And not just that movement, but she looked like she should be on one of those high-glam reality shows, though definitely not *Housewives of Dens Road*. Bright yellow nails that were like the cat's fully extended claws, and accessorised with a thin yellow scarf. Tight black track-pants showing off well-developed buttocks and toned abs. And really showing it all off. Flaunting it. Like she was trying to draw the male gaze to her.

Amy, Vicky's supposed pal and she still had no idea who she was. Maybe she'd lost a lot of weight since school, but... Christ.

She smiled at Vicky and something like recognition sparkled in her. 'Oh look at you, honey. You look divine.' She hugged the cat to her and grabbed Vicky's free hand and pulled her inside the flat. 'We've got *so* much to catch up on.'

Not the actions of someone who's just heard their kid sister was in the mortuary.

Vicky managed to shake free of her grip in a fancy kitchen. Glossy units and worktop, looked a million pounds more expensive than a Dens Road flat should be. 'I'm here about—'

'Marianne. Mum called me and told me what happened.'

'Right. Are you okay?'

'It doesn't feel real. Sorry.' She leaned against the counter and tugged her hair back over her shoulder. 'Can I get you an espresso?'

'I had a coffee with your mother.'

'Uh huh. So why are you here?'

And Vicky got another glimpse of someone she recognised, something in the way she frowned maybe. 'I need to speak to your father.'

'Oh, him.' Amy stood there, fists placed carefully onto her wide hips. 'Trust me, nobody wants to speak to him.'

'I need to break the news and, you know the drill. Find out if he has any idea why someone would kill his daughter.'

'Man like that doesn't think he has any kids, let alone a daughter.'

'All the same, if you—'

'He's in Turkey.'

'Turkey?'

'Uh huh. Used to run a pub, then he owned one, then he owned three. Sold the lot to a brewery and moved out there. He's letting me keep it. After what he put us through, it's the least he could do.'

'So, can I get his number?'

'It doesn't work.' Amy folded her arms. 'Just tried it when... when Mum called me. He must've changed it, or he's dead, or who cares?'

'Right. Then I need to ask you a few questions about your sister, is that okay?'

'You really don't remember me, do you?'

'I don't, sorry. Your mother said we were at school together.'

'In Carnoustie.' Amy snorted. 'Glad to be away from that place.'

'Your mother was playing the same game with me. Kept me guessing. She taught me in primary. And sorry, Amy, I don't remember you.'

'We sat next to each other in Geography. Remember Mr Harrison?'

'Wait a second...'

'Uh huh.' Amy tugged her hair back until it was flat, her jawline tightening to a grimace. 'I was called Martin at school. Martin Brewer.'

And now Vicky remembered her. Him. Her. She took another look at Amy and started to see features she definitely recognised, hidden under make up and maybe surgery. Whatever she'd done, Martin was long gone. Maybe traces of his perpetual frown or his nervous smile, but this person was now fully Amy.

She could still see her friend in there; maybe the closeness they'd shared was not externalised somehow. The raucous sense of humour, the kindness, the darkness. All still there.

'Wow.'

'You're not the first person to say that.' Amy pranced over the kitchen floor and wrapped Vicky in a hug. 'It's good seeing you.' She smelled amazing, like she'd shopped at the most exclusive Dubai scent palace. Maybe she did. She pulled away, still holding Vicky's hands. 'You've aged well, sugar.'

'Sorry I didn't recognise you.'

'That's kind of the point. Our school was brutal. I mean, can you remember anyone who was even gay?'

'What about that boy who got pissed and shouted about how he fancied David Beckham?'

'The one who got hospitalised, you mean?'

'Right.'

'I'm Amy. Always have been. Part of being transgender is accepting that who you were born as to the outside world doesn't have to be who you are. At school, Martin was bullied for being a "poof". I mean, if they knew...'

'I remember.'

'You always stuck up for him.'

Vicky laughed.

Amy's glare tore her apart though.

Vicky held up her hands. 'I'm sorry. I'm finding this difficult.'

'Don't be sorry. People find it tough, but maybe it gives a little window into poor Martin's life. And he's history now. It's okay to mourn him. When Mum went back to her maiden name, I thought what the hell, that can be my maiden name too. And Amy Gall was born.'

Vicky felt a flicker of tears in her nostrils. 'Either way, Amy is very vivacious.'

'Uh huh. Always was, just in my bedroom.'

'I'm sorry we lost touch.'

'It's called university.'

Vicky smiled. 'Where did you go? Glasgow, right?'

'Strathclyde.' Amy shook her head. 'It was okay, but... The people were good, the course was good, but I wasn't. I dropped out, worked at a call centre in Dundee. Then I found myself, accepted who I was, and here I am. I work as a rape crisis counsellor.'

'Wow.'

'Hey, you're the one who has to catch those fucks and prosecute them.'

'I don't do the prosecution bit, but okay, I'll take the compliment.'

'Well, even so. It's horrible what you have to do.'

'Tell me about it.' Vicky stroked the cat now marching along the worktop. 'Were you and Marianne close?'

'As close as we could be with that sort of age gap. Martin was, well, having trouble when she was still just a rugrat. And he just didn't have time for her. I moved out when I went to uni and Mum was a typical Dundee wifie, like you.'

'I'm not married.'

'It's the Dundee bit I'm referring to.'

'Right. But I get it. She was hard on you both.'

'And worse on Marianne. She was ten years younger than you and me. After... After all the stuff I went through, Mum didn't take it well. So she doubled down on Marianne. Pushed her until she broke. She didn't go to uni, just got a shit job. But I was on the scene now, and I rebuilt our relationship. In a lot of ways I was like her big sister.'

'When did you last see her?'

'Christmas. You know how it is. Round the table with Granny and Granddad, both asking me deep and personal questions about my nether regions without asking why Mum put up with that animal for so long.'

'You keep calling your dad an animal.'

'Right, I know. It's just so raw. I mean, I could play him, could get what I wanted out of him. It's come in handy over the years. He paid for my operation, gave me this place, but that's it. End of the line. And Marianne never had that training. I mean, I pretty much raised her. Mum was useless. Just drank gin and felt sorry for herself.'

'I had no idea.'

Amy inspected her long nail and Vicky saw a flicker of Martin's old torment again. 'Nobody did.'

'Your mother said your sister didn't talk to her about her affair.

Did she with you?'

'No. I guess it's a Brewer trait. That side of the family just don't talk. But us Galls? Try shutting us up.'

'Did Marianne talk about anyone she was seeing?'

'Oh, him.'

'So she did?'

'Right. She mentioned someone at Christmas. Derek, I think his name was.'

'You know how they met?'

'So you know him?'

'He's on our radar.'

'Did he kill Marianne?'

'No.'

She was leering now. 'I smell bullshit, Victoria.'

'Come on, Martin, that's—'

Amy flinched like she'd been slapped.

Vicky let out a sigh. Come on, she had much more important stuff to worry about than what bloody name to call her.

And she caught herself. That wasn't for her to say. She could see Amy's lifelong struggle and hurt reflected in that flinch. And here she was, being ignorant enough to dismiss her hurt when it would cost nothing but a moment's consideration to spare her feelings.

'I'm sorry, Amy. I shouldn't have deadnamed you.' Vicky raised her hands. 'You called me Victoria, and it just took me back to us in the classroom, arguing over stupid shit. It just slipped out.'

'Apology accepted.' Amy came over and wrapped her in a hug.

Vicky met her embrace. 'Look, I'm not used to this yet. But I am proud of you. It can't be easy.'

'It's a different world now, Vicky. It's crazy. I've got a friend who's a teacher in Forfar and there are four kids transitioning that I know of. In *Forfar*.'

'Wow.'

'You keep saying that.'

'Sorry.' Vicky laughed again. 'I forgot how much fun we used to have. We should go for a drink sometime and catch up.'

'That'd be good.' Amy walked over to an expensive-looking espresso machine and fiddled with the controls. Some thumping and hammering later and the machine was hissing away, dribbling out perfect-smelling coffee into a small cup. 'So the last time I saw my sister was just after my op and...' She leaned back against the counter and sipped at her espresso. 'Well, all Marianne was telling me about this guy was...' She put the cup down. 'Are you sure you don't think he killed her?'

'We don't believe he did.'

'Why?'

'Because he died before she did.'

'Christ.' Amy shook her head. 'This is that case on that golf course out past Carnoustie, right?'

'Right.'

'The papers think it's a copycat of that Atreus guy?'

'The papers can think what they like.'

'Is it?'

'Can't say either way, Amy.'

'Right, well. This Derek guy seemed like a typical sleazeball. Married, kids, just like my old man. And he put her up in a shagging pad in Carnoustie.'

The flat where Craigen's family were living now. Where his wife died.

'Did she say anything about him? Anything that you might think, now, oh that doesn't stack up?'

Amy shrugged. 'Marianne worked as an escort.'

'An escort?'

'Right. I mean, I don't *think* she was a hooker, but she was hired out to rich oil men in Aberdeen and American golfers in St Andrews and Carnoustie. She *always* looked much younger than she actually was. I guess for some, that's what they wanted and they'd pay extra for. Most of the thrill with none of the fear of getting nabbed by you lot. But the way she told me it, this Derek guy hired her once, then he got obsessed with her, persuaded her eventually to stop doing that gig. He paid her money, put her up in that shagging pad, told her a load of bullshit about how he was going to leave his wife.'

'He did.'

Amy raised her perfect eyebrows. 'Seriously?'

'Push came to shove. He got caught, moved your sister into his big mansion, put his family up in that flat.'

'Christ.'

'You got an address for this agency?'

'Why?'

'Well, it's possible—'

'You think some old dirty pervert has killed her?'

'Not really, but I need to check it out.'

Amy tossed her cup into the sink and walked over to the dresser. 'My sister, bless her, gave me a card for them.' She held it out to Vicky but didn't let it go. 'She wondered if I wanted to do some work for them. People don't understand. I am Amy Gall, I'm a person, I'm not some sick weirdo's sexual fantasy.'

'I know you are, Amy.'

'Thanks.' And she let the card go. 'And I'll give you Dad's number. See if he wants to talk to you rather than me.'

31

The address was an office in West Ferry, in a long row of upmarket townhouses looking across the Tay towards the north Fife coast, all lit up in the afternoon sunshine. And nowhere did the signage mention anything about escorts, not that it was likely to. Just seemed to be a high-end taxi firm, promising Mercedes and limousines.

Vicky tried the number Amy gave her again. She assumed the dialling code was for Turkey, but it wasn't something she'd ever had to know before.

And it was answered. 'Martin Brewer?' Sounded like he was in a pub. Someone sang *Hound Dog* over a karaoke system.

'Sir, my name is DS Vicky Dodds. I'm based in Dundee and—'

'This is about Marianne, isn't it?'

So someone had managed to get through. Or he'd listened to Amy's voicemail.

'I'm afraid so, sir. Is there anyone who you can be with just now?'

'Eh? What are you talking about?'

'To help you cope with your daughter's death.'

'Right, right. Well, I'm fine. I barely knew the kid.'

'Sir, we need to—'

Click, and he was gone. What a heartless bastard.

She tried again but he bounced the call. Superb. Just superb. Made her appreciate her old man. And her mother. No matter how much bullshit she'd thrown at them, they'd been there for her. She'd always have a safe haven from the world.

Not everybody did.

Vicky sucked in a deep breath and gave it one last go but Martin Brewer wasn't picking up. Despite the heat, she shivered. Maybe he'd been called up to the karaoke machine. Singing something utterly horrible like *Wonderful Tonight* by Eric Clapton. She got out and walked over to the door, then grabbed the handle.

'Wait up!'

She turned round to see MacDonald jogging towards her. What the hell? 'Euan, how did you—'

'Forrester told me to join you.'

'Why?'

'Well, he wasn't happy about you speaking to people on your own. An old primary teacher of yours, and some girl you went to school with. So here I am.'

'Remind me not to mention anything to him in future.' Vicky twisted the handle.

But MacDonald blocked the door with his foot. 'Back up a bit. Why are we here?'

'We aren't here. I am. I identified our first victim and I need to know everything I can about her life.'

'Right. And she was a hooker?'

'An escort. There's a difference. And a sleazy wanker like you should know.'

'Charming.' MacDonald picked at his teeth. 'So you think she was still turning tricks?'

'I don't know, Euan. How about we ask?' Vicky stomped on his foot and pushed through the door.

It looked more like an undertaker than a taxi firm and it was freezing in there, with the kind of air conditioning you got in America. A man in his sixties lounged behind a desk, dressed in that silver grey suit you'd occasionally see toffs wearing at races, but it was all untied and loose. 'Howdy.' Raw Hilltown accent, like an open sewer. 'You guys need a car?'

Vicky walked over to his desk and could smell the booze halfway across. 'Looking to speak to the owner.'

He hiccuped, then blinked a few times. 'That's me, darling. I can drive you.' He made to stand up but collapsed into his seat.

'Not in that state.'

'Fair enough. Let me call Johnny in.' But he just yawned into his fist. 'Won a bit of money on the golf this afternoon.'

'That was yesterday.'

He frowned. 'Was it?' He reached over and poured a good measure of whisky into his glass. 'Well, whatever. Slainte!' He sank it then wiped a shaking hand across his mouth. He tried to get up again, but his legs still weren't co-operating. 'So where can I take you?'

'Police, sir.' Vicky opened her warrant card and held it out, but reading seemed to be a bit beyond his capabilities just now. 'Need to speak to you about Marianne Gall.'

'Oh, Marianne.' He pursed his lips. 'One of my favourites.'

'I take it she didn't drive a cab for you?'

'Correct. Working girl.'

'You mean escort?'

'Something like that. She was the best, though. Always did what she was told. Popular with the Yankee-doodle-dandies.'

'Any local favourites?'

'Oh hells yeah. Had a few repeat customers. Big earners round here, they'd keep on coming back, asking for Marianne, but I had to keep telling them how she's no longer on the payroll. Have to pass them off to Kelly or to Lorna, but they're not the same, are they?'

'I don't know. Does Marianne still do any work for you?'

'Never. Some sleazy bumhole basically bought her off me. I hooked them up, even drove her down to his shagging pad in Carsnooty, and this boy thanks me by getting her to jack it in. I mean, I've offered her a king's ransom and just for a cheeky wee hand shandy off some Yank, but nope. No dice. Some of these lassies, they don't have the stamina for this. Just want to be some clown's trophy wife. What can you do, eh?' He reached for his bottle and splashed more onto the counter than into his glass.

And right then, Vicky's phone blasted out into the ice-cold room. 'Sorry about this.' She looked at it just long enough to see it was Rob, then bounced the call, then back at the owner. 'We're going to need a list of these clients.'

'List!' He bellowed out a laugh. 'There's no list, hen. I just get boys to drive people around.' He sank his latest measure and focused on her, or as close to focusing as he could manage. 'Let me see that warrant.' As pissed as he was, he still knew where to draw the line. Or that he had to draw it somewhere.

'We don't have one.'

He made little legs with his fingers. 'Well, why don't you bugger off out of here and come back when you do?'

But Vicky doubled down, resting her hands on the desk and staring at him. 'Marianne was murdered.'

He burped, then finished his whisky. 'You think she's the first of my girls to pop her clogs? Bugger off!'

Vicky took a look at MacDonald but just got a shrug from the useless wanker. She rapped a knuckle off the desk. 'We'll be back.'

'No you won't.' He took a betting slip out of his pocket and kissed it.

Vicky was sorely tempted to rip it out of his grasp and hold him to ransom. Or just tear it into a thousand pieces. But MacDonald was there and was likely to grass on her. 'Come on.' She stomped out of the door and stood outside in the baking heat. 'Well?'

MacDonald's gaze followed a bus hurtling along the main road, dragging a wave of traffic after it. 'I doubt we'll get a warrant.'

'Yeah, me too.'

'Still, taxi company with a sideline. Very shifty.'

'You're one to talk.'

'Eh?'

'You're a shifty sod, Euan.' Right then, her phone rang again. Rob. 'Better take this.'

'Who is it? Forrester?'

'My partner.'

'Partner.' He smirked. 'Why don't you say boyfriend?'

'Because people in their thirties feel silly saying boyfriend when they've moved in together and their partner's kid calls you Mummy.'

'Well.' He flashed up his eyebrows. 'I still like you, Vicky.'

'Euan, you're married. You're going to be a father.'

'I've made a mistake.' He sniffed. 'And I'd get out of it in a heartbeat if I knew there was something to get into.'

'Get over yourself. You sleazy prick, I'm in a relationship. With a nice guy, not a cheating bastard like you. The world's full of lost and lonely kids whose fathers were selfish pricks that couldn't handle responsibility. Don't be another one.'

But he just stood there. 'Charming.'

'You're all mouth and no trousers.'

'You felt the bulge in my trousers when we kissed, Vicky.'

'Is that what it was? I thought it was a very small Yale key. You're married, you slimy prick.' She walked off towards her car and got out her phone.

But Rob had rung off.

Superb.

But MacDonald had followed her over to her car. 'Sorry, but I need you to follow me.'

'Excuse me?'

'DCI Raven asked me to escort you to Bell Street. He wants a word with you.'

32

Vicky knocked on the office door and stepped back, heart in her mouth. A male voice droned through the wood, someone talking on the phone.

'You okay?' MacDonald was trying to smile, but it wasn't coming off as genuine, at least not to Vicky. Narrowed eyes, clenched jaw.

'I'm just fine and dandy, Euan.' Vicky stood there, the butterflies in her stomach flapping harder and harder. She still had no idea what this was all about, what Raven wanted and why he'd sent MacDonald to fetch her.

Well, maybe she had an inkling. Several of them. Her dad, Alan, MacDonald himself.

'Sod it.' She opened the door and MacDonald tried to stop her, but she brushed him off and powered in.

DCI John Raven was sitting at his desk, speaking on the phone, but sweeping a glower across Vicky. 'Carolyn, I'll call you back. Thanks.' He eased the handset down on the cradle, then took a sip of coffee. 'Mac, thanks for ferrying her here.'

Vicky stood there. Didn't even give MacDonald the satisfaction of eye contact. 'What's this about, sir?'

Raven pointed at the chair in front of the desk. 'If you wouldn't mind?'

Vicky took the seat and badly wanted to nibble at her finger-nails, but she resisted it. 'Is there a problem, sir?'

Raven walked over to the machine bubbling away by the window overlooking the car park and refilled his cup. 'Coffee?'

Vicky shook her head.

'Wouldn't mind one, sir.' MacDonald was still by the door.

'Bet you wouldn't.' Raven sat back down with a laugh, and cradled his mug. 'You can go, Mac.' He shot him a brief wink, then slurped at his coffee, waiting for MacDonald to leave them to it. 'Now, Sergeant, I'm looking for an explanation and it better be good.'

'What am I supposed to have done, sir?'

'As you should be aware, Superintendent Ogilvie from Professional Standards is investigating who's been leaking to the press. If I'd known it was you, I'd have—'

'What?'

'Okey-doke. Denial, is it?'

'Of course I'm denying it. I've not leaked anything to anyone!'

Raven took another drink of coffee. 'So the name Alan Lyall doesn't mean anything to you?'

This was going even worse than how she expected. That little creep was getting all over her professional life now? And she caught herself nibbling the nail on her left index finger. 'If this is about who was leaking to the press, it's *not* me.'

Raven looked right at Vicky, those dark eyes drilling into her. 'But he is your ex, right?'

'That's immaterial.'

'And Alan Lyall is the father of your child?'

'I shouldn't have to endure this.'

'Aye, you should. Your coat's on a really shoogly peg here, Sergeant. You're acting like you don't think the rules apply to you. A member of my team made me aware of the connection between you and this Alan Lyall.'

'DS MacDonald told you.'

'Why is that?'

Vicky snarled at him. 'Because he's a brown-nosing bastard.'

'You know what I mean...'

'I find it really interesting how DS MacDonald is grassing to you.'

'*Grassing*. You're not at school here, Sergeant.'

'It feels a lot like it. Did DS MacDonald make DI Forrester aware of this allegation?'

Raven just stared into his coffee mug.

'So he's got a direct line to you, right?'

Raven raised his eyebrows. 'You and this Lyall were an item. Your daughter is his child. Stands to reason.'

'Believe me, the last thing I'd ever want to do in my life is speak to him.'

'And yet you have. You let Mr Lyall photograph the Craigen crime scene, didn't you?'

'First, it wasn't a crime scene, it was just a victim's home. And second, DI Forrester was informed of that. Said you'd approved it.'

'I did, did I?'

'Are you saying you didn't?'

'No, I approved it, but it's interesting how much you're helping your baby daddy.' Raven took a sip of coffee, grimacing at the taste. 'I'll schedule some time with you, me and Superintendent Ogilvie tomorrow morning.'

'The complaints? Seriously?'

'I suggest you work on your story before then.'

She punched the desk. 'I've got nothing to hide here. Euan MacDonald seeing me chatting to my ex is enough to get me in the shit with the complaints? This is complete bullshit.'

'Would you rather it was any other way? If I just let you get away with this, this place would be absolute chaos. Just like when your old man was serving.'

'You should be *very* careful what you're saying.'

Raven sat back and finished his coffee with a long slurp, dumping the mug on the table. 'I'm giving you one last chance before I throw you to the wolves. Have you been leaking to the press?'

'No.'

'Okay, another last, last chance.'

'No, I haven't been leaking anything to anyone, sir.'

'Do you know who might have been?'

Vicky had a good idea, but there was no way she was grassing to him. 'No, I don't. Listen to me, Alan Lyall hasn't been part of my life for a long time. Over seven years. I unfriended him on social media, blocked his phone, all that jazz. He's never even met his daughter. He's dead to me.'

'Well, if that's how you're playing it, I have to say I'm disappointed but not surprised. You probably want to wear a suit to work tomorrow.'

Vicky took one last look at Raven and realised he was a lost cause. 'Good evening, sir.' She went back out into the corridor and slammed the door behind her. The hallway felt like it stretched miles south, all the way to Edinburgh, maybe even London.

She was sure she could hear buttons being pressed on the phone through the door. Raven calling his contacts in the complaints, piling more on the file. Maybe DCS Soutar, updating her on an emerging vacancy in the Dundee MIT.

She knew in her heart it was Considine leaking. Stupid bastard didn't know what he was doing. And it was all hitting her.

Vicky needed to put a stop to it.

~

VICKY TWISTED the bottle lid and let it fizz up slowly, easing it off with a hiss until the bitter dark smell hit her. Not a drop spilled and it was a lot flatter. She took a sip of the ice-cold drink and looked around the canteen.

Time was, this place would be jumping about now, the servers dishing up burgers and chips to anyone and everyone. But things being what they were in Police Scotland, it was almost deserted, just a few isolated pockets of cops eating on their own. Night shift probably getting stuck into something before they started.

No sign of Considine.

'I'd kill MacDonald, fuck Raven and marry Considine.' A familiar voice drifted over, way too loud to be getting away with that. 'You?'

'Definitely kill Raven, fuck MacDonald and marry Considine.' Another voice, one that should be a lot busier. They both should.

Definitely two someones who knew where Considine would be.

Vicky put the cap back on her bottle and wandered over to the table. 'Ladies.'

Karen was fiddling with a white headphone cable dangling from her mobile. An Ashworth's sandwich wrapper was crumpled up in front of her. 'Hey, Vicky.'

Vicky rested her bottle on the table but didn't sit down. 'Have either of you seen Considine?'

Jenny Morgan was sitting opposite, dropping soy sauce onto a sushi roll, looked like avocado and cucumber rather than raw fish. 'So what order would you do them? MacDonald, Raven, Considine.'

Karen smirked at Jenny. 'Fuck. Marry. Kill. Definitely.'

'Oh hells yeah.' Jenny picked up her sushi with chopsticks but just held it there instead of eating it. 'Though I think she'd marry Considine. That mothering instinct.'

'Haven't you two got any work to get on with?'

Jenny nibbled at the sushi, daintily slicing off half and chewing slowly. 'Wait, marry means you don't get to fuck them, doesn't it?'

Karen scowled at her. 'Eh, no?'

'Of course it does. Otherwise you'd... Anyway, I reckon Vicky would actually fuck Considine.'

Vicky slumped down in the spare seat and tore the lid off her drink. 'Right now, I would kill all three. But I'd start with knowing where the hell Considine is.'

Karen tilted her head to the side. 'What's he done now?'

'He's fucked me over.' Vicky tried to cover her simmering rage with taking a sip, but it wouldn't get past either of her two friends. 'He's been leaking to the press. And now Mac's grassed to Raven, saying I've done it. And I've got a session with Ogilvie from the complaints tomorrow.'

Jenny opened a pickled ginger sachet. 'That mean you're off the case?'

'Probably.'

Karen sat back. 'So I've been listening to that podcast for no reason. Great.'

'Hardly. Look, Raven didn't explicitly say I'm off the case.'

Karen raised her eyebrows. 'If you've got a meeting with Ogilvie tomorrow, then you need to tread carefully.'

'And where's that likely to get me?'

'Have you spoken to Forrester?'

'Not yet.' Vicky sat back and swigged cola. 'So, have you seen Considine?'

'He was at that hotel, last I heard.' Karen started wrapping her headphones around her mobile. 'Doing God knows what, but what else is new?'

Vicky reached over and tapped her phone. 'How's the podcast going?'

'Slow.'

'Slow good or slow bad?'

'Well, not good. The audio quality is shocking, so it's really hard to make out what they're saying half the time. It's like she recorded it with two tin cans tied together by string.'

'So you've got nothing?'

'I'm getting there.'

'But nothing?'

'Christ, I'm starting to feel sympathy for Considine. No, nothing.'

'Right.' Vicky took another drink. The only way out of this deep hole was to either murder Alan, nail Considine to a cross and get him to squeal, or to solve the case. So she stared at Jenny. 'What about you?'

'I was thinking I'd probably have to fuck Considine.'

'I mean, have you got anything on the case?'

'Other than a packet of supermarket sushi, no. I'd kill for—'

'Jenny.'

'No, we haven't got anything since you last pestered me.'

Vicky leaned over and kept her voice low. 'Seriously?'

'I don't know what you expect me to say here.'

'Something like you've found the knife from the Broughty Ferry crime scene. That'd be like all of my Christmases in one go.'

'That's a lot of—'

Jenny.

She smiled and popped a shaving of pickled ginger into her mouth. 'Vicky, I don't know what you expect here. The records are still missing.'

'And that's it? You just can't find anything?'

'Well, no. I mean, I can see that the knife was stolen. Also, that prints were done.'

'Prints? From the knife?'

'No, from the Tay Bridge. Yes, from the knife. Taken from the initial dusting at the crime scene.'

'How can you tell that?'

'Back then, they didn't have anything automated. You needed to book time on the computer and do it by hand.'

'And someone did?'

'Right, but that's part of what's missing. And the results aren't there either.'

'Christ. That's all I need.'

'What are you trying to achieve?' Jenny grabbed her wrist. 'I know what you're doing. Trying to exonerate your old man. Trying to prove that he didn't mess up. But it's not fair on him, Vicky. What happened, happened.'

Vicky sat back and sucked on her cola. She should've gone for the sugar-y one. Full fat, as her dad would say. Not that it wasn't anything other than full of as many sweeteners as the diet one these days.

Sanderson was their guy. A serial killer. Drugging pairs of adulterers. Raping the women and murdering their partners in front of them, showing them the error of their ways. Casting judgement on them and their decisions.

But was that the full picture?

'Humour me here. Did Jim Sanderson kill these people?'

'What other explanation is there?'

'Pretend you're on the stand. What would you say to the jury?'

Jenny thought about it, drizzling some more soy sauce over a block of rice. 'I'm telling you the DNA evidence matches Sanderson. He was the rapist.'

'How do you know that?'

'Okay, so we had DNA evidence on file. Semen, found in Susan Adamson's vagina. Back then, it was early days and it wouldn't stand up in court necessarily. Also, it would take as long to run as it must seem to you cops. Months. And it would be done by some guy up at the university, too, on a favours basis. And it was pioneering tech back then, so the number of false positives was pretty shocking.'

'And did they run it?'

Jenny smirked as she put a red pepper nigiri in her mouth and chewed. 'Didn't have to. He died on remand, remember.'

'But?'

'One of my guys has just finished processing the DNA.' Her look darkened. 'Sanderson was definitely the rapist.'

Vicky put the cap back on. 'Marianne wasn't raped, was she?'

'Nope. Neither was Louise. Our copycat is only going part of the way.'

Just then, MacDonald walked into the canteen, talking on his phone. Probably grassing on her to Raven, or getting an update. He shot her with pistol fingers and left the room. Didn't seem to want to know how it went with Raven. Or maybe he already knew.

And it hit Vicky, hard and right between the eyes like a stress headache. 'What if Sanderson was doing it with someone else?'

Jenny and Karen shared a look. Puzzlement, maybe, or frustration.

'He raped them, but someone else killed them. Am I going mad here?'

'Not really, no.' Karen put her phone in her pocket. 'Look, that podcast, one episode had a chat with the old SOCO guy. The one who lost the prints... What was his name...?'

Jenny looked over. 'Willie Orr?'

'Him. I just listened to his episode and he alluded to stuff he couldn't talk about. Louise Craigen tried to make a big thing of it, like there was some hush-up, tried to get it in the papers, but it didn't stick.'

'Can you speak to him?'

'I've tried. Can't find him.'

'I know him.' Jenny carefully placed the lid back on her sushi box. 'Used to be an officer before they made them all civilians in the eighties. He resisted the dark side of the force and stayed on in our area. Willie took me under his wing when I started here. Good guy, one of the really old school. No-nonsense, and he used to get so much grief for being called Willie.'

'Can we speak to him?'

'You can try.' Jenny sighed. 'He's got Alzheimer's. Poor guy. Barely clinging on. I mean, you're welcome to speak to him but I gather it's not pretty.'

Vicky got to her feet. 'Then we need to at least try. We need to know if he ran the prints. Where is he?'

'Lives in a care home in Carnoustie.'

33

Vicky trailed Karen down the new road in to Carnoustie. Her satnav was a lying bastard, though, telling her to go along the main road, but that was going to be clogged up with traffic at this time of night.

And Karen fell for the trap, taking the left along Barry Road.

Vicky pulled up at the roundabout just as her phone rang. She reached into her bag for it, eyes on the rearview to make sure she was clear of anyone approaching from behind.

Rob calling.

She answered it with a frown.

'Vicky.' Rob sounded stressed, breathing hard. 'You need to come home. Right now.'

'What's up?'

'It's Alan. HOY!' And he was gone.

Shit, shit, shit.

Vicky kicked it into first and swung across the roundabout, heading home. She tapped redial but Rob didn't answer.

What the hell was going on? Alan? What was he doing?

Another right, then another and she was onto Corby Drive, just a left and she was home, but Rob *still* wasn't answering.

She drove into the street and hit the brakes hard.

Alan was standing in their driveway, laughing.

Rob stood in his way, fists clenched.

Vicky pulled up and got out, then ran over to them.

Rob stepped forward, not quite going head to head with Alan, but not far off rutting stags. 'Of course I know Bella's your daughter, but this is my house and these are my size twelves, so I suggest you leave my house if you don't want them lodged in your backside.'

'I'd love it.'

Vicky stormed across the driveway and got between them, jabbing a finger at Alan. 'What the hell are you doing here?'

Alan was still grinning. 'Hey, Vicks.'

She pointed away from the house. 'Go. Now.'

But he just stood there. 'Is this your way of saying I can't see my own daughter?'

Vicky wanted to grab his arm and twist it until he squealed, but that was exactly what he was playing for. She took a deep breath. 'Of course you can see her, just not right now. We need to talk this through.'

'What, so you can get even more of your poison into her skull?'

'My *poison*? Alan, this needs to be done properly, and by me. Not you. It's taken me two years to get her to the point where she'll accept Rob in her life. You can't just come in here and muddy things like this.'

'After all the help I've given you on this case?'

'There we go. You knew I was up in Dundee, didn't you? So you came here, waited until they got home and—'

'Get real.' Alan shook his head. 'Vicky, I just wanted to see Bella. That's all.'

Vicky felt sick to the stomach. 'This is the last time you'll see her without a court order.'

Alan stood there, rasping his stubble and smirking. 'You think you'll win?'

'You might get rights, but they certainly won't include seeing her completely unannounced like this. So I need you to leave, now.'

But he wasn't looking at her. He was staring to her side. 'So that's Rob? Your latest beta male cuck?'

'And you're such an alpha male.'

'You're not denying the cuck part. Is that why you were at an escort agency today? Hiring a hooker to—'

She raised her hand to slap him, but stopped. That was what the little shit wanted. No, she had better ways to make him suffer.

'Vicks?' Colin Woods was by his front door, surrounded by the din of children running wild. 'Everything okay?'

'No, Colin. This arsehole is trespassing and won't leave.'

Colin's police officer's instinct was kicking in. 'Sir, if you don't clear off...'

Alan stared at Colin, then Rob, then back to Vicky. 'Okay.' He turned his back on her and walked up the street.

Colin was walking over. 'Who was that?'

'Bella's dad.'

Colin shared a look with Rob. 'Oh.'

'Aye. Thanks.'

'I know you can handle yourself, but sometimes you just need another witness. Right?'

'So true.' She clapped his arm and watched him walk back to his house.

'You okay?' Rob was in the drive, frowning at her.

'I'm not, no.' Vicky let out a slow breath. 'How are you?'

'Rattled.' Rob wrapped her in a hug and held her there.

She looked up at him. 'Where's Bella?'

'Inside.' Rob took her hand and led her across the slabs to the house. One last look at the road and he opened the door for her.

The place was quiet, just the distant swooshing of Jamie playing his video games in the living room.

Vicky followed Rob through to the kitchen.

Outside, Bella was running around, hair in pigtails and chasing after a football, dribbling the ball through a maze of imaginary defenders. She kicked it, with way more grace than any of the boys her age, and it arced through the air and bounced off the window. Her hands shot to her mouth, eyes wide.

Vicky beckoned her inside.

Bella trudged over the grass and opened the door. She was wearing her Dundee Utd replica kit, even the bright-orange socks. 'Sorry, Mummy.'

'It's fine, Bells. Just go and play with Jamie, okay?'

'But he's playing Mario Kart and he won't let me—'

'Tell him I told him. Okay?'

'O-kay.' And she huffed off through the house.

Vicky let her shoulders go. Now Bella was inside, Vicky started to feel centred again. In her home, *their* home. A family. Mum, Dad, two kids.

She looked over at Rob. 'Thanks for doing that.'

'I'm a teacher. I can handle myself with useless wee wankers.'

'And I'm still sorry. You shouldn't have had to deal with him.'

'Vicky, we're in this together, okay? You, me, Bella, Jamie. Whatever happens, we've got each other. Okay?'

She wrapped him in a hug. Pulling him tight. 'Thank you.'

He nudged her back, but still held tight. 'So, what's Alan playing at?'

'He's playing games with me. I just don't know what. He's been sniffing around this case and now he's here and getting at you and Bella and Jamie and...'

'It's fine.' He held her that bit tighter. 'It's just... What did you ever see in him?'

'I really don't know. That part of me died a long time ago, I swear.'

'And he wants access to Bella? Now?'

'I don't know. It's hard to tell with him. And if he does... it'll be impossible to fight, especially given that he's her father. And I kept it a secret from him for way too long.'

'How did he find out about her?'

She didn't have an answer to that. 'I've no idea. But we need to be really careful here. This can have a long-term effect on Bella.' She grabbed his hand. 'As can not having a long-term father figure. We're in this together, okay? Warts and all.'

'Okay.' Rob sighed. 'Come on.' He led her through to the living room.

The kids were lying on the floor in front of Rob's massive new telly, tummies on the ground, looking up at the little figures racing around a cartoon world. Time was Vicky and Andrew did exactly the same on his old Nintendo thing. And he hated it when she won.

'Mummy!' Bella held the blue controller and weaved around like she was controlling her own movements. 'And he keeps using the shells on me!'

'Bella, it's all part of the game.' Jamie adjusted his glasses. 'You can use them on me.'

'How?'

'Oh come on! I keep telling you!'

Vicky looked outside and there was no sign of Alan.

But there was a car sitting in the parking bays round the corner, idling. A Ford Mondeo. And Alan was behind the wheel, talking to someone on his phone.

He'd been following her all day, but she could flip his tail and follow him, see who's been talking about her.

Find out if it was Considine. Maybe that's who he was on the phone to.

'I need to speak to him. He's interfering in this case. And someone's leaking to him about the case, and about me. About us. I need to stop him tormenting us like this. I want to protect Bella and Jamie from him.'

The exhaust plumed and Alan tossed the phone onto the passenger seat, then eased off along the street.

'Following him?' Rob nodded slowly. 'He'll have spent all day looking for your car. Take mine.'

'Good idea.' Vicky leaned over and kissed him. 'And I love you, Rob.'

'Love you too.'

34

Vicky kicked Rob's car down and sped up, following Alan's Mondeo as he drove along Barry Road. Instead of heading out of Carnoustie, he passed over the roundabout.

She put her phone to her ear. 'Control, can you get me an update on those plates?'

'Just running them now.' Sounded like the operator was chewing something. 'Registered to an Alan James Lyall of Pipe Street, Edinburgh.'

'Anything outstanding on it?'

'Nope. Clean as a whistle.'

Well, that wasn't what she wanted, but maybe what she expected. 'Okay, thanks.' She killed the call and followed, keeping at a safe distance, keeping it slow, which wasn't difficult given the amount of double parking going on. Something in the warm weather brought the numpties out in droves and made them think that parking like a normal human being was optional.

Alan pulled round the corner and she lost him briefly. Looked like he was speaking to someone on his phone.

Round the bend and Vicky had to slam on the brakes. A police car shot down from the old police station, now all but permanently closed down, blocking the road.

A few metres ahead, Alan leaned back and stared up at the heavens. The blocking car powered on, and Alan sped off along the straight high street, a narrow Scottish artery thick with cars instead of fat and cholesterol. He took a right at the Stag's Head pub, and powered on down the side street, heading towards the golf course.

Vicky was on home turf, knew all of these roads inside out.

She took the right by the chip shop and ploughed down in parallel. At the end, a cheeky bastard in a Volkswagen SUV tried to pull out but the big sod caught her glare and stayed where he was, flicking the wanker gesture at her. She turned left onto Kinloch Street and, through the heat haze, she could see Alan at the end, cutting across the junction. She kept her distance, kept her focus on him as she slowed for the junction.

A blue Nissan was hurtling towards her, the red-faced driver shouting at something or nothing, so she floored it and cut across in a blaze of horns and squealing brakes.

Alan was indicating, still heading towards the golf links at a fair old lick.

She followed, having to go faster than she'd like on quiet streets like these, and she cut through the short tunnel under the train line and out the other side, then drove up to the junction.

The rest gardens sat to one side, with the leisure centre just beyond. An old hotel sat opposite, long since turned into flats. The golf course lay further over, but the stands were half down, with giant trucks blocking any view along that way.

She'd lost him.

Shit, shit, shit.

No, wait. The Black Slab lurked under the sky, the sun silhouetting some dog walkers. Almost tea time, so the lack of cars made sense. Perfect meeting place.

Alan's car was the only one she could see, trundling over the asphalt until it parked between two flat-bed trucks. Made things much harder for her approach.

Vicky followed him, but parked at a distance and kept an eye on the sneaky bastard. She leaned her head back against the headrest and waited.

All this was because of her father. And she was bringing Alan back into their life. Or rather, he was forcing his way in. Either way, it was endangering Bella's future and risking Jamie and Rob.

Her phone rang again. Karen. 'What is it?'

'Are you okay?'

And that hurt Vicky worse than anything. She had no idea how she felt. 'What do you mean?'

'Just spoke to Colin. Said there was something happening at your house?'

'It was Alan. Trying to get in to see Bella. Rob stopped him, and... I'm following him.'

'Following him? Have you lost your mind?'

'Probably. But he's got a mole and I'm determined to find out who it is. Where are you?'

'At the care home. But the nurses aren't letting me see Willie Orr.'

The old SOCO. Right. Felt like a million years ago. 'Can you come to the Black Slab?'

'In Carnoustie?'

'Right.'

'I'm two seconds away.'

'Okay.'

'Stay there.'

Vicky ended the call, but she couldn't sit still.

A door slammed and Alan walked along the Black Slab, hood up with a maroon baseball cap poking out. He slipped between another two lorries and disappeared.

She got out and nudged the door shut until it clicked. The warm wind cut through her hair and she had to fight it back into place. She checked she had her baton and set off.

Christ, the number of times she'd sat in cars here. First with older boys, then with her mate Lizzie, shouting along to Alanis

Morissette, then alone in her car, then bringing Bella to play in the park.

She reached the first lorry, but the clattering of the workmen drowned out any sound. A deep breath for luck and she crept along the side of the lorry. She stopped at the end to peek round.

Alan was kneeling on the passenger seat of a blue Subaru.

Vicky pulled back and pressed herself flat against the truck.

A Subaru. Idiots. Alan was meeting Considine.

She'd seen them at the hotel, laughing and joking. And the twat had denied knowing him, kept calling him Constantine. How much was Considine getting as a backhander? How could he give up all that information on Bella?

She needed to get in there, confront them.

But the Subaru drove away, rally style, sliding into a reverse then screeching off.

Christ, she couldn't see who was behind the wheel.

She ran back to her car, gunned the engine and powered off, wrapping the belt around her until it clicked, then wrestling with her mobile, dialling Karen.

'What now?'

'I need you to man-mark Alan's car. A blue Ford Mondeo parked between two lorries. 67 plates.' Vicky shot across the road in the Subaru's wake. She spotted Karen coming from all the fancy new golf apartments along the seafront, but soon she was gone as Vicky hurtled back the way she'd come.

Blink and you'd miss it, but the Subaru shot left at the top end onto Dundee Street without indicating.

'Can you find out who's got the pool Subaru now?'

'You think it's Considine, don't you?'

'Just do it. Please.'

'Okay...'

Vicky dumped the phone on the passenger seat. At the top of the road, she had to wait for a long queue of traffic so she checked that Karen was still on the call. She was.

The Subaru sat by the Stag's Head pub, indicating right, but caught up by a long wave of traffic coming from Dundee, weaving in and out of the parking bays. Carnoustie High Street was still a nightmare for cars. And the town's stupid layout didn't give Vicky any opportunities to head them off at the pass.

Well, she could double back, go up Queen Street and along Terrace Road, but by the time the Subaru had—

No, she had a plan. She took the left down Links Avenue then along Kinloch Street, unpicking her earlier trail, then squaring the circle up Camus Street.

Made her smile to think that Alan had thought it was named after the French philosopher rather than a raiding Viking warlord from a thousand years ago.

Her gamble paid off — the Subaru was still there, stuck between two parking bays. It cut in front of a bus and tore off up West Path.

And Vicky lucked out again. The bus screeched to a halt, but the oncoming traffic didn't immediately shift to fill the gap, so she ploughed over the high street and followed the Subaru up West Path.

As she drove, she put her phone to her ear. 'Karen, still there?'

'Yeah. Apparently MacDonald signed it out this morning, but Considine has had it all afternoon.'

'Typical. Call him.' Vicky ploughed on up the hill, Borrie's Brae or whatever it was called, but the Subaru took the sharp left along Braefoot.

What the hell?

Vicky followed the car round onto Wallace Street, all streets Vicky had walked as a school kid, when these quiet back streets swarmed with children for ten minutes every night, just like the golf crowd over the other side of the train line.

And she now had no idea where Alan was going.

Oh, wait a sec.

Christ, he was heading for her mum and dad's.

Why? Had he been speaking to her old man?

Dad had turned up pissed the other night at her house, around the same time Alan had made his move.

Shit, shit, shit.

Bingo. The Subaru pulled up at the end, indicating right. Postwar council houses on both sides, pockmarked with recent developments in all the gaps that they used to play in as kids way back when.

Vicky slowed and waited for a car to navigate the curve, then turned into Bruce Drive. She stopped at the end and watched it take the left.

Definitely heading for her parents' house.

Obviously to speak to her dad. But why?

Vicky set off, following the exact path and, sure enough, they were parked outside. Alan and Considine.

What the hell were they up to?

Vicky pulled up two houses away, where the circuit completed, just in case they made a run for it. She put her phone to her ear. 'Karen, have you got hold of Considine?'

'Nope. Phone's off.'

'Interesting. Stay there.' Vicky killed the call and got out onto the pavement. She snapped out her baton and walked over to the Subaru.

The engine was still running, coughing out sickly fumes. Vicky sneaked up the driver side, every step made her think it was going to jerk away from her and escape. She opened the door and snapped a handcuff on the hairy wrist. 'Stephen, you've really done it now.'

But it wasn't Considine.

35

M acDonald just sat there, shaking his head at her, full of disappointment. 'What do you think you're playing at?'

Vicky got in the back, in the middle, leaving the door open, just in case. She didn't say anything, just let this play out.

'What have you got on me?' MacDonald looked round at Alan in the passenger seat. 'Sitting in a car with a journalist? It's not a crime.'

'You were just going to chat to my old man about the golf, were you?'

Alan sat back, arms folded, and laughed. His limp fringe was hanging free, down to his jawline.

But she couldn't look at him. Not yet, anyway. 'Euan, you've been leaking to him about an active murder investigation. Two pairs of bodies. Four deaths, all in. And your actions are in danger of fucking that up royally.'

'You've got the wrong end of the stick here.'

'But I am holding one end of the stick in question and I'm going to smack it across your face. Several times.'

MacDonald just sat there, scowling at Vicky, drumming his fingers off the wheel.

'Euan, what has he been giving you?'

'Nothing.'

'So what have you been giving him?'

'Come on, Vicky. After I helped you connect the dots with that victim and her poor, poor mother, this is the thanks I get?'

She turned her attention to Alan. 'What have you got on him?'

He paused. 'Nothing.'

Meaning there was something.

'So what was going on back there at the Slab? Dogging?'

MacDonald just sat there, his lips twitching. He was looking right at Vicky, eyes narrowed to little black coals burning away. 'Hardly.'

But Vicky had a good idea what Alan might have on him. 'Come on, Euan. There had to be something. Money, drugs, jelly babies. What was it?'

'I'm not talking.' And he was shaking his head.

'You've got more money than a DS should have. Flash car, nice flat.'

His eye was twitching. 'It's not money.'

'So what is it?'

He just sighed.

'You need to talk to me here, Euan. I can be on your side.'

'Yeah and you can throw me to the wolves.'

She wasn't ready to strike yet. 'You told him about Bella, didn't you?'

'That wasn't your secret to hide from him.' MacDonald shook his head. 'How can you keep the fact that you had his kid from him?'

Christ. Alan wasn't even looking at her, but he was getting at her. Using MacDonald to attack her.

'You want to tell him, Alan?'

He still didn't look her way.

Vicky leaned forward on the seat. 'He knew I was pregnant and he left me. So you shouldn't feel any sympathy for him.'

MacDonald looked over at Alan, but it didn't look like he was going to lash out. So he was definitely being blackmailed here.

'So what does he have on you?'

'You could've got a transfer and be working in the Edinburgh MIT by now. Your old mate Scott would put in a good word.'

Vicky felt a shiver, saw the goosebumps spreading up her bare arms. 'Hardly. Scott was a DC.'

'Not any more.'

She sighed. 'The truth is, Alan, I just couldn't be arsed with you anymore. You left me here in Tayside and it's fine. I'm fine. Bella's fine. It's not been a picnic, but I can't imagine how bad it would've been with you in the picture. No father is better than an absent one.'

He stared into space.

'How did you identify Marianne?'

'You really want to know?' Alan leaned back, grinning so wide that Vicky wanted to smash his teeth in or pull them out with pliers. 'Someone at the paper was doing an investigation into this escort agency. Chance thing, but Marianne Gall was covered in a story about them. One of her "clients"—' He even did the rabbit ears. '—got caught in a sting and spoke on the record, and gave us some photos of her. Never used in a story, but when I got hold of the photo of your victim, I ran it through our facial recognition tech, which is badass.'

'Euan gave you that photo?'

Alan craned his neck to look at her. 'I'm not answering that.'

'Okay, so you were merely blackmailing a police officer, then?'

He turned round, shaking his head. 'That's bollocks, and you know it.'

'Really? Because I know you've got something on him.'

And MacDonald's neck was burning red, just a few shades shy of Forrester's sunburn the previous day.

Vicky left a long pause.

Alan wrapped his long fringe behind his ear, but he crumpled first. 'Well he shouldn't be such a dirty bastard, should he?'

'Seriously, shut up.'

Alan smirked. 'What, you don't want me to tell her what you've been up to?'

MacDonald looked like he was going to smack him one, but looked over at Vicky with his wrists raised. 'You mind taking these off?'

'I do mind, but seeing as it's you.' Vicky reached over and undid them.

'Thanks.' MacDonald got out of the car and slammed the door behind him.

Vicky kept an eye on him. Last thing she wanted was for him to do a runner. Maybe letting him go was a bad move.

Alan looked round at Vicky. 'I heard about this website where married men can date on the sly. Hooks in to Schoolbook so there's a trust thing too. Sign NDAs with the girls, so they think they can get away with it. But my source told me it had a few politicians on there. So I went on and started catfishing.'

'Catfishing?'

'I pretended to be a woman looking for men.'

Normally Vicky would make a joke about it, but speaking to Amy earlier... Well. 'I imagine that was easy for you given how good a liar you are.'

'Anyone could've done it, Vicks. It was like shooting fish in a barrel with a rocket launcher. Their guard was as far down as their trousers. I was running a sting, tracking about fifteen MPs and MSPs, and boy did I luck out.' Alan waved at Euan outside. 'Turns out it wasn't Ewan MacDonald, the MSP for Galloway and West Dumfries, but one DS Euan MacDonald.' He sat back and beamed wide. 'Stupid prick here just turned up in a hotel room, expecting to shag this young model.'

'Was the model there?'

'Well, obviously. It was all above board. Had to actually hire her. Five lassies, all in, used their photos to snare these stupid twats. She was in the hotel room, pretending to be who I was pretending to be on that website. What was her name again? Crystal. Crystal McKay. And it was actually her birth name. And it sure didn't take Mac here long to get her into bed. Glass of champers and bingo.'

'What, you burst in with a photographer?'

'Give me a little bit more credit, Vicks. No, the whole thing was recorded.'

'That's blackmail.'

'Vicks, Vicks, Vicks, you know me better than that. We met up and I gave him a chance to put his story across, and boy did he start singing. Offered me *anything* in exchange for keeping his identity secret.'

Vicky gripped the seat back like it was the only thing that would stop her from leathering Alan. 'That's still technically blackmail.'

'No. See, I've got copy filed with my editor, ready to go at the push of a button. "Dundee Cop In Online Vice Sting". And I know the law. He's a source now.'

'A source of what?'

Alan just shrugged.

Vicky wanted to throttle the smug bastard. 'What did he give you?'

'More what he didn't.' Alan shifted his chair round to look at her. 'I just sat back and listened while he sang his heart out.' He gave that look, the one that told her he was on to her. 'He told me all about your team. Forrester. Considine, Woods, Buchan, Summers. All of them. What really happened to this lad Ennis who was here before him. And he was talking about someone called Vicky or Victoria that he worked with, and who he was in love with.'

Vicky felt like spiders were crawling all over her skin. 'He's not in love with me.'

'Try telling him that.' Alan raised an eyebrow. 'Doesn't seem like your type, though.'

'Yeah, I go for creepy weirdos.'

'Funny. No, I mean I've seen his wife.' Alan whistled, leering like a sex case. 'And he's got a kid on the way? Shagging around like that? It's fascinating, though. What makes a guy like that do it? Naughty, naughty, very naughty. Didn't stop you snogging him.'

Vicky's glare shut him up.

'And I asked him about you, but I eventually found out you

had a daughter. Vicky Dodds. Victoria. My Vicks.' A snarl cut across his lips. 'The woman who cut me out of my daughter's life for literally no reason.'

So Alan had MacDonald by the short and curlies. He'd blabbed, put Bella at risk.

'Wait here.' Vicky reached for the key then stepped out into the heat.

MacDonald was standing there, head bowed. 'Sorry.'

'You stupid, stupid bastard. You've got a gorgeous young wife who's having your kid and you're—?'

'This isn't the right time for us to have it.'

'It?'

'Them. Him, her. I'm not up on personal pronouns like you are.'

'You're a fucking idiot.'

MacDonald looked at her and moisture filled his eyes. 'I can't do this. I'm not ready.'

'So you've been meeting desperate women online? You make me sick.'

'Vicky, I'm just...'

'Divorce her. Be a single guy and pay her to raise your kid. Be yourself. Don't make her suffer. Don't make your child suffer.'

'I can't do that either.'

'You're just going to live a lie?'

He wiped at his eyes. 'It seems better than any alternative.'

'How's that going to impact your kid? At least give Zoey the choice here.'

'I... Maybe you're right.'

Vicky pointed at Dad's house. 'Why are you here?'

MacDonald just shook his head.

Vicky stared at him. How could he let them down so badly? 'Stay out here. Call Forrester and tell him to come.' She got back in the car and sat behind the wheel. 'What do you want from my dad?'

In the passenger seat, Alan was smoothing his hair over and over. Vicky wanted to cut it all off.

'You were just going to doorstop him?'

'That was the plan, aye.'

'Alan, I know you. Better than you think. You've got something. Spill. Now.'

'Only if I can speak to your dad.'

It didn't feel like she had a choice, but Vicky wanted to run a hundred miles away. But she needed to know what they had. 'You're not getting anywhere near him without spilling the beans to me first.'

'Fine.' Alan folded his arms. 'Trouble is, you've got two pairs of victims killed by a serial killer who died years ago. Real big mystery, huh? You hear they're shutting my old paper?'

'The *North East News*?'

'Right. "All the best coverage of Tayside, Angus, The Mearns and Grampian." Hardly the *Press & Journal*, not even the *Courier*, but it sold well. Until it didn't, so they're shutting the offices. This lad I know from way back when, he's in charge of closing the Dundee and Aberdeen offices, centralising all the print and editorial operations in Edinburgh along with the *Argus* and the *Strathclyde Star*. Lucky they're not merging it with the *London Post*, but hey ho.'

'This got a point?'

'Anyway, the Dundee office has a treasure trove in their vault. Shug knew I was working this case so he dug out what we had on Atreus from back in the day. We have evidence that Jim Sanderson wasn't Atreus.'

Vicky couldn't speak. 'Shut up. We've got his DNA. It was him.'

'Aye?'

And the doubts nibbled at her. 'What do you have?'

'Your boss prosecuted the right man, but for the wrong crime. Sanderson raped them, sure, but he wasn't the killer.'

'So who was?'

Alan wagged a finger in front of her. 'You want what I've got? I get my interview with your old man. No questions.'

36

Vicky knocked on the door and stepped back.

MacDonald was sitting in the Subaru like a good boy, without the key. No sign of Forrester's car on the street behind them, but then no messages from him warning her not to go through with it.

Alan was nosying through the front window. 'Remember when you brought me here to meet your parents?'

'Quit it.' Vicky's mouth was dry now. Her voice sounded like somebody else's.

'Well, I thought this place was a crap heap, but I can see why you still live here. It's a nice town. Quiet, safe. Well, safe enough. I can see how you've turned out like you have. I can see why you didn't come through to Edinburgh with me. And I can see it's been good for Bella.'

He was getting to her, and she couldn't help but feel that thickness in her throat.

'She's a good kid. Think she could be a footballer.'

'Let's just see what she wants to be.' She glanced at Alan and it felt nothing like that time when she'd brought him down from Dundee to meet them. Then she told herself she was in love with him, but now...

Now she saw right through his bullshit.

What the hell did she ever see in him?

But that was the wrong way round, wasn't it? When they first met in that pub in Aberdeen, he was all over her. Charming her, getting inside her head, making her depend on him emotionally. Three years together, then breaking up and her becoming a cop back in Tayside. And he became a reporter in Dundee and he opened the door again, deepening the hold he had on her. Another three years, then just like that he was off.

But she was on to him now. Stronger and wiser. And, given his blood flowed through her veins, Vicky was astonished that Bella was turning out so well.

The door opened and Vicky's dad stood there, glasses dangling from the chain round his neck. 'Vicky? Your mother's not here.'

'Through in Glasgow, right?'

'Stuck in traffic. Told her to avoid the Erskine Bridge, but would she listen?'

'Typical, eh?' Vicky gave him a grin and a few seconds. 'Dad, I—'

Alan stepped forward. 'Hi, George. It's been a while.'

Dad jolted backwards. 'What's he doing here?'

'Long story, George.' Alan grinned at him. 'Just the small matter of having evidence that Sanderson wasn't the killer.'

'We know that, son. He's dead. Vicky's hunting a copycat.'

'No, I mean back in the day. It wasn't Sander—'

'What?' Dad stepped out and looked like he was going to crack him one. 'Vicky, what's he talking about?'

'Dad.' Vicky grabbed his arm. 'He's got proof.'

'Have you seen it?'

'That's the thing. He wants to speak to you first.'

'Cheeky little shite. Well, I'm not speaking to him.'

Alan smiled wide. He knew he was getting at them. 'George, if he can prove Sanderson wasn't Atreus, then you were right.'

'And how's that any use to me now?'

'It's not. But there's someone copying him now. Four victims down and...'

Dad stared at him, but his anger had fizzled out. 'Through here.' He led them inside and opened the study door.

Alan walked inside, hands in pockets like he owned the place. 'Nice paint job, George. Do that yourself?'

Vicky stayed standing by the door. The low light level meant she didn't have to focus too hard on the little creep.

Alan took the chair, facing her, eyebrows raised.

Dad stood by his murder board, now completely covered in prints and connections. Despite what he said, his obsession was deepening. 'So, let's see your evidence, then.'

Alan smirked like a schoolboy. 'Not so fast.'

'Son, I'm really not in the mood for your bullshit.'

'The deal is you go on the record and—'

'Or you won't share the information?' Dad looked at Vicky. 'You want to hold him while I beat the living shite out of him?'

She smiled back. 'More than happy to.'

Alan folded his arms, the glint back in his eye. 'Suits me. I'll get a decent pay-off.'

'You have to still be breathing, son.' Dad cracked his knuckles. 'Doubt there'll be many people at your funeral.'

Alan blinked hard a few times.

'Son, I know you've enjoyed making my daughter feel like shite as part of this whole thing. So you can't just sit there and act like I'll share anything with you. This comes one way, you to me, then if you're a good laddie, I'll *maybe* speak to you.'

'I'm not a good laddie and I'm not—'

Dad lurched forward, grabbing Alan's right shoulder with his left hand, and drove his right thumb behind Alan's ear. Vicky knew the exact spot, where the jaw connected to the skull, had seen it used a few times. Sickening pain and no marks.

Alan crumbled onto his knees, fingers scrabbling at Dad's hands. 'Let me go!'

The stupid prick had misread the whole situation. He was used to dealing with modern cops, people like Vicky and stupid arseholes like MacDonald, not with monsters like her old man.

'Now, son, are you going to play nicely?'

Alan nodded, fast and strong like a kid promising not to kick his ball over the wall again.

Dad let go of him and stepped away. 'Out with it, then.'

Alan opened and closed his jaw a few times. Then wiped a tear away. It hurt like hell, they all knew that, but he didn't want to show it. 'Okay, so like I told your daughter, I found some evidence at the *North East News*, dating back to the 1992 case in Broughty Ferry.' Alan was rubbing behind his ear. 'The way I see it, someone was working with Sanderson.'

Dad looked like he was struggling to keep his cool. 'Sounds like shite. Smells like shite.'

'You can taste it if you like.'

Dad was staring at the murder board now, shaking his head.

'George, you were a convenient scapegoat for the bungles on the case. And Sanderson dying inside, that wasn't suspicious to you?'

Dad swivelled round. 'What are you saying?'

'It's possible Atreus was a cop.'

'Son, I'm this close to swinging for you.'

'Cool. Go for it.' Alan held his gaze. 'I have something you definitely will want to see.'

'Oh, fantastic. What is it, a new entrance to Narnia?'

Alan reached into his pocket for his phone and fiddled with it for a few seconds before holding out the screen. 'No, it's the catalogue sheet for this knife that went missing. The prints, and who ran them.'

'How the hell did you get this?'

'In the archives. They had a copy of the entire discovery for the court case from the defence side. It's got full copies of all the police files. Someone at Sanderson's law firm must've leaked it.'

Dad looked up at Alan. 'Why didn't anyone come forward with this?'

'I wondered that myself. Turns out my editor worked the story. Douglas Johnstone. Know him?'

'I did. Reporter, right?'

'Was, but he moved on up to Edinburgh and climbed the slippery pole and now he's the editor of ten papers, all one big happy family.'

'And he knew all along?'

'He didn't, no. It was all locked away in a vault in Dundee, like I say. I mean, it was marked for destruction ten years back. But it wasn't destroyed. The old Dundee editor carked it in 2008. Heart attack on the golf course.'

Dad got to his feet, slowly, and towered over Alan. 'You're full of shite, son.'

'Dougie thinks his predecessor was keeping it as leverage.'

'Against who?'

'I don't have the full story here.'

'No, you clearly don't. Six constabularies were involved in that case. You're saying there was a UK-wide conspiracy? And they knew that the killer was still at large?'

'No. You lot needed to close it down. A serial killer hitting different cities was close to causing mass panic. Nobody knew where he would strike next. Sanderson was good for the other cases. Apparently there was some sort of forensic match that put him there. So they threw the book at him. It was in everyone's interests to secure a conviction — the press could switch from scaring people to covering the trial, and the cops could take credit for the collar.'

'He denied them all.'

'And he died on remand, so the problem went away. And I know who made it disappear.'

Dad's mouth hung open. 'Who?'

37

Vicky stood in Barry, a gentle dusting of traffic whizzed past, making her ponytail flail around like it was attached to a horse. She needed to cut it short, despite what Rob wanted.

She caught that smell of chicken shit from the farm down the road. She could tell the time by it now. Bang on five o'clock. Every night. It stank of shit half the day, so no wonder a high school PE teacher and a cop could afford one of the better houses in Carnoustie.

Syd Ramsay's house seemed empty, like it hadn't been lived in for years, even though she'd just visited that morning. The gates were pulled back, no sign of the cars.

Forrester parked just ahead and got out, his face like thunder as he stormed over to her. 'What cars were here earlier?'

'A Honda, I think.'

'You think? Come on, Doddsy. You're better than that.'

She got out her notebook and searched through it. Damn. 'No, it was a Volvo. A blue SUV. 67 plates.'

'Attagirl.' He thumbed over the road. 'That one there.'

Certainly matched her note.

Forrester tried to wrestle the gate open, but it didn't budge so he kicked it and got it. 'Syd Ramsay...' He started crunching along the diagonal path towards the front door. He stopped to ring the bell. 'The old bastard knew how to get away with it. He's just unlucky that he didn't take his secret to the grave.'

'We can stop him doing any more.' Vicky walked over and peered through the side window. Seemed empty. She looked back at Forrester. 'He's not here, though.'

Forrester banged on the door, loud and hard. 'Police!' He kicked it now. 'Open up!' He held the bell down but clicked his tongue a few times. 'This is no bloody use.'

'So, what do we do?'

Forrester shrugged.

Vicky took another look inside, like she was searching for an answer as much as a person. 'You got a better idea than breaking in?'

'Nope.' Forrester was scowling at the door. 'Syd bloody Ramsay... Christ, he probably arranged for Sanderson's death inside. It's... it's *brutal*.'

Vicky had to agree. 'But serial killers just don't stop like that, do they? They keep going until they get caught or killed. Syd just stopped.'

'See what you mean.' But it didn't look like it. 'Not long since Janice died. And his cancer. Getting diagnosed, maybe it awakened something in him.'

She held his gaze until he looked away. 'But they weren't raped, were they?'

Forrester frowned, creasing his burnt forehead. 'No, but he's killing again, just without his wingman to rape them first.'

'What the hell do we—'

Something smashed. Sounded like it came from round the back of the house.

'You hear that?'

'Aye.' Forrester was walking across the pebbles, heading away from the entrance, the opposite direction from the way they'd come. 'You go round that side. Meet you at the back.'

Vicky retraced her steps until the small gate leading to the garden. No sign of anyone.

Another smash. Glass tinkling. Definitely came from over there.

She snapped out her baton, opened the gate and stepped through onto the lawn to dampen her approach. At least the sprinklers were off. She crept along the side of the house but couldn't hear anything except her soft footsteps and her breathing. She stopped at the end and peeped round.

Someone was standing on the patio, facing away from her. A man, but she couldn't tell who. He wore a raincoat, with the hood pulled up. Two bottles of beer lay smashed across the slabs.

'Police! Identify yourself!'

He didn't move. Sounded like he was saying something.

She stepped forward onto the pebbles.

'This is all wrong. I've got to end this. Yes. Yes.'

'Stop!' Vicky took another step, brandishing her baton. Not far away from him now. Another step and she was in striking distance.

But the man jerked towards her. She swung blindly towards his shoulder but he sidestepped and drove a low kick into her shin followed by an uppercut to her chin.

She went down, sliding across the pebbles.

She tried to move but all she could do was groan. Footsteps raced away from her. She tried to get up, but everything felt distorted and dampened, and she just couldn't even move.

And she must've blacked out, maybe, because an engine kicked into gear and a car shot off with squealing tyres. All she could think was it was heading away from them, back towards town, back towards Rob and Jamie and Bella and her parents. She knew that at least.

Vicky got up, but her shin was burning, and it felt like she'd lost half her teeth. She had to check, but a full set of teeth bit into the fleshy part of her hand.

Was that Syd Ramsay who attacked her? An old man who'd just undergone chemo? Had he really battered her and got away?

She tried to look over at the patio, to where he'd been standing, but her head was on fire. Made her think she...

No.

Shit, shit, shit.

Syd Ramsay sat on a rattan chair like he was at a barbecue, but his white shirt was reddening, blood spreading out from his heart.

38

Vicky stood over the body, phone pressed to her ear. 'No, he's very much dead. Christ, you know how many crime scenes I've visited?' She shook her head. 'Get as many as you can from the golf course. And an ambulance, even though it's probably too late. Thanks.' She stabbed the screen and killed the call.

So it wasn't Syd after all. Who the hell was it?

And where the hell was Forrester?

She raced along the other side of the house, her shin burning worse with each step. A jagged rose bush caught her arm.

Hard panting came from the side.

Vicky slowed to a stop, tightening her grip on her baton.

Forrester lay there, moaning. He looked up at her. 'Vicky? Ah, shite.'

'Christ, are you okay?'

'Very far from okay.' He gasped. His black trousers were a mess of torn fabric and blood. He screamed.

Vicky inspected the wound with her fingers. Small and tight, but deep. Blood pooled out now, soaking the fabric.

'Hold still.' She reached over and tugged his polo shirt over his head. She folded it and put it over the wound. 'No major arteries or you'd be dead by now, so he's just cut muscle. Hold that tight, you'll live.'

Forrester shut his eyes and clenched his jaw. 'In the name of—'

'There's an ambulance on the way.'

Forrester was grimacing like he was trying to ignore the searing pain in his thigh. 'I let him go.'

'Did you see him?'

'No. He hit me from behind.'

Shit, shit, shit.

Voices came from the road, but they didn't have the telltale rhythms of police chat, so most likely the paramedics.

'Stay here.' Vicky raced down the path and through the gates. She flagged down the paramedics. 'He's up there!'

Both of them hurtled past her, big brutes both carrying half a hospital each.

On the street, the Volvo had gone, leaving just Forrester's car and the Subaru.

Lying back there after she'd been attacked, it sounded like the car had headed towards Carnoustie. Vicky could get in the Subaru and follow it.

But he could've taken either road towards Dundee. She was in the dark here.

She got out her notebook and her fingers were covered with Forrester's blood. Jesus Christ. She rubbed them together, drying most of it off. Then rifled through and found the page, then tapped the licence plate into a message and sent it to Karen, then called her, putting her phone to her ear. 'Can you get me a location on that car? It's a Volvo.'

'What car?'

'I texted you it.' A wave of shivers ran up Vicky's spine, making her teeth chatter. She needed to pull herself together and fast. 'Run the plates. Please.'

'Now?'

'You can listen to that podcast while you do it, can't you?'

'Christ. Fine. Bye.'

Vicky killed the call and walked over to the car. She opened the boot and found a bottle of half-drunk water, lukewarm and putrid. She tipped it over her fingers and started washing the blood away. She dried her fingers on her trousers, but they still had that lingering redness.

She checked her phone again like it'd make Karen call her, but nothing, nothing, nothing, so she walked back up the path. She stopped next to the paramedics dealing with Forrester.

The knife lay in a pool of blood. Not the usual thing she'd find in a Menzieshill flat, but more like the kind of scalpel she'd see in Arbuthnott's lair.

She got out her phone and called Jenny. 'You about?'

'Just about to clock off for the night. Why do I get the feeling that's about to change?'

'Can you get down to Carnoustie? We've got another body. Found a knife, need to confirm if it's the same one as the other four victims.'

'Right.' A long sigh distorted the speaker. 'Text me the address.'

'It's in Barry.' Vicky crouched down to inspect it. 'It's a surgical knife. I think. That's what we're looking for, right?'

'Sounds like it. Be there soon.'

Vicky ended the call and stood there.

The nearest paramedic looked up at her. 'Hear you've got a body?'

She pointed towards the patio. 'Up there.'

'With you in a minute. You mind keeping an eye on it for me?'

'Sure.' Vicky made her way up to the crime scene, her heavy footsteps thumping on the pebbles.

Syd Ramsay still sat on the chair, tortured and dead.

Vicky took a deep breath and crossed the mossy patio until she was close enough to cast her inexpert eye over him. Wild slashes cut across his face, across his forearms too. The cuts on his eyelids looked the same as the three other victims, but she just didn't know for sure.

Whoever did this was still out there. And why had he done this? Why kill Syd?

And now she was up close, she could see another knife,

plunged into his heart. They had evidence. Whoever had done this, the person who'd attacked her and stabbed Forrester, they'd left the knife behind. Jenny would get prints off it. They'd find them.

Just like her old man thought he would way back when...

The blood still poured down his face, and now soaked into his shirt.

Wait a second...

Vicky reached over.

Syd jerked forward and slapped her hand away. 'Who the fuck are you?'

He was alive!

Vicky cupped her hands around her mouth. 'Need some help here!'

Syd tried to winch himself up to sitting, but couldn't. 'You're Dode's girl?'

'I am. We met at your golf club at lunchtime.'

'Christ.' Syd was staring at the knife in his heart. 'What the hell?'

'Stay still!' Vicky grabbed his wrists and tried to stop him pulling the knife out. Probably the only thing keeping him alive was where it was sitting.

'What's going on?'

Something clattered behind her. Vicky wheeled round, reaching for her baton.

Someone stumbled over a rattan chair. 'Christ on a bike!' The paramedic managed to shake it off with a final kick.

'My head's pounding.' Syd tried to push himself up again, then tumbled to his knees with a scream. He held up his arm. All of the fingers on his left hand were bent back.

The paramedic barged between Syd and Vicky and started inspecting his wounds. 'Christ.'

Vicky sat next to him on the sofa. 'Do you know who did this?'

Syd winced as the paramedic popped the buttons on his shirt. 'John.'

'John? John Lamont?'

'Aye.' Syd flinched again, pulling his head away from the para-medic. He tried to stand up, but the paramedic held him in place. 'I need to—'

'You need to sit still.' The paramedic spoke into his radio, deep and inaudible to Vicky.

Vicky took Syd's hand. 'You need to tell us everything. Starting with John Lamont. Why was he trying to kill you?'

'You need to record this. I'm not long for this world.'

Vicky had her phone still in her hand. She started the voice recorder app. 'DS Vicky Dodds with Sydney Ramsay.' She put it in front of him. 'Go on.'

'Atreus was two people. Jim Sanderson and John Lamont. Jim raped them, John killed them.' Syd looked around the paramedic at Vicky. 'They were old schoolfriends who worked together for Kjaer Oil in Aberdeen. The way John told it, they were in the bar at a conference in Birmingham in 1988, when Sanderson spotted this woman. She worked in their Birmingham office and was known to chase anything not in a skirt at conferences, broke up a marriage or two. Lamont was sickened, said she needed to pay the price. So Sanderson waited until she pounced on this young lad, followed them to their room and he attacked them. Knocked the lad out, then raped her. John was watching, but it wasn't enough for him, no. He realised they were only targeting half of the equation, so they cut off her eyelids so she could watch them murder the poor lad. Then he killed her.'

'Jesus.'

'And they didn't talk about it until they were in Newcastle a year later on a boys' weekend. Down in the quayside, and they see this boy take off his wedding ring and hit on this woman in a bar. She was married with kids. An unhappy marriage, but that's no excuse. The guy struck gold and they followed them and repeated the trick. Lamont cut off his eyelids, then forced him to watch as Sanderson raped her, and he plunged the knife through the guy's heart as Sanderson... finished. Then Lamont got to murder the woman. And they kept on at it. Inverness and Carlisle, getting closer together in time.'

'What about the Ferry?'

'The male victim was Lamont's stepfather. Alec Mitchell. And his new girlfriend, Susan Adamson. She was much younger than him. Lamont broke their code, and killed him before Sanderson was finished with her. It threw him, and he noticed the condom had burst. They argued, and Lamont ran off. As far as he knows, Sanderson tried to clean the crime scene as best he could, but he left DNA inside her, didn't he? And that knife your dad found? It was never lost. We had it, and I got the prints fast-tracked, my eyes only. And they matched John's. He was on the system for a fight at the football in Dundee. Never charged with it, but his prints are there.'

'I don't get why?'

'John was married to Irene, my kid sister.' He shuddered. 'I'm very protective of Reenie. I couldn't tell her that John... That he... He'd killed ten people. It would've destroyed her.'

'So you framed Sanderson?'

'No, he was equally culpable. And the conviction would've been solid if he hadn't... If he hadn't died.'

'You had him killed?'

'Hardly. I'm not that powerful. He was unlucky. We were lucky. Some arsehole from the Hilltown was in the cell with him, got into a fight and ended up strangling him. But don't feel bad for Sanderson. That sick fuck had been raping women at conferences for years. It's all in the case files, the glue that would hold the conviction together. But...'

'But what?'

'This is all my fault.' Syd slumped back in the chair. 'I spoke to John, and we agreed to just blame Sanderson, and he accepted he needed to stop. The deal was he sold up and moved to Canada. And he did, in November 1995. He got into property development over there, bought up loads of land and built like there was no tomorrow. Then it all boomed. He stopped killing.'

'But he's started up again.' Vicky grabbed him by the lapels. 'Lamont has killed again. You could've stopped him!'

'Don't you think I know that?'

'And all it took was ruining my dad's career.'

'Your dad was a powder keg. Only a matter of time before he exploded.'

Vicky ended the recording and checked it was saved and synchronised to the cloud, then hit dial. 'Karen, can you get me a location on John Lamont?'

'Is that before or after the plates on that car?'

'Have you got anything on the car?'

'No!'

'Right, well, call me when you do. Get Considine to help.' Vicky killed the call but kept her distance from them. 'Do you have any idea where he's gone?'

'You don't understand what's going on in his head. All these stressors and triggers here. Building that golf course was obviously too much for him.' He slumped back on the sofa. 'And John's mother died and he moved back here. Left his old life behind and trying to build a new one, but...'

'What happened with Irene?'

'Irene met Buddy at their country club, and she divorced John.'

VICKY POWERED ALONG THE ROAD. In the distance, the Carnoustie Hotel was almost lost in a sea of temporary stands. The long, empty expanse of the eighteenth baked in the sun. She caught up with the last of three buses full of arsehole golfers riding convoy along Carnoustie's promenade, and she just couldn't even get past one, let alone all three.

Shit, shit, shit.

The coaches powered past the Carnoustie Hotel, a big part of the whole Open machinery, but at least the security had slackened off, so Vicky pulled off into the car park, half-full of cars.

And holy shit, there was Syd's Volvo.

So Lamont was here.

She reached over for her phone and tried to dial Considine as she drove. 'Stephen, have you—'

'I'm at Lamont's house now, Sarge. Nobody here.'

Just perfect. 'Okay, get over to his hotel, would you?'

'Will do. Oh, I called Control and they said they're struggling to get units over there. Something to do with an incident in Barry?'

'It's the same one! Get them to redirect those cars. Tell them the order comes from DI Forrester. And if that doesn't work, tell them it comes from DCI Raven.'

'Sure thing.'

'Thanks.' Vicky killed the call.

She found it hard to believe Lamont was a serial killer. He'd managed to turn off the blood lust like a tap and stop for, what, twenty-four years? No telling what had happened in Canada, though. But now something had changed and he'd snapped back to his old ways.

And Syd Ramsay... Helping Lamont cover it over. Just to protect his kid sister?

Inside the hotel, the natural light from the giant windows overlooking the course cast the plush furniture into stark relief. Gentle electronic jazz played over the speakers, barely louder than the bubbling fish tank. Smelled like someone was barbecuing steaks.

And no sign of Lamont.

Vicky walked over to the reception desk and kept her voice low. She unfolded her warrant card and slid it across. 'Need to speak to two of your guests. Irene and Buddy Schneider.'

She tapped the keyboard. 'Sorry, but we don't—'

'Might be under Donald Schneider.'

'Okay.' More keyboard abuse. 'Got them.'

'Are they still here?'

'I think so. Hard to tell.'

'Has anyone asked to speak to them?'

The receptionist stood there, smiling. 'Sorry, I've just started my shift.'

'Can you speak to whoever was here before you?'

She nibbled her lip. 'Give me a second.' She picked up a phone and put it to her ear. 'Hey, Rach? Yeah.' She turned away and Vicky couldn't hear the rest of it.

The front door slid open and Abby from Abbey Catering pushed a trolley inside, singing to herself. A guard appeared from a side door and raced over to her.

And the receptionist was back, cracking the handset down on the cradle. 'So, I just spoke to Rachel? She was on. He asked to go up to their room, but they didn't let him.'

'When was this?'

'Ten minutes ago?'

So Lamont was close. And the Volvo was still there. He was here to murder his ex-wife and her new husband.

She smiled at the receptionist. 'Can I see your CCTV?'

'I can't just—'

'Listen to me. I can't tell you why, but it's incredibly important that you do it. That man... We need to speak to him. Urgently.'

'O-okay.' She swivelled her screen around and showed it to Vicky. 'This is ten minutes ago.'

And there he was in black and white. John Lamont, arriving at the hotel, eyes glazed over with the look of a man about to murder. The man who'd attacked Vicky and stabbed Forrester.

Another car pulled up behind and a man got out. In a flash, he was on Lamont, pressing a knife into his back and forcing him back into the Volvo.

Francis Sanderson.

39

Vicky walked across the hotel car park and she gripped her phone tighter.

Shit, she had it the wrong way round. Francis was the aggressor here, pressing the knife into Lamont's back.

Why?

Did he attack her at Syd's? Stick the knife in Forrester's leg? Why?

Taking revenge against Lamont, his father's partner in crime? The one who'd got away with it. The one whose trail Syd Ramsay had covered over. Who'd lived a lucrative life in Canada.

The call was answered with a yawn. 'Jenny Morgan.' Ice queen voice.

'Jenny, it's Vicky. Are you at your desk?'

'Eh, no? You asked me to get to Barry?'

'Shit. Sorry. Look—'

'What do you need?'

'Get me a trace on that number I just texted you.'

A sigh. 'I've pulled in. Running it now. Give me a minute.' She was quiet, just the swooshing of passing cars. 'That phone's off.'

But why were they here? And where had he gone?

Vicky got in the car and started the engine. 'Can you get his last location?'

'Okay, got it. Can you deal with a GPS code?'

'Text it.'

'Done.'

'Thanks, Jenny. And can you check on Sanderson.'

'Francis Sanderson?'

'Please.' Vicky ended the call just as her phone buzzed. A new text message. She tapped the link and the maps app opened up. Lamont's last-known location was just down the road.

Vicky strapped in and set off, racing along Links Parade, a row of posh houses overlooking the golf course, big Victorian things in that brown Angus stone, some now hotels and guesthouses, some just second homes.

Her phone chimed — she'd arrived.

She killed the engine and got out into the heat.

No sign of John Lamont or Francis Sanderson.

Vicky swivelled round. Hers was the only car in the car park, closed off for the Open. The golf course was wide open to the south and the west, and completely empty. The road continued on, so maybe they'd gone that way?

To the north, a short street had a weird triangular modern house halfway up, leading up to Golf Street Halt, as her mother would call it. One of Carnoustie's three train stations, though barely used.

She checked her phone. Another text from Jenny:

"Last location for Sanderson's phone is at the train station, by the looks of things."

Bingo.

Vicky set off up the street. Had to be here, they just had to be. She stopped at the end, the train line blocking the path ahead. Platforms on both sides, a metal bridge to the left. Long gardens sat on the right.

But two figures were up on the railway bridge, silhouetted in the bright day, one leading the other over to the middle, pressing a knife into his back. She couldn't see which way round it was.

Vicky stepped closer and a car pulled up over the other side. Karen got out, waving recognition at Vicky. They had him trapped, at least.

And she knew she had to do this. She had to get up there. So she started up the stairs, gripping her baton tight and loading it firmly onto her shoulder. She wouldn't be surprised this time.

But footsteps came from behind her.

Dad stood there, eyebrows and hands raised.

'What are you doing here?'

He held up his phone. 'I tracked your location to Syd's place. Then followed you here. What's going on?'

'Dad, I need you to stay there.'

'Vicky, you know I'm not going to do that. You need to tell me what's going on here.'

She didn't have a choice. After all that'd happened, he deserved the truth. 'It wasn't Syd working with Sanderson, Dad. It was John Lamont.'

'Christ.' Dad looked up the stairs. 'What's going on?'

'I think Francis Sanderson has him.'

'His son?' Dad shut his eyes. 'I'm going to crack his skull op—'

'No, you're going to stay here. You're not a cop any more. Not even a consultant.'

'So you're just going up there on your own?'

'I've got back up heading over. And Karen Woods is over the other side. Wait here for them and brief them.'

'And yet you're going up there alone. Chip off the old block.' He wrapped his arms across his chest. 'Fine. Go on. Do your bit.'

She thanked him with a smile and set on up the stairs, wondering whether this was the right move. Knowing it wasn't, but not exactly having any choice. The last few steps now, so she crept and stopped at the corner.

'Don't you see?' Sanderson was standing in the middle of the bridge over the rails, at the peak, the vivid blue behind him bleaching all the colour. He had a knife in his hand, different from the one he'd stabbed Forrester with and cut Syd's eyelids off with, the one left buried in Syd's chest.

This looked like a Stanley blade, perfect for cutting football hooligans or packaging.

'Please.' Lamont's voice was a thin gurgle. 'Please, stop this.'

'Aren't you listening to me?' Sanderson spotted Vicky. He gripped Lamont tighter and pressed the knife against his throat. 'Stay right there.'

Vicky tightened her grip. 'Francis, you don't want to do this. Please!'

'Of course I do. This sick bastard ruined my life. Killed ten people. And now another four. It's clear what I've been put on this earth to do. I need to rid the planet of him.'

'That... That wasn't me.'

'So who was it, then?'

Lamont shook his head. 'Craigen got what he deserved. They all did.'

Francis pressed the knife against Lamont's eyes. 'This isn't the kind of blade for it, but I should just repeat what you did to them, shouldn't I? How would you like that? What do you say, John, an eye for an eye? That's almost biblical isn't it?'

Vicky stepped up one. 'Just let him go and it'll all be fine.'

'Fine?' Francis aimed his glare at her. 'How can it be fine? How can anything be fine again, Victoria? Fourteen people are dead!'

Vicky stepped closer to him. Still a long way to go. Four steps up to the junction, then half of the middle section. But she was getting there. 'Francis, why don't you—?'

'All those years, I wanted to believe my father was innocent, that he was framed by this vermin here. By Syd Ramsay. But Alan helped me.'

Oh God, what had he done now? Speaking to Francis behind her back. No wonder he knew what was going on.

'Alan helped me figure out it was Syd Ramsay who helped this loathsome animal, and covered up all those deaths.'

Halfway across now. 'Francis, please, just let him go.'

'You police let him go, Victoria. My father had his faults, but this man played God, he took lives away and that is not the domain of man. My father raped all those women, but this animal here, he murdered them. He punished them for their sins. Who has the right?'

Another step up to the junction.

But Lamont was pleading. 'Don't you see, Francis? Me and your father, we were doing God's will. All of those sinners! And Craigen and his whore were cavorting around like it was all fine. At my party! Acting like it was just fine!'

'And God has let me down, John. I know what you did back in the eighties and nineties with my father. But God has chosen me to set that right again John, I am an instrument of his will.'

'You don't know anything!'

'But you stopped, John.' Vicky took another step. 'Moved to Canada.' And another. The baton was on her shoulder with her elbow up and the butt of it facing Francis. Her left hand outstretched, trying to calm him and gain his attention. But neither was working. 'You can stop again.'

'No, he can't! Don't you see? It didn't work. He always felt the urges. He thinks he's doing God's work.'

Another step. Not close enough to consider attacking, but getting there. 'He stopped, Francis.' And another. 'He kept them in check for years.' She stopped. She could hear the lines ringing. A train was coming. She couldn't tell from which direction. The track bent here, so you could only see it when it was upon you. She took another step. 'Francis, why don't you let him go?'

'Because I can't. I know my purpose. He's killed four people since Saturday. You'll just let him go again.' He stared at Lamont. 'You know what he was doing at the hotel? You were going to kill your ex-wife, weren't you?'

'My wife... BUDDY.'

She took a shorter step now, timing it with Sanderson's glance.

'I had to leave Canada, after what they did to me. I came back here to Carnoustie, and my golf resort... All that stress, and for what? So Craigen and his whore can drink my champagne in a goddamn lighthouse?'

'That's not your call to make!' Francis pressed the blade against Lamont's cheek. 'Nobody has that right!'

A short, shuffling step. 'You don't have to do this, Francis. Let him go. We'll prosecute him.'

'After what he did, my father deserved what he got. Dying in jail like that. I know that was God's will. But how is it right that this sinner gets away, scot free? That Syd Ramsay helped him, but not my father?'

'Because he—'

'Because the Almighty has plans for you, and for Syd Ramsay.'

'I killed him. Syd. He's dead.'

'Francis, you need to let him go. Tell us everything and we *will* convict him.'

'You think I've got any faith in the criminal justice system? I have my faith in a much higher court. You don't know what my father told me.' Sanderson tugged at Lamont's hair and pulled a good clump out. 'About how John Lamont was the other half of Atreus. How he killed them.'

'Let's just get this all on the record and we'll sort it all out.'

'No. He told the police. Told your father and Syd Ramsay. And nobody believed him, nobody did anything. They just let John give a statement to the police, framing my father.'

Vicky wanted to step forward again, but he was keeping his focus locked on her. 'You don't want to kill him.'

'It is *His* will.' Sanderson let the knife go from Lamont's throat and pulled him up taller. 'Making him pay for his sins, making him pay for my father's sins... It's the only thing that makes any sense. My divine purpose.'

Vicky stepped closer. The air was starting to shift now, to her right, turning into a stiff breeze. And she recognised it — an Aberdeen to Glasgow train, non-stop from Arbroath to Dundee, so a good fifty miles an hour, at least.

Was that his plan? Push Lamont in front of the train? Why?

'Francis, you should listen to your faith.'

'Oh, I am.' Francis pulled Lamont's hair back and pushed the knife against the side of Lamont's neck. 'I hated my dad for what he did, all my life. Didn't believe what he told me. But God helped me realise that I should devote my life to help others. Help my community. But my faith was only so strong. I wasn't certain I could do what God asked of me, but now I know I can.'

'Please, Francis. I'm caught up in this just as much as you. This affected my father. There's only so much we can do to protect them, to stop the past from ruining the present. But you need to trust me here, Francis. You need to let me help. We can convict him, Francis. We've got evidence.'

Francis stepped away and let Lamont go. He stood there, head bowed, the wind rustling the nearby trees. Then he drew the blade right across Lamont's throat from ear to ear.

Vicky jerked forward and hit Sanderson's wrist. The Stanley hit the ground. But she was too late. Way too late.

Blood sprayed out like a fountain, coating Sanderson and Vicky in seconds. Francis stepped back, covered in the blood of his father's friend.

Lamont lay against the side barrier, eyes bulging, gurgling, blood seeping through his fingers as he tried to put his bloody neck back together. But he couldn't do anything except die, eyes open.

No need to check his pulse. Lamont was gone. Dead.

She had failed.

Lamont needed to pay for what he'd done. The old murders, the new ones. And Syd Ramsay. But not like this.

Francis stood against the rail, arms raised, staring at the blood dripping from him. 'What have I done?'

'It's over, Francis.'

'It's not. Don't you see? I have been tricked, this was not God's will; this was the devil's work, how could I not have seen? I've murdered. I have become a punisher. I have sinned.'

'He was going to kill you, son.' Dad was just behind Vicky now. 'That was self-defence. I'll back you up. Vicky will too.'

Francis stared hard at him. 'I don't know what to believe anymore.'

'Son, that wasn't on me. I was sidelined by then.' Dad glanced at Lamont's bloodied corpse. 'I followed the party line and your father suffered for it, son. I'm truly sorry. He should've faced justice. Like John Lamont here. He should've spent the rest of his life behind bars, but we failed.'

Vicky saw the sorrow and rage swelling up. She raised her hands and walked towards Francis. 'If anyone understands what it's like, what you and your mother and your father went through, it's us. Me and him.'

Francis stared at her, nostrils spread wide. 'How can you...? How can you even...?' His gaze shifted between them, then to Lamont's corpse. 'I'm just the same as my father.' He looked along the rails, towards the oncoming train, then lifted himself up onto the railings at the edge of the bridge, the short barrier blocking the tracks.

Vicky darted forward, trying to stop him, but he jumped down. She tried to follow him down, like there was something she could do.

Dad pulled her back. 'Vicky, no!'

And the wind pushed her back into his arms and the train shot past below them.

40

Vicky sat in the car and looked over at the railway tracks and shivered. Despite the bright daylight, the crime scene tape flapping in the breeze was glowing.

She focused on it, watching each individual movement behind it. The investigation was already underway, securing Francis Sanderson's remains. A whole stretch of train line knocked out by one man's desperation.

Dad wrapped an arm around her shoulder. 'You okay?'

'Not really.' Vicky sipped the sugary tea and looked up at the blue sky. 'Why did he have to do that?'

'We were there. He couldn't live with himself.'

'Poor guy. Can't even imagine what he went through. Knowing your dad was a serial killer. Or worse, having that doubt in your head, thinking that he wasn't. That he was a patsy. That somebody else had done it, only for him to be snuffed out and the case closed.'

'He went through hell because of what happened back in the past. Not the first, sure won't be the last either. I just...'

'Alan was all over this, Dad. He was leaking to him as well. Pouring his poison in his ear. Feeding him all those stories. I should've stopped him, should've stopped Francis.'

'There was nothing any of us could do, Vicky. What happened, happened. No reason behind any of it. Syd made sure a guilty man was going to be convicted of the wrong crime. While others... They helped the other half get away with murder.'

'Just to protect his sister...'

A car pulled up and Raven got out, followed by MacDonald.

'Here we go.' Vicky finished her tea and tipped the mug out onto the pavement.

'Sergeant.' Raven smiled at Dad. 'Give us a sec, George.'

He got up and tried to walk but put a hand to his back. 'Ow, you bugger.' Something clicked in there and he scuttled off.

Vicky looked over the golf course, the green almost glowing in the evening light. 'I didn't stop him in time.'

'Happens.' Raven took Dad's seat in the car and let out a sigh. 'If you hadn't done what you did, we'd be none the wiser. And it saves us the cost of a trial.' He shook his head. 'After what happened back in the dim and distant, I'll be glad to avoid that.'

'There'll be an FAI, right?'

'Sure will.'

'I'll be in the shit, won't I?'

'I love your sunny optimism.'

'A pessimist is never disappointed.'

'You have DC Woods and your old man there, Vicky.' Raven folded his arms. 'We've got that confession from Syd Ramsay.' He scowled. 'I can't believe it.'

'How is he?'

'He didn't make it.'

'Right.'

'And Forrester?'

'He's in the hospital. Squealing like a pig. He'll be fine. Might limp like your old man, though.'

'And me? We still got that meeting with Ogilvie tomorrow?'

'Can't back out of it now, I'm afraid.'

Vicky shut her eyes for a few seconds, trying to calm all the noise down. 'I did nothing wrong.'

'Don't worry, Sergeant. Nothing bad's going to happen to you. I just want to make sure there's no blowback.' Raven nodded over towards the train line. 'You see what happens when people take the law into their own hands, when they cover over their tracks. You've done nothing wrong and Ogilvie will find that out.'

'What about Euan MacDonald?'

'Now that's a different story entirely. He should be investigated. And will be.'

'He told me he was following your orders, sir.'

'To a point. But I didn't realise what your ex had on him. MacDonald was bloody stupid and careless. It's going to be a tough fight for him to keep his position.'

Vicky actually felt sad for him. Stuck in a position he didn't want to be in. Tough.

Raven stood up. 'I'll manage things here, okay? You get yourself to the station, have a shower, change of clothes, then get yourself home.'

~

VICKY WALKED through the door and listened hard. No signs of life. She checked her watch. Hours late and wearing someone else's clothes. 'I'm home.' She walked through to the kitchen.

Rob was standing at the counter, headphones on, and kneading a dough on the counter. He looked round at her and smiled. 'Hey.' Speaking way too loud.

Vicky reached over and paused his music. 'You okay?'

He dolloped the dough into a bowl. 'I'm fine.'

Vicky stayed there, hands on hips. 'Kids in bed early?'

'No, Colin's running a Mario Kart tournament. Ours and theirs.' Rob rolled off the dough from his fingers into the sink, then draped a tea towel over the bowl. 'Bella was winning, last I heard. Once she figured out how to use the shells, there was no stopping her.'

'So, why are you here on your own?'

'Well.'

'That sounds ominous. You're not just making bread, are you?'

'Vicky, we need to have a talk.'

There it was. He was here alone because he was breaking up with her.

She collapsed into a dining chair. 'Rob, I'm sorry. I shouldn't have rushed off like that. Earlier. It's just Alan, he's... He's a total dick. You're right. I've no idea what I ever saw in him, but he knows how to press my buttons and I saw a chance to take him down.' She shut her eyes. 'We caught the guy, but he died after he killed someone and...' She broke off with a sigh.

He wasn't saying anything, just stood there at the sink. 'I know, Vicky. Colin told me a few hours ago, Karen called him.'

'Rob, I'm sorry about how I treat you. I'm such a selfish bitch and you don't deserve it. As much as I love you and Jamie, if you want to—'

'Vicky, I wanted to talk about your house.'

'What?'

'And the last thing I want to do is split up with you.' He sat next to her and grabbed her hand in his, still damp. 'But you do keep so much in your head. All that shit with Alan? I want to help. I'm here for you, okay?'

'I really do not deserve you.'

'That's true. You deserve a slimeball like Alan.'

She laughed. 'What about my house?'

'I... got a call from the letting agency. Whoever it was staying there, they left a bomb site.'

'How bad is it?'

'Bad bad. But the agency has withheld the deposit. Means we can get the new flooring in there and maybe sell it?'

'That'd be good.' Vicky collapsed into his arms, but the prospect of getting new floors in her old house filled her with as much dread as hunting a serial killer. No, more. 'I'm so sorry, Rob. I've let you down. I just upped and left to go after Alan.'

'Did you catch him?'

'Long story, but yeah. But I don't want to be all Machievellian about this. I don't want my stupidity to cost you, Rob. I feel so bad.'

He pushed away from her. 'Look, that shit with Alan, dangling Bella in front—'

'But I didn't dangle her.'

'No, I'm saying that he did. I never expected it and this is as much on me as it is on you. You're Jamie's mum now, just like I'm Bella's dad. She's Alan's flesh and blood, but she's our daughter and we're raising her together. She's got a brother, a mum and a dad. Okay?'

God, he was right. And Christ, she really didn't deserve him. 'Okay.'

'Okay? I was hoping for more than that.'

'Well, after the day I've had, "okay" feels like "pure dead brilliant".' She leaned in for a kiss. 'So, given the kids are away, how about an early night?'

EPILOGUE

Alan checked through the last paragraph again. He knew not many readers would get that far through it, but the ones who did would be important. A story like this had national attention and, boy, having someone from the *Guardian* or the *Times* read it, even a colleague in the *London Post*, well. That would open doors.

It was perfect, even if he did say so himself.

He pulled off the headphones and rested them on the cradle next to his keyboard, the carved wooden head-shape that held them when he wasn't using them. He stretched out his neck as the newsroom's noise swelled up around him. The TV in the corner played some news from America, inside a courtroom somewhere. Alan nudged Rich next to him. 'Pub?'

Rich sat back. Skinny bastard had that haunted look that ladies loved, that made them just want to mother him. But he was only interested in the fathers. Wealthy ones. Sugar daddies, but Alan didn't think there was any cash passing hands. 'You finished it?'

'Just giving myself five to make sure it's *ready* ready, then yeah. It's done.'

'Doug know?'

'He's read the first draft. Tore it apart.'

'I meant, does Doug know how you got it?'

'Course.'

'You're a snide fucker, Al. What did you tell him?'

'What he needs to know. I got the story. That's it.' Alan got out his wallet and pulled out a crisp fifty. 'Come on, my shout. Might even get some Colombian marching powder, if you're a good boy.'

Rich rubbed at his nose. 'Maybe, then.'

'It'll be a night of wild celebration.'

'It's ten in the morning.'

'All the better, Rich. All the better. I got the story and, believe it or not, I got the girl too. I'm the hero.'

Rich stopped putting on his coat. Always wore a jacket. The skinny fucker would shiver in the Sahara. 'I thought that copper didn't want to have anything to do with you? Wasn't she trying to get you charged?'

'Not that girl. No, Richy boy, it turns out I have a daughter. Bella.' Alan reached over to his machine and clicked Publish. 'And it might take me a couple of years, but I'm going to make Vicky's life a misery for keeping me out of Bella's life.'

AFTERWORD

Hey,

First, thanks for taking the time to read this book. Second, if you bought and enjoyed Vicky's first outing, then a huge thanks for that and I hope this did justice to the character, the area and that book.

It's taken me a while to get here, so thanks for your patience. When I wrote the first cut of SNARED, back in April 2014, it was my first novel as a full-time author and I wanted to turn it into a series. Thomas & Mercer published that book in April 2015 and did a fantastic job of getting it in readers' hands. While I had a deal for a sequel, provisionally entitled FALLEN, the success of the first two Fenchurch books led to a desire for a third, so that got swapped out. By the time of the fourth and fifth, SNARED had gone quite cold, so I bowdlerised some of that idea into the fifth Fenchurch book. Part of that deal was that I got the rights back to SNARED, which I re-edited (*heavily*) and republished TOOTH & CLAW.

So, a fresh start in June 2018, with an outline for FLESH & BLOOD, including some of the subplots you've just read. But then things got out of hand and I had to write other books instead. FINALLY, in March 2020, I had the time to do this justice. Writing against the backdrop of the pandemic was weird, and being able to escape back to July 2018 was actually pretty nice, though I doubt the me of July 2018 could've foreseen that.

Anyway, it's done and I'm going to definitely do a third Vicky book for next summer. If you were paying attention to the second Cullen & Bain book, you might've picked up on some strange happenings in Dundee… There's actually a lot of stuff left from FALLEN that I didn't steal that will give me a nice leg up. Anyway, I hope you enjoy it when it comes!

Thanks to **Kitty** for helping with the initial idea, alpha reading and moral support throughout; to **James Mackay** for the procedural analysis, development editing work and so much more; to **Allan Guthrie** for fixing the language of this book, and for being the best agent I could hope for; thanks to **John Rickards** for the fantastic copy editing; to **Vicki Goldman** for the sterling job proofing it at such short notice; and to the many beta readers, thanks for all your help and support.

Thanks to Colin Scott, you know who you are and what you do for the mental health of me and my friends, though you're to blame for our livers being worse.

Oh, and to Millie, this book's for you. You can't change the past, but I hope you can enjoy the present as much as possible. And the future's yours.

If you spot any typographical errors, please either report them on your Kindle or email me at ed@edjames.co.uk. Thanks!

Finally, if you enjoyed this book, please could I ask you to leave a review on Amazon? It's a massive help to indie authors like me and helps people find my novels.

Ed James,
    Scottish Borders, June 2020

ABOUT ED JAMES

Ed James writes crime-fiction novels, primarily the DI Simon Fenchurch series, set on the gritty streets of East London featuring a detective with little to lose. His Scott Cullen series features a young Edinburgh detective constable investigating crimes from the bottom rung of the career ladder he's desperate to climb.

Formerly an IT project manager, Ed began writing on planes, trains and automobiles to fill his weekly commute to London. He now writes full-time and lives in the Scottish Borders, with his girlfriend and a menagerie of rescued animals.

OTHER BOOKS BY ED JAMES

SCOTT CULLEN MYSTERIES SERIES

Eight novels featuring a detective eager to climb the career ladder, covering Edinburgh and its surrounding counties, and further across Scotland.

1. GHOST IN THE MACHINE
2. DEVIL IN THE DETAIL
3. FIRE IN THE BLOOD
4. STAB IN THE DARK
5. COPS & ROBBERS
6. LIARS & THIEVES
7. COWBOYS & INDIANS
8. HEROES & VILLAINS

CULLEN & BAIN SERIES

Six novellas spinning off from the main Cullen series covering the events of the global pandemic in 2020.

1. CITY OF THE DEAD
2. WORLD'S END
3. HELL'S KITCHEN
4. GORE GLEN
5. DEAD IN THE WATER
6. THE LAST DROP

CRAIG HUNTER SERIES

A spin-off series from the Cullen series, with Hunter first featuring in the fifth book, starring an ex-squaddie cop struggling with PTSD, investigating crimes in Scotland and further afield.

1. MISSING
2. HUNTED
3. THE BLACK ISLE

DS VICKY DODDS SERIES

Gritty crime novels set in Dundee and Tayside, featuring a DS juggling being a cop and a single mother.

1. BLOOD & GUTS
2. TOOTH & CLAW
3. FLESH & BLOOD
4. SKIN & BONE

DI SIMON FENCHURCH SERIES

Set in East London, will Fenchurch ever find what happened to his daughter, missing for the last ten years?

1. THE HOPE THAT KILLS
2. WORTH KILLING FOR
3. WHAT DOESN'T KILL YOU
4. IN FOR THE KILL
5. KILL WITH KINDNESS
6. KILL THE MESSENGER
7. DEAD MAN'S SHOES
8. A HILL TO DIE ON
9. THE LAST THING TO DIE (December 2022)

Other Books

Other crime novels, with Senseless set in southern England, and the other three set in Seattle, Washington.

- SENSELESS
- TELL ME LIES
- GONE IN SECONDS

- BEFORE SHE WAKES

VICKY DODDS WILL RETURN

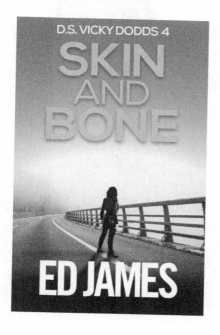

A dead boy. A missing girl. A dark mystery.

When a teenage girl is abducted from a Dundee street in broad daylight, DS Vicky Dodds and her team are put on the case.

When the body of the girl's teenage boyfriend is found, battered and broken, with just one clue — a sheet of paper clutched in his fist, containing an inscrutable code.

Vicky must hunt across Dundee for the girl, drawing on old friends and family, and probe the deep corners of the dark web.

Out May 1st, 2021. Preorder now at https://geni.us/EJD3back
By signing up to my mailing list, you'll get access to **free, exclusive** content and be up-to-speed with all of my releases:

Made in the USA
Las Vegas, NV
07 March 2024

86823061R00177